The SECRETS OF THE LOST VINEYARD

The SECRETS OF THE LOST VINEYARD

ERIN PALMISANO

MOA PRESS

Published in New Zealand and Australia in 2026
by Moa Press
(an imprint of Hachette Aotearoa New Zealand Limited)
Level 2, 23 Victoria Street East, Auckland, New Zealand
www.moapress.co.nz
www.hachette.co.nz

A catalogue record for this book is available from the National Library of New Zealand.

The authorised representative in the EEA is Hachette Ireland, 8 Castlecourt Centre, Dublin 15, D15 XTP3, Ireland

ISBN: 978 1 86971 873 2 (paperback)

Cover design by Christabella Designs
Cover image courtesy of Getty Images
Author photo by Victoria Vincent
Text design by Bookhouse, Sydney
Typeset in 12.7/20.4 pt Garamond Premier Pro by Bookhouse, Sydney
Printed and bound in Australia by McPherson's Printing Group

The paper this book is printed on is certified against the Forest Stewardship Council® Standards. McPherson's Printing Group holds FSC® chain of custody certification SA-COC-005379. FSC® promotes environmentally responsible, socially beneficial and economically viable management of the world's forests.

To Dan. Always my leading man.

PROLOGUE

On a planet with 195 countries and a population of eight billion people, there are a lot of places to see and a lot of stories to tell. For many of those billions, the sun rises and sets, routines take place, and the world exists for each person in a pleasantly expected way. But there are also unexpected moments, joys and sorrows, plans embarked upon, mistakes made, and life becomes a story within a story within a story. Such is life and such is our existence that we live our own beautiful story all the time, every moment of every day.

This particular story takes place on a very small, very unique piece of land called Las Viñas, near Mendoza in Argentina. It is very small as there are only forty-two people that live in and around the village of Las Viñas, and it is very unique because its fifteen acres of lush vineyard are cursed, and have been for the past fifty years, since a woman asked Las Viñas to hide a secret.

The woman's name was Luce Anyas de Alveras, and she came from a line of women who knew how to speak to the land, how to become one with it. To Luce and her mother before her, and her grandmother before that, this gift was natural, though to us it might seem a little bit like magic.

The moment this story begins, on a Wednesday at 4.06 pm, a teenage girl is sneaking into the vineyard with some friends.

'Pia, what are you waiting for?'

'Shh – quiet,' Pia replied. 'Las Viñas doesn't like the noise.'

'Is it really cursed, the vineyard?' Julio asked, sneaking in closer to Gabi, Pia's best friend.

'Do you see any grapes growing, moron?' Alex said, rolling his eyes.

Pia knew she could get in a million years of trouble if she was found taking people onto the neighbour's property, but who was going to know? Luce Anyas de Alveras had died a few months ago and the house sat empty, devoid of any occupants.

'It's been cursed since the 1970s,' Pia said, taking them through the vineyard. 'No one knows why or how.'

'I bet there's a tragic love story involved,' Gabi whispered.

'You think everything is a tragic love story,' Pia muttered.

Pia was taking them to the top of the highest hill, to a single vine called La Abuela, or the grandmother vine.

They reached La Abuela just as the sun began to set behind the Andes, the magic moment. Pia admired the vine, so old, so majestic. Nothing grew for about six feet around her on any side.

'So what do we do?' Julio asked.

'Pia?' Gabi asked.

Pia shrugged. 'Nothing. It is said the curse will break with the last Anyas de Alveras. Or something like that. Today was the first bud break of the season, and old lady Luce passed away a few months ago. She was the last. So maybe it will just . . . wake up?'

'Well, I brought this, since we're here anyway,' Julio said with a cheeky grin, pulling out a bottle of cheap red Malbec. He took a swig straight from the bottle, then passed it to Gabi.

They shared the bottle around, playing games while they waited. The sun dropped behind the mountains and the sky turned pink.

'Nothing,' Gabi said, trying to sound disappointed. She wasn't. Gabi knew, just as Pia did, that nothing was going to happen, but it was exactly how she'd hoped the night would unfold with Julio. Now they could walk together in the dark and hopefully he'd take her hand and hold it, perhaps even kiss her when they lost Pia and Alex in the acres of vines.

'Sorry, guys,' Pia said, standing and feeling relieved to be leaving. 'But I suppose . . .'

A sound interrupted, like a sneeze.

'Bless you,' they all said at the same time, then turned to one another, looking confused.

'I thought that was you, Pia,' Gabi said.

Pia shook her head. The others did the same, each denying they'd made the sound. Finally, slowly, they all turned to La Abuela.

The great old vine looked as she had moments ago. Pia walked towards her, her eyes narrowed, looking for something, anything that would indicate that the sound came from the vine. A bird, a rabbit, a snapped branch. There was nothing.

But just as Pia was turning to laugh at their fright, there was a shift in the air, as if the land around her was sighing. Suddenly, though there was no wind, the vines around them began to sway towards the north-east, to where the city of Mendoza was – an hour away.

'I'm outta here,' Julio said, taking Gabi's hand and leaving quickly the way they came.

Alex ran behind them, calling back, 'Sorry, Pia!'

Pia turned back and sucked in her breath. La Abuela was there, but something was different. Something had changed. Pia leaned in, and suddenly there was a tiny green bud, almost as if it had opened its eye to look at her.

'Dios mío!' Pia cried, stumbling back and running home as quickly as her legs could take her.

'Mama!'

'Pia? What is it? Where have you been?' Marilena asked crossly, looking at her daughter who had come racing into the house with scratches on her arms, dirt smudged on her cheek, and her eyes wild.

'Mama! La Abuela,' Pia said, out of breath. 'Come, look.'

Marilena's heart raced. Was it happening? Luce, God rest her soul, had been buried for three months. Luce was the last. That Las Viñas's curse hadn't been lifted yet was a mystery. But now . . . now perhaps their luck was changing.

Marilena knew that even though Las Viñas was cursed, the vines weren't actually dead. She had once pulled the rootstock out and it was perfectly healthy and thriving. Las Viñas grew, had life, but never flowered and never produced fruit.

But when Pia pulled Marilena to the vine of La Abuela, there it was – a *bud*.

And in that moment Marilena knew one thing in her heart – the curse of Las Viñas was lifting.

And so begins the story of Las Viñas, the cursed vineyard, and the secrets beneath her vines.

CHAPTER ONE

'Ms Bishop, did you need me to repeat the question?' The reply was silence. 'Ms Bishop?'

'Victoria?' a familiar voice now asked.

Victoria turned her attention to her ex-fiancé, Michael Griffon. She stared at the man with whom she'd spent the last six years of her life.

He'd been boyish at twenty-six, when they'd met. Big, soft blue eyes with long lashes, dirty blonde hair grown slightly too long. Victoria remembered the day he first walked into her life, a fresh young wannabe actor who'd just signed with an agency Victoria worked with often. He didn't have much experience, but Victoria's gift, as her boss Levi always said, was her ability to see the potential in a person and their talent.

'Our aim here at LGM, or Levi Gold Management, is to help you on your way to having the career that best suits you,' Victoria had said.

'Let me take you to dinner tonight,' Michael had interrupted.

Victoria rarely blushed, but she did then. 'I, um. Thank you, Michael, but if I plan to be your manager, that will not be possible.'

'Then don't be my manager,' he'd said, leaning forward. 'Let me take you out instead.'

Victoria had sat back at her desk and crossed her arms, pressing her lips together to keep from smiling. 'No.'

When they came out of the office, Monique had said to him, 'Ah, Victoria's latest project! Welcome to the team.'

Now he was thirty-two, his blonde hair darker and cropped short, his frame filled out, and he'd had a beard for the past five years. He looked like a man. He *was* a man.

And he was also a successful actor because of Victoria's belief in him six years ago, despite the unwise decision to start a personal relationship. But she'd seen his potential, she took him under LGM's wing, and he was now their biggest and most successful client to date. He'd been on a popular Netflix show for the last four years and recently been cast in his second feature film role, though he was yet to take the lead.

'Ms Bishop,' the mediator between them asked her again. 'Do you need me to repeat the question?'

'Yes please,' she answered, hating the way her voice cracked. She should have brought someone with her today, but instead it was just her, her ex-fiancé and their mediator, looking at lists of their life to divide up between them. Not a shared life anymore. Not a them; not a we.

The mediator was a woman in her forties named Pen, who was all business, no nonsense, but Victoria saw a flash of sympathy in her eyes. 'This has all been easy so far – thanks to you both for your willingness to work together. You each have your own income, your own vehicles, and you have agreed upon your personal assets within the house. So now, it is just the house.'

The house. The beautiful 1920s Spanish-style villa on 15th Street in Santa Monica they'd purchased a year ago. Until then, they'd both lived in apartments in the city. A four-bedroom house with an actual yard, in the perfect school district, was part of Victoria's dream to start a family.

The longing for what could have been – what she'd lost – suddenly made her choke up and she turned her head, blinking fast and tilting her face to try and stop the tears. She refused to break down now.

'Victoria,' Michael said. 'I'm sorry. I want you to be comfortable and able to move on. I will buy you out, so you don't have to worry about the mortgage or any of those things.'

His voice was kind and genuine, and for a moment she felt like he really was doing this for her. After all, he was earning much more than her now and he had paid for most of the house already. To offer her half was generous, even though it was probably the law. But she looked up suddenly.

'You want the house?'

It was Victoria who wanted the house. *She* was the one who wanted the family so desperately.

Michael had been surprised back when Victoria said she was ready to start a family young. She'd had to explain to Michael that as a person who was adopted, even though her adoptive parents were amazing, to have her own child and family and lavish them with everything wasn't just a dream, it was a necessity. After actively trying for over a year, when nothing happened, she finally went to see a doctor.

'It's called anovulation,' the doctor had said. 'It is when the ovaries don't release an oocyte during the menstrual cycle. It would explain your infrequent periods since you were a girl.'

'So how do I fix it?' she'd asked, trying not to allow the fear to infiltrate her blood. She *had* to have children.

'We'll do tests, but often the cause can be guesswork. If you are actively trying to get pregnant, a woman with anovulation's best effort is to start with ovulation induction, and if that doesn't work, IVF.'

After five cycles on Letrozole, the maximum her doctor and their budget would allow, they started IVF.

Michael didn't seem too enthusiastic about the cost or the fact that the doctor said that the chance of it working for her was under thirty per cent, but he agreed. As treatment started and hope bloomed, they bought her dream house. Victoria planned the decor as she stabbed herself with hormones twice daily.

When that also failed, it was like her sense of who she was and her purpose in life failed as well. She'd fallen into a depression for a time, had become someone Michael didn't recognise. Someone Victoria herself struggled to recognise, too.

But soon enough she was getting up and deciding to try again. Michael, however, said no.

'Michael, we've only tried once!' she cried. 'We can try again.'

'Vic,' he'd pleaded. 'You know what the doctor said, that you are—'

'Don't you say that word!' she'd yelled, covering her ears. But it was in the air and they'd both heard it. *Infertile.*

He came to her, trying to take her in his arms. 'I don't want this to be our life. Either you accept that we will move on together and whatever happens between us with or without children is enough for you, or not.'

She'd cried in his arms and nodded, but she knew it was not enough. Something in Victoria broke then, and things between her and Michael just . . . fell apart.

'Why do you want the house?' she repeated now, feeling an impending doom in her belly, heating her from the inside.

'Victoria . . .' he said, hesitating.

'It's an old character house that you never even liked. You wanted something modern up in the Palisades. Why do you want the house now?' she repeated.

He turned his eyes away and ran his fingers through his hair. The truth punched her in the gut.

'Oh god, is there someone else?' she asked.

He ran his fingers through his hair and wouldn't meet her eyes. 'I didn't mean for it to happen so soon, but yes, there is someone else.'

'And she wants my house,' Victoria whispered. 'A four-bedroom house for a family.' The pain in her gut was so strong, she suddenly felt sick and stood up.

'I think perhaps now would be a good time for a short break,' Pen said calmly, not getting out of her seat, as Michael put his face in his hands.

'I think now is a good time for us to finish this mediation,' Victoria said.

'Yes, we can re-schedule for another time that suits to finish,' Pen started.

'No, I want this done today. I accept Michael's offer to buy me out at the market rate, based on my own lawyer's assessment, if Michael's lawyer agrees.'

Pen took notes and got the paperwork ready for her to take with her.

'Victoria,' Michael said quietly, but Victoria glared at him.

'I want you out of my life.'

~

Victoria was in a state of shock and grief when she got outside.

'Está bien, Victoria?' Javi, the driver from LGM, asked her.

She and Javi only ever spoke in Spanish. Despite the fact that her adoption was closed, what little her parents knew, they shared. Victoria's birth mother was Latina, though they didn't know where from. So, they ensured that Victoria was bilingual from birth, hiring babysitters that could speak Spanish, even though they themselves couldn't. Spanish came naturally to Victoria, and she spoke it as often as she could, which was easy enough in Los Angeles.

'Javi, gracias por esperarme, thank you for waiting for me. I think I'll walk back today,' she said.

'But you're in your favourite heels! The Loubsomethings!' he called.

'You're right. Can you please take my shoes back to LGM,' she said, handing him the red-soled heels Michael had bought her for her last birthday. At the time, she'd thought it was such a generous gift, but it occurred to her today that she hated heels. She never wore them. So why did Michael buy them for her?

She was tempted to tell Javi to throw them over a cliff, but knew he'd have to get at least to Malibu for that to happen.

'Oh, and this,' she added, handing him a folder. 'Give it to Ange. Shoes to Monique.'

'Please, Victoria, I beg of you to not do this,' Javi said, with tears in his eyes.

Victoria suddenly looked down at herself and what she'd handed Javi and realised what it looked like. She couldn't help but laugh.

'I'm just walking back along the beach, I promise,' she assured him. 'No search parties needed.'

Javi didn't look convinced. She appreciated the support she had.

She took pity on him and showed him her phone. 'Here,' she said, opening the location app and sharing her location with him. 'Now you can find me with your phone, and so can Ange and Monique and Levi.'

He looked relieved.

'Thank you,' he said. 'Also, Victoria?'

She turned. 'Yes?'

'Whatever it is, it will get better, okay? You'll be okay, I promise,' he said.

She smiled genuinely for the first time that day.

'Gracias, Javi.'

~

As she expected, when Victoria arrived back at the office a half hour later, Levi and his wife Ange, her bosses, were sitting with Monique at the big dining table they had in the common kitchen area, a spread of just-delivered food on the table.

'We ordered Gjusta, just for you, Vic,' Levi said.

'That's my favourite,' she said, the walk having calmed her slightly. 'Did you get the burrata flatbread?'

'And the Tuscan kale salad,' Ange said. 'Victoria, our food budget has gone up tremendously since you've worked here.'

'I take that as a compliment,' she said, sitting across from them. She picked up a piece of the flatbread and nibbled on it. She wasn't hungry – not with so much emotion rolling around inside of her – but they'd gone out of their way to make her feel better and she owed it to them to try to enjoy it, especially considering what she was about to do. Levi had no idea what was coming.

She managed another bite of the bread and put it down. They all watched her movement.

'Levi,' she began, but he stood abruptly, and the table shook.

'No, I refuse to accept your resignation.'

Okay, so he did know what was coming. Not that she should be surprised. She and Michael had tried not to fall in love when she was still his manager, but they had. They'd managed to keep it a secret for a few months before finally deciding that they wanted a future together and had to come clean. Levi had shrugged – it was common in Hollywood – but he started managing Michael himself. Still, it was a small, intimate company, and they saw one another at the office almost daily.

'I'm sorry, Levi, but I cannot continue here, knowing I'll see him all the time, and . . . with *her*. He's with someone else,' she finished.

'Already?' Monique gasped.

'How do you know?' Ange asked at the same time.

Victoria slouched lower in her seat. 'When he told me he wanted the house—'

'The Spanish-style house that you loved and he never liked before?' Monique asked.

'Yup,' she said, extending the 'p'. 'I guessed. He confirmed it was true.'

'Who is she?'

Victoria shrugged. 'I don't know.' She turned back to Levi. 'I signed Michael, I nurtured his career, and even though you are officially his manager now, this is a small company. Do you honestly expect me to wake up every morning and come into work and keep telling the world how amazing he is, after everything we've been through?'

Levi sat. 'No, I don't, Victoria. But nor do I expect you to throw away a long, lucrative career that you love. Surely there is another solution.'

'Drop his sorry ass,' Monique said, her teeth clenched. She was never Michael's biggest fan, but finding out about another woman? That was a cut-off for Monique, even though Victoria didn't know all the details yet.

'We can't lose Michael,' Ange began, her eyes wide. 'He's our biggest client – he's probably paying for all Victoria's lunches.' The joke fell flat, but Victoria knew she meant well.

'No, you definitely can't lose Michael as your client – he's too important to the business. So the only solution . . .'

'It is not the only solution; it is simply the only one you are seeing right now, Victoria. Take a week off,' Levi said, nodding. 'In that time, we'll figure something out.'

Victoria resigned herself to giving her friends the time to think it over, but a week ahead with no plans and no work made her suddenly feel panicky and anxious.

'But what will I do?' she asked.

Monique put her arm around Victoria. 'Take a break, relax, go through that goal planner I gave you, remember?'

'Okay,' Victoria nodded. 'I'll take the week off, but when I come back, I can't promise that any solution is going to be one that works for me – I need you to understand that.'

Ange and Levi nodded. They'd been married so long they even nodded at the same pace.

Victoria pulled off a piece of flatbread, smiling suddenly. 'I can try cooking again! I just know with some time and practice, I could be a good cook. How about a dinner party at mine, say, Monday? Do you have plans?'

They all answered at the same time with great enthusiasm.

'Air hockey tournament.'

'Amateur night at the Comedy Club!'

'Actors showcase,' Levi said.

'Wow, good one, boss,' Monique whispered to Levi.

'You both work in talent management and air hockey and amateur night are what you came up with?' he whispered back.

'Wow, really?' Victoria said, impressed and not noticing their whispers. 'I should write those down for my list. There are actual air hockey tournaments? That is so cool! Okay what about Tuesday then?'

'Bingo night!' Monique called, at the same time as Ange's 'book club' and Levi's 'bat mitzvah.'

Victoria looked at them shrewdly. 'Are you guys going through the alphabet making excuses not to come to my house for dinner?'

'No!' they said at the same time.

'We'd love to come, Victoria,' Ange said. 'I mean, obviously not Monday or Tuesday, but later in the week, maybe we can have a potluck at ours?'

'But I want to cook for you guys!' Victoria said. 'I know the last time was a disaster, but—'

'And the time before that,' Levi pointed out.

'And the time before that, too,' Monique reminded her.

'Yes, well,' she said, getting frustrated, 'I was busy then. Distracted. Now, I'll be perfectly focused on one thing only. Cooking. Wednesday is out, but what about Thursday?'

'Date night,' Levi and Ange said together, as Monique was left silent.

Victoria crossed her arms, raised her eyebrows, and looked at Monique.

'We were up to C, for cheaters,' she muttered discreetly.

Levi shrugged unrepentantly. 'She skipped Wednesday. Fair game.'

'Great,' Victoria said sarcastically. 'Monique, my ex-best friend, wins the prize of coming to my house for dinner.' She rolled her eyes. 'Oh, come on. I'm not really that bad, am I?'

'Yes!' the others said as one.

CHAPTER TWO

The week felt endless to Victoria, which was surprising considering how productive she was.

For Christmas one year, Monique had given her a journal called *My Goal Planner*.

'But I do so much already!' Victoria had laughed, flipping through the book.

'You *work* too much, that's for sure. But outside of your job and Michael, what have you really done for fun for yourself in the past few years?' Monique had asked. 'This is supposed to be about the stuff we always say we'll get around to and we never do. Come on, we'll fill some out together.'

She had indulged Monique, but this was around the time she and Michael were talking to the doctors about the IVF treatment, and Victoria, always the optimist, was certain that by the end of the winter she was going to be pregnant.

On the first morning of her forced week off, she went to find that goal planner, but realised she didn't know which box it was in.

During their last fight, Michael had told her that he didn't love her the way that he used to. And that was it for Victoria. She'd fought hard for their relationship, but she didn't want to fight that. She didn't think she could bear it. She'd moved in with Monique while she looked for a new apartment. The house she'd loved was for dreams that could and would never come to be now.

She'd been so excited to decorate the villa to make it a cozy home, but she hadn't even been there long enough to start. After that last devastating revelation from Michael, she'd packed her boxes and eventually moved them into her new rental. They sat there now, largely untouched. It was a nice apartment with a courtyard, close to Venice in Santa Monica, but she'd had no motivation to unpack, let alone decorate it. Until now, with a long week off work ahead of her.

Normally Victoria would be fully invested in a new project, but this didn't feel like a project – more of a quick fix to get to something else, so she went to IKEA, the easiest place to go in and pick out furniture for her one bedroom. By the end of that first day she'd selected new furniture, had it delivered and put it together herself, decorated the apartment and unpacked her few boxes.

She looked around and could barely bring herself to smile. It was so lifeless. So barren.

Like you, she thought to herself.

She shook her head free of the negative thoughts. 'No, Victoria, think positive. Now your apartment can actually be of use. People can sit here now.'

She texted Monique.

Come over for a champagne?

Tinder date. Be there Thursday for dinner. Please don't burn your house down. Or poison me. Uber Eats?

Ha. Ha. Ha. Have fun, get laid! And I will impress the shit out of you with my mad cooking skills on Thursday!

She tried to ignore her gnawing disappointment in the prospect of being alone the next few days with all this time on her hands.

She opened the goal planner she'd found when she unpacked her books. Victoria couldn't help but smile as she went through the list she and Monique had created.

1. Take a hot yoga class (Monique insisted Victoria was the only person in LA who hadn't).
2. Learn to cook (something, anything, without burning it, yourself or your house, Monique had added).

3. Go to a sacred place.
4. Eat out by yourself every night for a week at places you haven't been to before (she never dined out alone).
5. Travel somewhere for at least a week (a month, Monique had corrected, or more!).
6. Do Ancestry.com (finally, one was checked off!).
7. Take a surf lesson.
8. Become a mother.

She sighed. It wasn't as if she'd spent her whole life waiting to have babies and be a mother. The truth was, she hadn't thought about it too much through her twenties, but after a couple of years with Michael, she'd realised that she was in a happy relationship, she was in love, she was engaged and she was nearing thirty. She knew that women could have children much later now, but she didn't know anything about her medical history. She'd always had very irregular periods, and she knew that every year over thirty lessened her chances.

It was still only the beginning of her week off, and Victoria was feeling depressed and aimless. She could beg Levi to at least let her work from home so that she'd have something to focus on, but she knew that wasn't the solution. She loved where she worked and had loved her job, but now Michael was out of her life with absolutely no chance of coming back into it, she had to think about her future.

She managed her own clients who would come with her to another management company, but was that what she wanted? Her career and Michael's had been intertwined for so long she hadn't even really thought about whether she still loved being a talent manager the way she had when she was fresh to LA, or if it was Michael who had excited her. She'd made a career out of seeing the potential in others and working that potential into lucrative careers for her clients.

But what of her own potential?

Her phone dinged.

Just got back from our cruise, Bicky – we wish you could have come with us! Catching up on everything now but we love you! Mom and Dad

Victoria smiled. She didn't have the energy to call her parents yet, but just reading their text made her feel better. She texted them back and then picked up her goal list, deciding it was what she was going to focus on.

'Alright, Victoria, let's get some of these things ticked off the list,' she said, opening her computer. She typed *surf lessons in Venice Beach.*

'Starting with you . . . .'

CHAPTER THREE

'Knock knock!' Monique said in lieu of actually knocking when she arrived on Thursday night.

'Jesus, you scared me to death!' Victoria called from another room. 'That spare key was for emergencies – normal people wait for an invitation!'

'I defy all vampire rules,' she quipped. 'Where are you?'

'Bathroom, be right out. Have a seat!' Victoria said enthusiastically.

'I can see why you invited me around. I finally have somewhere to sit that isn't on top of one of your boxes.' Monique looked around. 'What did you do, rob IKEA?'

'More like IKEA robbed me,' Victoria said, coming out of the bathroom. 'I literally went in and found a kitchen, bedroom and living area, took photos, went to the front and said, "give me these."'

Monique howled with laughter, and Victoria joined her with a chuckle. 'I wish I was joking.'

She stepped into the light to hug Monique, but Monique jumped back. 'Jesus, what happened to your head?!'

Victoria grabbed the champagne bottle that Monique held and took it to the kitchen. 'Number seven.'

'Huh?'

'Look down.'

Monique looked down to Victoria's goal list, her eyes lighting up at number seven. 'You took a surf lesson?! That's awesome!'

'Oh yes, it was brilliant,' Victoria said sarcastically. 'Did you know you can still manage to get six stitches and not stand up on the board, not even once?'

Monique grimaced. 'Well, it's still a cool thing to try. And I mean, battle wounds usually look kind of cool . . .'

But she didn't finish as Victoria sat down beside her with two glasses of champagne. 'I look like Frankenstein, I know.'

Monique pressed her lips together and took the glass Victoria offered. 'Well, I see a lot of ticks here. Let's see. Number one, hot yoga – you finally did a class! Now everyone in LA has, you've rearranged chaos. Well done. How was it?'

Victoria crinkled her nose. 'Hot. And smelly.'

'Ah, someone in there with BO? That sucks.'

'No, farting. What's up with all the farting?'

Monique laughed. 'Girl, you are getting the shit end of the stick on this goal list so far.' She looked down. 'Go somewhere sacred is ticked off. That can't have been too bad?'

'Tried to go to a synagogue,' she said, downing her champagne and pouring another one. 'They didn't let me in.'

'Why? Because you're not Jewish?' Monique asked, confused.

'Neither is Kristen Bell and she got Hot Rabbi on that show we binged,' Victoria said, gracing Monique with a ghost of a smile.

'Well, it's only been a few days, so I know you haven't gone on a big trip, but at least you have your place furnished so you could sublet it at the drop of a hat. Tell me you've had luck at least with some of the food parts. You love eating!' Monique said.

'Considering I once almost burnt down your apartment trying to make two-minute noodles, the eating out at different restaurants part has been a highlight. I *finally* went to Felix, that Italian place on Abbot Kinney. Remember I wanted to go for my birthday, but Michael had stopped eating carbs and started doing that whole protein thing?'

Monique nodded.

'Yeah, that sucked, so I finally went the other day and ordered two pasta dishes back to back because I couldn't decide which one I wanted. It was awesome. Oh! I also went to this new place where they have a set menu only, so I booked for the set menu, and I get there, and they're like, but you're alone? I joked that my invisible friend was with me but not hungry that evening.'

Monique snickered.

'Right?! It's funny! Nobody laughed, and they got all snooty that the set menu was a shared style for a minimum of two people. "So feed me for two," I said to them.'

'What happened?'

'I sat down by myself, put my napkin in my lap and ate a six-course degustation for two. Every. Fucking. Bite.'

Monique raised her glass. 'Represent girl, represent,' she said, toasting Victoria, who was now pouring her third. 'You gonna share that bottle?'

'I poured the cheap stuff first so you can enjoy your nice bottle once I pass out.'

'Class act, Bishop,' Monique said, raising her glass again. 'Oh,' she said, pulling out a stash from her bag. 'I brought your mail.'

Victoria looked at the pile still addressed to her at the house. 'Did you see him?' she asked. 'Or her?' She lowered her voice inadvertently.

Monique shook her head. 'No, they were just on my desk the other day. He hasn't been in and there hasn't been any tabloid stuff or gossip about whoever she is. Yet. Sorry.'

Victoria didn't say anything, so Monique started going through her mail. 'Jeez, haven't you opted out of paper? Huh, this one is big. From Argentina. Remember that night we went to the bar and had way too much tequila and . . .'

'Yes, we came home and drunk-called my parents for all the details and filled in my Ancestry.com,' Victoria finished, pointing to the old ticked-off item on the goal list.

That tequila night, she and Monique had come home and paid for Ancestry.com, then filled it out. A week later, she got her assessment, which didn't tell her much. It said that Anyas, which was the last name on her birth certificate, was a first name of Incan origin, and as a surname, would likely have come from the Andes region of South America, namely Peru, Argentina or Chile. She'd made her profile public, just in case, but nothing ever came of it.

'I know nothing came of it then, but this is from Argentina. Don't you want to open it?' Monique asked.

Victoria got up to check on their dinner. 'Go for it.'

Monique opened the letter and read it. 'Victoria, I think you should read this.'

'Why?' a muffled voice called.

'Do you need help in there?'

'No! Just . . . um . . . give me a minute. So what does it say?'

'It's a pretty official-looking letter from a lawyer in Argentina named Santiago Ceres, who would like you or your lawyer to contact him about a possible inheritance.'

Victoria came back in with the next bottle of champagne, rolling her eyes and topping her up. 'Don't you think my parents would have been the first contacted if anyone knew anything about my heritage?'

'Not if it came from the Ancestry.com thing – remember we made your profile and details public in case anyone had any information.'

'I don't remember leaving my home address, so I say throw it in the fire and drink more champagne!' Victoria said, and burped. 'Scuse me.'

Monique raised an eyebrow and took the champagne bottle, pouring herself one. 'You don't have a fire.'

'Then throw it in the effusively burning pile of my rage and pour me more champagne!' Victoria laughed.

Monique sniffed. 'Actually, what is that smell?'

'My chicken?' Victoria asked. 'I just checked on it. I'm not really sure what it should look or smell like now, but it was a little glassy looking.'

Monique looked at her sharply. 'Tonight, you decide to go for number two?' She stood up and went to the kitchen, Victoria following her.

'Well, it's not like I was trying to make anything special. I went to the supermarket and got the ready-to-cook chicken you told me to get last time, the one that even I couldn't mess up . . . I got it at Whole Foods, so I got mashed potatoes and veggies from the salad bar and threw them in the dish with the chicken,' Victoria explained.

Monique opened the oven door, and the smell overwhelmed the kitchen.

'Good lord!' she said, pulling the tray out. Monique could see different colours dying the chicken. 'Victoria, please tell me that you didn't cook *this* chicken in the plastic bag.'

Victoria's eyes went wide. 'But isn't that what ready-to-go in a bag means?' she asked.

'Oh sweetie,' Monique said, turning off the oven and covering the ruined dish with water until it cooled enough to be tossed out. 'It does, when you get the one in a bag meant to go in the oven. This one is just ready to cook, as in, it is marinated. The bag was just . . . a bag.'

Victoria looked as though she was going to cry.

'Come on, let's go finish our champagne, order takeout and watch a programme.'

'Hot Rabbi?' Victoria asked, tearing up.

'Sure, Hot Rabbi sounds great.' They sat on the couch and Monique ordered Uber Eats. Suddenly Victoria was snoring softly.

Monique took the glass from her and put it on the side table. When she was certain Victoria was asleep, she opened the letter from Santiago Ceres.

'Dear Ms Bishop . . .'

CHAPTER FOUR

A ping from her phone woke Victoria the following morning. She was on the couch, a pillow under her head and a blanket covering her. Courtesy of Monique, she assumed, groaning when she remembered the plastic chicken. She sat up and groaned again as her brain seemed to pound against her head.

'Ugh, champagne,' she muttered, standing up and wobbling slightly as she went to the bathroom and poured a glass of water, taking two ibuprofen. Looking up, she caught her reflection in the mirror. Her mascara was smudged under her eyes, and the still-fresh stitches on her forehead were bleeding slightly.

'Well, Victoria, you officially look as bad as you feel. Well done.'

But she didn't feel like she'd done well at all. In fact, she felt like crawling into bed and not coming back out again for a very long time. Her phone pinged again, and she finally picked it up to see a text from Ange asking her to pop into the office that afternoon.

She didn't bother dressing for work – she was still on leave, and she wanted to go in looking relaxed, like she was enjoying her goal list, even though she wasn't. So, it was in her lululemon tights and sweatshirt, with a tray of everyone's favourite coffee in her hands, that she reached the door to LGM and found herself face to face with Michael and *her*.

Her was a twenty-two-year-old actress named Skye, of all names, an actress that Victoria herself had just recommended Monique sign. She was younger than Michael by a decade, with long dark hair and a mouthful of quirky teeth. She was chock-full of potential, which was probably because she was the daughter of a wildly successful Hollywood director and his actress wife. Skye was a winning deal.

And now she had to walk in every day to see Michael and *her*, LGM's two biggest clients. Together.

'Victoria!' Michael said, pulling his hand from Skye's. But he knew she'd seen, and he ran his fingers through his hair, glancing at Skye.

'Hi, Victoria,' Skye said in acknowledgment. She gave a ghost of a smile and glanced at Michael. 'I'll see you back home?'

Home. The casual way the young actress talked about Victoria's house, *her* home, *her* unrealised future, resonated in her head. Victoria's home was now Michael's. And Skye's. Her hand began to shake.

'Here, let me take the coffees,' he said, taking the tray, then opening the door with his foot and letting her in first.

Once she was through the door, she turned, held the door and took the tray from him.

'Victoria . . .'

But she let the swinging door slam into his face.

'Victoria!'

~

'Why didn't you tell me they were going to be here?' she hissed once she was in Ange's office.

'Because I didn't know,' she said softly. 'I'm sorry. We only just found out.'

Victoria brushed her tears away and took a deep breath. 'I brought you coffee.'

Ange smiled and took the cup.

'You see why I can't stay? This is what it will be like, every week. I need to move on, Ange. I need closure.'

'Yes, I understand . . .'

'And I can only get that if I—'

'You take a sabbatical,' Ange finished for her, overriding her words. At Victoria's confused look, Ange pulled a folder off her desk. 'Six months fully paid. I already got Levi's okay.'

'But I won't come back here,' Victoria said. 'I can't.'

Ange opened the door to check that no one was listening, then closed it, turning to Victoria with her voice lowered.

'How do you know that? Michael and Skye could leave at any time, go to a bigger management company. But even if they didn't, do you have any idea how hard the market is out there right now in the middle of a recession? You have to protect yourself.'

Victoria dropped into a seat and looked up at Ange. 'I cannot even begin to tell you how grateful I am to you both for thinking of me and my future, but a six-month sabbatical? What would I even do?'

'That's exactly why I asked you to come in today,' Ange said. 'Does this look familiar?' she asked, holding a big envelope.

It did look familiar, but Victoria didn't know why. 'Vaguely, why?'

'Because,' Ange said, handing her the envelope, 'Monique brought this to me early this morning and asked me to have a look at it, since, you know, I'm a lawyer. And I can confirm, it is legitimate.'

Confused, Victoria took the envelope. 'What's legitimate?'

'That you have, in fact, inherited a property in Argentina,' Ange said. 'Mendoza, to be precise.'

Victoria gasped. 'But that's impossible. My parents spent years trying to find more information about my heritage and got nothing. You're telling me one drunken night with Monique on Ancestry.com and I inherited a property? That can't be true,' she argued.

'I know, it seems unthinkable,' Ange agreed. 'But this is the world we live in, where the internet and social media can and do actually connect us more than any tool we have ever had in the past. Believe me, that's why I have a job these days. And I took it upon myself to make sure that this information was legitimate before I contacted you. I called Santiago Ceres on your behalf as your lawyer. Thankfully, he speaks English – loudly, I might add – as I'm not fluent in Spanish like you are.' Ange glanced at her. 'Speaking of, Santi, as he calls himself, was quite interested to know how and why you were fluent in Spanish when I mentioned that fact.'

'My parents were adamant that I embrace as much of my heritage that we knew about as possible, so I've been speaking Spanish pretty much since I was born. They only hired Spanish-speaking babysitters and used to take me to all sorts of Central and South American restaurants.' Victoria couldn't help but smile, despite the weight of what she was hearing. 'They wanted me to feel at home when I finally learned something about myself.'

Ange grabbed her hand. 'They did a great job with you. And because of that, you are prepared. I asked Santi to send specs and photos of the land. He sent those, and the will of your grandmother, Luce Anyas de Alveras, who passed away a few months ago. You are the last living relative, and you have inherited a vineyard and house in Argentina.'

Victoria shook her head, but Ange leaned in, grasping her hand. 'I'll show you, but first, you should read the letter yourself.'

'Why?'

'Because this is the first introduction to your long-lost family, Victoria.'

~

Dear Victoria Bishop,

I, Santiago Ceres, and my father before me, have been the lawyers for the Anyas de Alveras family in Mendoza, Argentina, for many decades. Earlier this year, it came to the attention of my client, Luce Anyas de Alveras, that her estranged daughter, Camila Anyas de Alveras, had a child before she passed many years ago. Luce made it her life's mission to find you and introduce you to your legacy here in Mendoza. Unfortunately, she passed in her sleep some months ago, but with the peace that we believed we found you. We spent months tracing the whereabouts of Camila to send for adoption papers, but without knowledge of the year or state, seeing as the adoption happened in a different country, the search seemed ill-fated – until Luce was advised to try the DNA testing on Ancestry.com and see if it matched any public posts. It is here that we found you.

Upon confirmation of your kinship and who we think you may be, I would ask you to come to Argentina to assess your inheritance for yourself, and advise what you, the last of kin, would like to do with the property.

Warm regards
Santiago Ceres
Attorney at Law

'This is actually legit?' Victoria asked for the hundredth time. Monique and Levi were back from their meetings. 'From Ancestry.com?'

'I know, can you believe it?' Monique agreed. 'And we did that Ancestry.com while we were drunk, too. Are you sure it didn't mess with the DNA or something, Ange? I did my DNA test, too. Could they have gotten mixed up?

'Monique,' Ange countered, 'you repeatedly trace your family back to Nigeria for the whole of Black History Month every year. You know more about your family history than most of us put together. Do you really, truly think that your DNA got mixed up with an obvious Argentinian's?'

'No,' Monique answered quietly, sitting back in her chair.

'No, I didn't think so,' Ange said, suppressing a smile. 'It seems as though once they found out you actually existed, they looked for you for quite a while. I checked into the adoption records in Ohio, and they are pretty hard to get into. You have to have full proof that you are related to the person you want to contact before you can contact them, and that is *if* they want to be contacted. Your parents, of course, have your adoption on the open records to be contacted if and when anyone in your family wanted to. But because your birth mother is no longer alive, the family had to go through extra hoops to access your certificate. They had applied, but then, it looks like you and your grandmother both had the grand idea to use Ancestry.com, and that opened doors relatively quickly.'

'Not quickly enough,' Victoria said.

'What do you mean?' Monique asked. 'This is amazing news!'

'It is,' Ange agreed, glancing at Victoria. 'Unfortunately, Victoria's grandmother, Luce, passed earlier this year. Natural causes.'

Monique and Levi both turned their heads.

'I'm sorry, Victoria,' Levi said.

'I had Santi send me over some specs of the land and property. Shall we have a look?'

'Yes!' Levi and Monique said together.

Victoria and Ange looked at them, raising their eyebrows.

'I was asking Victoria,' Ange said, turning to her. 'Shall we?'

Victoria nodded, and Ange pulled up a file on her laptop titled 'Las Viñas'.

'Oooh, that sounds sexy and romantic. I wonder what it means?' Monique asked no one in particular.

'It means "the vines",' Victoria said, rolling her eyes. Then she leaned in. 'Is all that the land? It looks really big.'

'According to Santi, it's a relatively small property,' Ange answered, opening the same file on her phone. 'About fifteen acres of grapevines. It was a vineyard apparently, back in the day.'

'What does that mean, back in the day?' Victoria asked.

Ange shrugged. 'Santi was a bit vague on that front. But I looked at it on Google Earth. You are talking heart of wine country in Argentina. See,' she said, pointing to the picture on her computer. 'It looks beautiful, doesn't it? Santi said you had to come down and see for yourself.'

Victoria laughed. 'Seriously? Just fly down to Argentina and go check out some random land from some random person?'

'Once the DNA tests, which I've ordered and paid for, confirm things, then yes.'

Victoria looked back at the screen of the computer. It was unlike any land she'd seen before, the Google Earth picture highlighting the peaks of the Andes mountains. Her heart raced suddenly. The Andes region, where it was said the name Anyas came from. These mountains, this land that she was looking at on the screen. This was where she came from. Suddenly it was hard for her to breathe, and she reached for her chest instinctively.

'So, I was thinking,' Ange said quietly, coming to her side, 'that maybe you take your sabbatical and go to Argentina.'

'Victoria Bishop, our woman with a mission,' Levi agreed, standing beside them.

'The perfect project for the next few months,' Monique said, joining them and looking at the screen. 'Is that a house on the property?' she asked, pointing to an outline.

'A rather large one, I'm told,' Ange answered, glancing at Victoria. 'Victoria, the exchange rate on our dollar is excellent at the moment. I reckon if you make this one of your famous projects, you could sell this property for a value that would keep you comfortable for a while, especially if you took the time to get it well and truly saleable.'

'And . . .' Monique added.

'And what?' Victoria asked.

'And this might be exactly what you need right now, to move on from the most shit year of your life. Embrace the gift, Vic,' Monique pleaded.

As Victoria looked down at the computer screen, the blurred images of the green vines started to come to life, as did something inside her. It felt a little bit like hope.

~

Victoria was packing up the last of her personal things into a locked cupboard in her apartment, while Monique opened a bottle of wine and poured two glasses, handing one to Victoria.

Victoria looked at it with hesitation. Her hangover from Monique's last visit had taken two days to clear.

'Don't worry, I'm pouring tonight. And you know champagne always gives you a headache. You'll be safe with wine. Cheers, my girl,' she said, clinking her glass to Victoria's.

Victoria let out a laugh. 'What are we toasting to?'

'Hrm, what to choose?' Monique said, taking a sip. 'Let's see, I brought a Malbec, so we can toast to Argentina? Or finally being free of that douchebag Michael and his new super-tramp?' She looked around 'Or, subletting this sexy-ass apartment of yours straight away. I can't believe you own a property in Argentina. And that you're picking up and *going*. Respect, girl,' she said, raising her glass again. 'You've inherited like, a house, and a vineyard. In a different country. I feel like we're making a Lifetime movie or something.'

'I know, right?' Victoria agreed. 'But apparently it happens more often than you'd think. The property has been in my birth family for over a century.'

Victoria tried to sound casual, but Monique knew her too well. It was impossible for Victoria to even begin to comprehend, let alone share, the many things she was feeling right then. First, finding out she couldn't have children, then losing her fiancé. Then learning she had a family that had been desperately seeking her, only to find out she was the last of the line. She would never meet them, never know what it felt like to have a true blood relative. And if that wasn't enough, she wouldn't have anyone to pass this new legacy down to. The grief within her was sometimes consuming.

And yet, there was something else – a tingle of excitement, of knowing that even if she was the last, she came from somewhere. She had a heritage, and soon she would know more about it. She would be from somewhere. A place with a name. Even if she never connected with it, even if she went down and assessed the property and sold it, which was the logical thing to do, it still existed.

Monique took her hand. 'You know how much I hate it when people say that maybe this is for the best. I mean, it's like, the opposite of the truth, which is that people only say that when the worst thing that could have ever happened to you has happened.'

Victoria let out a choked laugh.

'So look, this is the worst year of your life. First the IVF, then Michael and the house, now the super-bitch. Worst. Year. Ever.'

'Is there a "but" in there? Anything positive at all?' Victoria asked.

'Nope,' Monique said, pointing to her glass, 'only this. Oh, and that perhaps someone taking your old life has set you free to live the life that you want instead.'

'But I don't know what I want,' Victoria said, sinking into her chair. 'Not now.'

'Maybe not right now,' Monique said softly, sitting beside her, 'but you are a strong, beautiful, amazing woman, and you will heal from this. I mean, this *has* to be you done for the year.'

Victoria let out a wavering laugh. 'Right, I mean, what could go wrong? I apparently inherited a vineyard in Argentina. Mr Santi Ceres is picking me up from Mendoza to take me to my "family home". I suppose I could just go down there and accidentally curse all of it?'

Monique smiled. 'There's my pragmatically dramatic and dark best friend. Always looking on the bright side. So are you going back to Ohio to see Frank and Joyce on the way?

Victoria nodded. 'My parents were so worried about me when I called that I promised I'd fly home for a couple of days before I went to Argentina.'

'Your 'rents are the best, man. So do you need a lift to the airport tomorrow?'

'Yes, please,' Victoria said. 'I don't know what I'd do without you.'

'I don't either,' Monique said, pouring them each another glass. 'But I do have the perfect toast,' she said. 'To new beginnings.'

'To new beginnings,' Victoria agreed.

CHAPTER FIVE

It was nearly 7 pm when Victoria landed in Cleveland, Ohio. Once she collected her bags, she went through arrivals to find a huge sign with her childhood nickname on it: 'Vicky Bicky'. At thirty-two years old, it should have embarrassed her, but instead she laughed as she saw her dad grinning abashedly. Frank Bishop looked nothing like her, which made sense given he was not her biological father. He was in his early sixties, fair skinned with curling salt and pepper hair, and a face that always understood, had laughter, had love. His was never a face that judged. She ran to him as if she were a child again.

'I love the sign, Dad,' she whispered, and tears unexpectedly came to her eyes. Like he always knew, he knew it then, and gently rubbed her back, holding her tight, until she stopped crying.

'Look at you!' he said, finally pulling back from her. 'Look how pretty my girl is! You don't look so healthy though – you need your mom to fatten you up. Come on, come on. I circled the lot and parked in the fifteen-minute zone, so we'll have to run for it.'

The drive to her childhood home was quiet. Frank liked the long silences, but as they got closer to home, he pulled the car over.

Victoria sat up, alert. 'Dad, what is it?'

'Okay, kiddo, me and you, we got a couple things we've got to talk about before we get home, because your mom is the world to me and I don't want to upset her.'

Victoria took a deep breath, waiting.

'I think your mom's got some sort of fillers or Botox or something. You can't tell, she looks just the same. But she keeps waiting for me to say something and I don't know what. So I just say to her every day how hot she looks and initiate the sex quite regularly.'

'Dad!' she yelled, holding her ears. 'Did not need to know!'

He ignored her. 'She thinks I'm reacting perfectly, but I know she needs a woman to tell her she looks great. I know you people. You think you're looking all pretty for us but really you're looking all pretty for each other. So that's the first thing you say to your mom, okay?'

'Yup, got it, Dad.'

They pulled up to the house a few minutes later. Joyce, Victoria's adoptive mom, was cooking dinner while singing and dancing to the latest P!nk song, her hair in a blonde bun.

'Hi, Mom!' Victoria called loudly over the music.

Joyce didn't seem to hear. She was swinging her hips and singing along. Frank tilted his head and stared at Joyce's bottom.

'Ugh, Dad!' Victoria complained.

'Don't worry, kiddo, I got this,' he stage-whispered, then went over to Joyce and tickled her from behind. Joyce screamed and the flipper flew out of her hand, the skillet of pancakes falling onto the stove with a heavy crash.

'Frank! You scared the bejeezus out of me!' she yelled, hand over her heart. 'Honey!' she cried, raising her arms and pulling Victoria into a warm hug, rocking her back and forth a little too strongly. 'My girl, oh we've missed you! Look, I'm making breakfast for dinner. That used to be your favourite, remember?' She kissed Victoria's forehead and Victoria relaxed into her embrace, something deeply coiled inside her releasing.

'It's still my favourite, and I've missed you guys too,' she said, winking at her dad. 'Mom, you look amazing! Have you been doing those face yoga apps I sent you?'

Joyce glowed. 'No, I got Botox, but your dad doesn't know! He thinks I'm growing this beautiful naturally. Don't tell him!'

she quickly whispered in Victoria's ear as Frank came past them, turning off the music and flipping the pancakes that were starting to brown too much on one side.

'I got that, Frank. Go sit at the table while I finish up here. I've got your newspaper open to the crosswords. You two used to love doing those together when you were little, Bicky. Do you remember?'

'Course I do. Do you still do it every Saturday, Dad?'

'Yup. Getting pretty good, too. Almost finished one a couple weeks ago without googling once. Not that your mom is any help.'

'She still as bad as ever?'

'I reckon she's gotten a lot worse, if you can believe.'

'I have not!' Joyce huffed. 'Occasionally I get a really good one.'

Frank and Victoria sat at the wooden kitchen table, the same one she'd sat at as a child. Frank had renovated most of the house over the years, but the kitchen and dining room looked exactly the same. It was comforting to Victoria.

Joyce brought them both iced tea, and Frank sharpened his pencil, rubbing his hands together, excited to get started.

'Okay, kiddo. One across. *Capital city of Brazil.*'

'Rio de Janeiro!' Joyce answered, pronouncing the J.

Frank scrunched his eyebrows and counted the boxes. 'Too many letters,' he said.

'But that's the capital of Brazil! That crossword is wrong!' Joyce complained, plating the pancakes on the side while she cracked eggs into the skillet.

'Brasília,' Victoria said.

'B – R – A – Z – ' Frank started, writing with his pencil.

'It's an "s" Dad,' she corrected.

'Damn,' he grumbled, erasing and correcting it. 'Hate erasing on the first word, it's bad luck.'

'Not even a real place,' Joyce muttered under her breath.

'Okay, two across. *Night sky observers*.'

'Stethoscopes!' Joyce called. Frank and Victoria both quietly chuckled.

'I think you mean telescopes, Mom,' Victoria said.

'That's what I said!' Joyce pulled the sizzling bacon strips out of a cast iron pan and plated them next to the pile of fried eggs. 'Grab some plates, Bicky, and some forks and knives.'

Victoria did as she was told as Joyce brought over the plates of pancakes, eggs and bacon. The syrup and butter were already on the table. Joyce made them all plates of stacked pancakes with eggs on top and bacon on the side like they used to have every Sunday. Victoria smiled and nibbled on some bacon.

'*Kama Sutra position named after a flower*,' Frank asked next.

'Lotus!' Joyce exclaimed, mouth full.

Frank looked closely at the page, putting his glasses on his nose. Impressed, he filled it in, nodding. 'By golly, she's finally got one.'

'Of course I did, and I'm surprised you even had to ask. That's the one we just tried last weekend, remember, after . . .'

'Mom! No sex talk over breakfast! Jeez, you two!' Victoria muttered, covering her ears.

'Okay, sweetheart, we'll talk about something else then,' Joyce said soothingly, taking a bite of her pancake. She winked at Frank and gave him a suggestive smile.

'Eye sex included!'

They both chuckled.

'Now then, honey, you know how thrilled we are to have you back for a visit, but we are worried. This news about a property in Argentina must have upset you so much. As parents, we always want to find out first, and we felt just terrible we were in Florida when this Santi person contacted you. We always did our best to make your information available,' Joyce said, twisting her fingers into knots.

Victoria pulled one foot up onto her chair. 'I know, and you did a great job. You've told me everything you know about my birth mother, but I thought we could just go through it one more time, and I could write it all down and refresh my memory before I go to Mendoza. Would that be okay?'

Frank put the paper down and glanced at Joyce, who had put her fork down. 'Of course it is, honey. We always wanted to find out more for you, but it was a closed adoption. That meant . . .'

'She didn't ever want me to find her or know who she was,' Victoria cut in. It had always hurt, that bit of information, when she was old enough to know what a closed adoption was.

'Oh, sweetheart,' Joyce said, stroking Victoria's hand. 'She was very young and not in a good place. We don't know much. We adopted you from birth at the hospital here in Cleveland. We'd been on the waiting list for so long, and finally, finally, it was our turn.'

'Never knew we could have got so lucky, Bicky,' Frank said, blowing his nose. 'You never even cried.'

'Ha!' Joyce huffed. 'You just snored too loudly to hear her. Cried all the time,' she said lovingly. 'Anyway, you were about two when we got the call from the agency that your birth mom had passed. They always had to let the other party know about the death of a parent. They said her name was Camila Anyas. From Argentina, but a US citizen by then. Not married, no next of kin. She died very suddenly in an accident so no time to have righted any wrongs. Otherwise, honey, we know she would have.'

Victoria knew all of this; her parents had always told her everything they knew. Still, she was frustrated and deflated, hoping that perhaps there was something she would have forgotten or missed, or that they had held back.

'She must have shortened her name to Anyas. The lawyer I talked to in Argentina, Santi, said my family name was Anyas de Alveras. I wonder what that means.'

'Well, you'll find out soon enough, honey. We're so proud of you for being such a beautiful person. I know that bad things happen to good people sometimes, like this year for you,' Frank said, moving his chair next to hers and wrapping his arms around her. 'But good things always end up happening for good people, too. I know that all this, all this new scary stuff about your family and your heritage, about Argentina, is shrouded in mystery right now, but I think it's gonna be a really good thing.'

'You do?' she asked, tucking her head into his shoulder and glancing up at Joyce, who smiled and sat on her other side, hugging her into a sandwich between her parents.

'We really do,' they said together.

CHAPTER SIX

After two days with her parents and a twenty-one-hour journey, Victoria arrived in Mendoza. It was a small city, with not many tall buildings, but instead more of a neighbourhood sprawl. The architecture surprised her, with a combination of old Spanish-style buildings similar to some in Los Angeles, modern concrete blocks and a surprising amount of 1920s art deco thrown in. It felt a bit mismatched yet filled with life. Her taxi weaved in and out of the gridded town, and as they reached the centre, the streets became wider, leafy, filled with parks and people dining outdoors and strolling. Some of the streets were pedestrian only, near where her guesthouse was.

It was a lovely little place called Pousada Luz, a classic Spanish house with only a few rooms, but a gorgeous courtyard garden for sitting and reading, a library, and shared dining spaces in the main house littered with antique furniture. The owners, Ignacio and Serena, greeted her and invited her to join the small table of other guests enjoying breakfast, even though she'd only just checked in.

Victoria replied in Spanish, and there was a collective cheer from the table.

'Yes! We got one!'

A woman in her early fifties hopped up from the table and took her arm. 'We've all been here for a couple of days and none of us, if you can believe it, speak Spanish,' she said in a very American accent, pointing to the other five people at the table. They all smiled warmly. 'Come, join us.'

'Oh,' Victoria said, 'thank you, but I need to get some sleep. Twenty hours travel . . .'

'No!' they all cried at the same time.

'You never sleep during the day, no matter how tired you are, don't you know that? That's how you get the jetlag. Come on, have some breakfast and push through the day. You'll thank us later,' the woman said. 'I'm Kelly, and this is my husband, Matt. We're on vacation from Florida. This here is a lovely young couple on their honeymoon from Germany, how sweet are they? Kristin and Felix.'

The younger couple waved and smiled. Victoria guessed they

were probably in their late twenties. The last two people were smiling blonde women in their forties.

'I'm Anne, this is my sister, Collette. We were in Buenos Aires for Collette's daughter's wedding and decided to make a holiday of it. Not a quick trip from Ireland either,' Anne said. 'May as well stay a while.'

'I'm Victoria,' she said, introducing herself. She did remember that saying about not sleeping during the day, so she had decided to try to relax for the next few days before Santi Ceres would pick her up. Perhaps she could even enjoy herself. It had been far too long.

'Lettie,' Anne said to Collette while getting up, 'get this poor girl a coffee. They make a mean French press, don't worry, you'll be right as rain in no time. Here, I'll introduce you to the best breakfast spread in Argentina.'

'Do you take milk in your coffee?' Collette, or Lettie, asked from the table.

'Just sugar, thank you,' Victoria said to a collective chuckle. 'Is that against the rules in Argentina?'

'Not at all,' Anne said, 'but you might want to make up your plate first. Argentinian breakfast consists mostly of sugar, sugar and more sugar.'

'And carbs!' Matt said. 'I went keto earlier this year to try to lose some weight. Not possible here.'

'Try the medialunas if you just want something simple and not too sweet,' Kristin said.

'Those,' Anne said, pointing to a plate of pastries. 'Like croissants but smaller and a bit more dense. Delicious. And these are churros. You'll probably recognise them, but they have a twist, and that is the most famous thing on the table – dulce de leche.'

'I didn't know that was Argentinian,' Victoria said.

'Don't let them hear you say that,' Anne said in a whisper. 'Here, dulce de leche is its own food group, and rightly so. And it's in *everything*. These are bolas de fraile filled with the stuff. Like donuts.'

'Balls of weakness,' Victoria said, smiling. 'That's what it translates to.' She picked one up, along with a medialuna. 'Half-moon.'

'Ah,' the group said, like it all made sense.

'This one is a librito,' Anne said, putting a filo-style pastry on her plate. 'What does that mean?'

'Libro means book,' Victoria said. 'So, little book, I suppose, though I've not heard that word before.'

'Excellent! I love that the names of the food match what they look like!' Kelly said, enthusiastically eating.

'There is also toast with cream cheese, Serena's homemade jam, and of course . . .'

'Dulce de leche,' they all said.

Victoria felt refreshed by the company and surrounded by sweet treats and the lure of coffee. She took a seat with the group.

Serena smiled and brought her an orange juice. 'Freshly squeezed,' she said.

'So, Victoria,' Collette said, 'tell us all about yourself. You sound like you're from the US, like Kelly and Matt?'

'Yes, I live in Los Angeles,' she began, then paused. 'But actually, I'm taking a six-month sabbatical to have a look at a property I just found out I inherited here in Mendoza.'

The group responded with delight and enthusiasm, and Victoria, for some reason, felt excited. What was it about being surrounded by strangers that suddenly made her feel like she was free to embrace this unexpected gift?

'What kind of a property?' Kelly said, taking a bite of her medialuna.

'Well, I'm not actually sure just yet,' Victoria said. 'You see, I'm adopted, and I never knew anything about my history or my family. And then, after my ex-fiancé decided to buy me out of our house so he could move his new young actress girlfriend in . . .'

There was a collective gasp.

'I know, right? Then I got news that my birth family was trying to find me because I have apparently inherited a house and vineyard here in Argentina. So then . . .'

~

'Do you think it might be one of these vineyards, Victoria?' Anne asked.

They all looked out the windows of the minibus that was taking them south of the city into a valley of vineyards with the mountains beyond them. Victoria had decided to join them at the last minute a few hours after breakfast, when her coffee and sugar high was wearing off and she was getting dangerously close to taking a nap.

She looked around at the manicured vineyards they drove past and shook her head. The beauty of the region was overwhelming. And she could feel something within her stirring, but she didn't know what it was. As they drove closer to the Andes, she had a distinct feeling, a pull, to a place she didn't know yet. Her arm drifted out of the open window, and it felt as though something was reaching out to her, something primitive and longing, that she wanted to reach back to with all of her soul.

'No,' she answered, pulling her arm back into the van. 'The map showed the property quite a bit further out of Mendoza than we are going today. Santi called it Las Viñas.'

'Las Viñas simply translates to The Vines,' Pablo, their tour guide, said.

'I know. I thought maybe it was a nickname of a place the locals knew about?'

Pablo shook his head. 'There is a very small village about an hour's drive from here that I think is called Las Viñas, but there were no working vineyards on it. Was there another name? A family name? That is what most of the bodegas are named after.'

'Anyas de Alveras,' Victoria said, looking at Pablo hopefully. The group all leaned in.

'Alveras, Alveras . . .' he said aloud. 'It is familiar, but of course it is a very common name.' He looked down at the vineyard map in his hands. 'I don't see it on here. I am new to the region, though, so don't take my word for it. The wine region here is quite old, originally planted in 1581 by Jesuit priests and monks from Spain for communal wine. But it wasn't until the mid-nineteenth century that commercial wineries started being planted and the region began to take itself more seriously, especially with the introduction of Malbec in 1876. It just took to the land so well, many believe, because of the terroir effect from the Andes. Some of the vineyards in Mendoza are planted at the highest altitude in the world.'

'Oh,' the group said, interestedly, glancing out to the mountains around them.

Victoria leaned forward to see the grandeur before her. The famous Andes mountains lay ahead, like a walled fortress surrounding the lush valley they were coming into, now that the city lay behind them. Snow was atop the mountains although it was early October.

'Is there always snow? Even this close to summer?' she asked.

'Not always, but often. The highest peak is Mount Aconcagua,' Pablo said, pointing ahead. 'If you are all here long enough, you should do a day trip to Parque Provincial Aconcagua, where you can take a horse trek or walk in the high country near the highest summit. My friend runs an expedition company that does a seven-day horse trek through the mountains to Santiago. You ride, you camp, meet fellow travellers. Plus, whether you do a day trip or an expedition, you have a traditional asado meal every night. Do you know asado?'

'That's like a big meat barbeque, right?' Matt asked, pulling up the pictures on his phone. 'That'd probably be keto, Kels.' They all looked at his phone.

'Hope no one is a vegetarian,' Pablo laughed. 'Not the best country for it. Though at the winery where we'll have lunch today, their specialty is the provoleta, which is a type of cheese.'

Despite being new, Pablo turned out to be an excellent guide, and Victoria learned an enormous amount about the history of the region and the wines that day, while having great fun with her new friends. They learned about the subregions of East Mendoza, San Rafael, the Uco Valley and Maipú, though they spent their afternoon in Luján de Cuyo, which was the original name of the wine region. They did wine tours and sipped award-winning red wines like Malbec and Cabernet Sauvignon, and whites such as Chardonnay and Torrontés.

When they got to the beautiful winery restaurant for lunch, they ordered a bottle of the crisp aromatic Torrontés that had been a favourite of all, followed by a rich yet minerally Chardonnay.

'Anyone want to share some things on the menu?' Victoria asked.

'Yes, please,' Felix said, and Kristin nodded. 'I love when people order for me.'

'Order away, Victoria,' Collette said. 'Only you can read the menu, and you should practice being a local now you're going to be here for a few months.'

'Buenas tardes,' Victoria said, turning to the waiter and ordering in Spanish. She wanted to order everything on the delectable menu. 'La provoleta, por favor, y las mollejas – se ven divines.'

'I got provoleta from Pablo telling us about it – it's that mozzarella-like cheese, right?' Matt asked.

She nodded.

'What was that second one you ordered, Victoria?' Kristin asked.

'Sweetbreads,' she said, hesitating.

'Oooh, I love that name, sounds tasty,' Kelly said.

Anne snickered, and Victoria grinned and continued. She ordered humitas – sweet and savoury corn cakes steamed in the husks of the corn itself – and added some spicy beef empanadas. The waiter began to walk away.

'Disculpe! Y el ojo de bife con chimichurri,' she added. She hadn't had the famous Argentinian steak yet.

'Good lord, Victoria, it's only lunch!' Matt said. 'What are you, a chef or something?'

Victoria laughed, refreshed by the glass of wine in her hand and the invigorating Argentinian air, but especially by the thought of all this delicious food coming out.

'Actually, anything but. I love food. I think I was born a foodie. One of my clients in LA is a chef and now has a cooking show on television. She is my absolute hero, and I am constantly getting her to send me recipes, but I am appalling. I swear, in my next life, I will be a chef.'

'Hey, maybe your vineyard could turn into a famous winery restaurant!' Kristin enthused. 'And you could start your new life as a chef.'

Victoria laughed. 'You're forgetting the "absolutely appalling cook" part of the story,' she said. 'Not to mention the fact that I am only here for a few months. I can't move to Argentina – my whole life is back in Los Angeles.'

'No,' Collette said, 'your old life is back in Los Angeles. You've got the rare opportunity that most people never get.'

'Which is?'

'You get the chance to start over. To have a clean slate. It might not have been pretty getting here, but now that you are, embrace it. You never know what life is going to throw at you until you open yourself up to taking the hit.'

At that moment, the waiter came out.

'Empanadas de carne, humitas, y la mollejas,' he announced, and Victoria translated.

'The empanadas, sweet corn cakes and sweetbreads,' she said.

'So what exactly are sweetbreads?' Kelly asked, taking a bite of one. They all did, moaning their enjoyment.

'Pancreas,' Victoria announced, biting into the delicious offal. 'And done to perfection.'

At that, there was a collective slide of unfinished plates to the middle of the table. But as the wine was poured, the group became more adventurous, and by the time the steak came out, they had finished every bite of everything Victoria had ordered. They savoured the complexity of the dishes and talked about each one, dreaming up the menu for Victoria's famous winery restaurant over a couple of bottles of wine. Victoria had to admit to herself that she hadn't felt this free in years.

Lying in bed that night, exhausted to the bones but happy, Victoria thought about how long it had been since she'd travelled for anything other than work.

In college, she and her girlfriends used to take trips around the US, Canada and Mexico on school breaks, and she always loved the food, but more than that, she loved the idea of becoming a person who was created by her own experiences and not by her past. Travelling had suited her. She'd gone on her first overseas trip to Europe with her friends after graduation. There were five of them, and they bought Eagle Creek backpacks and rolled their clothes into them while they took the trains and buses through Italy, Spain, France, Germany. They stayed in hostels and did silly things, had the best time.

When she got back from that trip, Victoria got the job at LGM. She had loved travelling and was thrilled when she realised she'd be travelling for her new job, sometimes every weekend. When she started managing Michael, they often had weekend trips together.

Thinking of Michael as she drifted to sleep, a memory came, unbidden, of her and Michael at South by Southwest in Austin, Texas. They'd spent the whole weekend at events like the premiere for an independent film Michael was in, and on the last night Michael wanted to ditch the after-party to go see an Irish band that he'd recently seen in Los Angeles. After the performance, they were sitting at the bar with the singer, a striking woman named Siobhan, who had the most amazing voice. They were all laughing and having shots of whiskey. Michael got up to go to the bathroom, and he tripped a little. Victoria caught him, laughing, and he leaned in and kissed her.

'Be right back, baby,' he said, slurring again.

She giggled and turned to Siobhan, whose eyes were wide and guilty. Her mouth was open.

'I'm so sorry,' she said. 'I didn't know. I thought you were his manager.'

'I am,' Victoria slurred, laughing.

'I thought you were only his manager. As I said, I'm sorry, I didn't know,' Siobhan said, taking her drink and leaving the bar to sit with friends.

Victoria had been confused at the time but brushed it off as soon as Michael had come back from the bathroom and kissed her again. But now she looked back and wondered. Had Michael been unfaithful to her with Siobhan? Had he been unfaithful to her with Skye or had they really met after Victoria and Michael had broken up, as he suggested? Everything about the beginning of their relationship was passionate and exciting – the parties, the travel, Michael's sudden rise to fame. And the slightly illicit sneaking around when they were home made it even more tantalizingly sexy. Had she been blinded by love, by the excitement, by Michael's charm? Had she created a relationship between them that felt more substantial than it really was because of her desire to have a family, to have this dream life she'd thought she wanted with him? Were they ever really in love, she and Michael?

Was this truly the start of a new life, a better one, as Monique had said?

She didn't even have the strength left to finish her thought as she fell into a dreamless sleep, on the last night of her old life.

~

'I'm still voting Bodega Victoria de Delicioso,' Matt said, after they finished breakfast the next morning.

'And in perfect Florida Spanglish no less,' Victoria teased, and they all laughed. Victoria was sad to say goodbye to her new friends, who had made this transition so enjoyable. 'Are you heading back home today?'

'Back to the ole US of A,' Kelly said sadly. 'What about the rest of you?'

Collette and Anne were headed to what they called an estancia in Las Pampas, to horseback ride for a few days before heading back to Buenos Aires.

'May the road rise to meet you all,' Anne said, kissing Victoria's cheek, then Kelly's and Matt's.

'Viel Glück, Victoria,' Kristin and Felix said together, doing the same.

'We are making our way down to Bariloche and the Lake District,' Kristin said. 'We missed the ski season in the lakes, but the springtime is supposed to be luscious with the flowers and hikes. You must look us up if you come down, Victoria.'

'I will,' she promised, returning their cheek kisses.

After saying goodbye to her new friends, she had a day exploring the city of Mendoza itself. It had a small but bustling centre with leafy avenues and plazas, although it was a desert town. There were fountains and city parks, the most famous being the Parque General San Martin with its lake and rose garden. Then there were the Church and Ruins of San Francisco, the central Plaza Independencia and the amazing views from the Cerro de la Gloria monument.

She filled her day with sightseeing and more food, strolling the lively Avenida Arístides Villanueva near her guesthouse, where the streets were bursting with outdoor diners enjoying the balmy evening. She tried juicy pears wrapped in locally cured ham, chicken livers from the grill and Patagonian lamb leg. Argentinian food, paired with amazing wine, suited her purpose – pure escapism from the reality she was to face the following morning.

CHAPTER SEVEN

Victoria was feeling incredibly anxious as she checked out of Pousada Luz, but when she turned to see a short man in a grey suit with a friendly smile, she gave a hesitant wave. His mouth opened to a wide grin, a few teeth missing in the back.

'Ms Bishop?' he asked.

'Victoria would be preferable,' she replied. 'Mr Ceres?'

'Santi would be preferable,' he said with the same easy grin. She smiled back, relaxing.

'Thank you for replying to me. I recognise it was quite an unconventional way to approach you,' he admitted. 'But I felt I was out of options.'

'I am lucky to have a lawyer as a colleague and close friend who was able to advise me. Even she agreed that while

Ancestry.com was unconventional in the past, it is the way of the future. I am . . . well, I'm quite overwhelmed, of course, but I am so happy that you found me,' she said sincerely, blushing.

'Though your grandmother never got to know you, the very knowledge that you existed made her joyful. She was thrilled to know that we thought we had found you. She died very peacefully because of that. I know it must not mean much to you now, but I assure you, had she known you, you would have brought her the greatest joy. Come, come, let's get to your property, shall we? You've come such a long way!' Santi said as he guided her to a small car outside, opening the door for her. 'Is this your first time in Mendoza?'

'Yes. First time in Argentina,' she said, putting on her seatbelt. 'You seem to know a lot about my family.'

'My family has been the Anyas de Alveras family lawyer for many years. My father was the family lawyer before me, back in the day when the vineyard was still thriving.'

'I've been asking around and no one has heard of Las Viñas. They just keep looking at me, confused, because Las Viñas . . .'

'Means "the vines",' he said, pulling out into the light traffic. 'It is actually the name of the small village around the vineyard as well. Though I doubt many outsiders would remember it. Back when this region was developing, the villages would grow around wherever offered the jobs. Las Viñas was one of the earliest working vineyards and created many jobs, therefore the village formed around it. That would have been in the 1920s and 30s, I imagine. This region has quite a long history, you know. Las Viñas was not the first place vines were planted by any means. That would have been somewhere back in the 1500s by some Spanish priest. But La Abuela of Las Viñas, she was special. It was the most successful vineyard in Mendoza for over fifty years. It wasn't until the early 1970s that the vineyard was nicknamed *Las Viñas Malditas*.'

'The cursed vines?' Victoria sputtered, startled. She'd made that joke to Monique, but it was just that – a joke.

'That's right, you speak Spanish. It will help,' he said, manoeuvring through the traffic. 'Las Viñas isn't actually cursed – well it is, but it isn't dead, as some think. The roots live and thrive; they simply don't go through the growing cycle. No bud burst, no flowers – which means no grapes. From what I hear, at least. One can never know with curses.'

'I should have known,' Victoria muttered, leaning back in her seat. 'A cursed vineyard. A cursed woman.'

'Oh, are you cursed, too?' Santi asked, winking at her. 'Perhaps then you are the one to lift the curse here. It is said only the last Anyas de Alveras would lift the curse. Or was it the last of the line? Or did the line have to die off? I'm sure none of us remember it exactly, but I am certain everyone will be very confused and very excited to meet you and see what happens with our cursed vineyard while you're here!' he said enthusiastically.

Victoria looked longingly back to the dwindling city of Mendoza behind them, when she'd been so excited earlier to meet her vineyard.

'There's a car at the hacienda,' Santi said, noticing her look. 'Your grandmother's. So you'll be able to come and go as you please. The property is about an hour's drive closer to the mountains from Mendoza,' Santi said, pointing ahead. 'The Andes. That's Aconcagua. You should do a trip. It would be beneficial for you in particular.'

'Yes, I heard about the trip through the mountains. Why do you think it would be a great opportunity for me *in particular*?' she asked, glancing at him as he pulled onto an empty back road.

'It is all steeped in mystery, your heritage, and that of your land,' Santi said. 'Alejandro Alveras was one of the Spanish immigrants that came through the Andes from Chile to Mendoza in the nineteenth century. He was lost in the mountains – his group gone, his horse dead – when a young woman found him. She was a daughter of one of the native tribes of the mountains, Inca-born, they say. Her name was Anyas, and she saved Alejandro Alveras and fell in love with him. When he recovered, he finished his journey through the mountains to the land in Mendoza, then called Cuyo, where they planted a vine he had brought over from Spain that Anyas had nourished with her gift.

'They called her the first vine, which we now call "La Abuela," and built a vineyard on the land, the Anyas de Alveras land. Or so it is said,' he smiled. 'Even though there are millions of vines now in Mendoza, to the few of us who know this story, she is still La Abuela of Las Viñas.'

Victoria took a deep breath as she absorbed the almost magical tale of her heritage. She knew, like everyone, that there had been people before her, that she had her own history. But it was almost as if she had cut that off as a child, separated from the blood that didn't seem to matter. What did it matter where you came from? It only mattered where you were going. Your bloodline is not who you are. You choose your family. So many quotes, so many years.

So many lies to herself.

It did matter. To her. Who she was. And now she had a history, and not only that of her mother and grandmother, but of a line of women who had a gift with the land, a passed-down magic. And a curse.

'Here we are coming through the first of the local villages before we get to Las Viñas,' Santi said, pointing out the window. 'This is the closest and largest township, San Alejandro. Back when Las Viñas was growing, this would have been the "city centre". Always in Mendoza towns there is the plaza, or the large square in the middle. This is San Alejandro's.'

He drove them around the square.

'That is BeBi's, and next door there is Reno's, a hardware store,' he pointed. 'Adriana's is the best local market for food and wine outside of Mendoza. Actually, people from the city come down to buy food from Adriana, who works with the best butcher in the area, Eduardo. There's a pharmacy too, and a church if you are so inclined. But very important to support the locals here, especially since . . . you know . . .'

'What?'

He shrugged. 'You're you.'

Victoria had no idea how to respond to that, so she asked her most important question. 'Did you know my mother?'

'Camila?' Santi asked. 'Alas, no. We would probably be the same age now, but Luce and Camila left the land in the early seventies and apparently went to America. Luce came back occasionally to check on the land, but never with Camila. There was a falling out, I heard, before Camila passed. I'm sorry, Victoria. I cannot tell you anything about your family, and considering you are just finding out that you had one, I am sure you desperately want to know more. I wish I had something I could share, anything, really.'

'Can you tell me about the house itself? The property?' she asked as they drove south, further into the southern valleys.

He brightened. 'That I can do! The house was built in the 1880s, so it has a lot of history. It is called a hacienda, built Spanish-style and quite beautiful despite being a bit run down. It has not been lived in full-time for decades, but the neighbouring house just there,' he said, pointing, 'is the home of the Silvas family. The Silvases have been on the land here nearly as long as the Anyas de Alveras family and have occasionally stepped up as caretakers of the land. Since Luce passed a couple of months back, Marilena Martinez – that's her married name, her maiden name was Silvas – has been keeping it tidy. The house has five bedrooms, which probably seems large to you since you have no family with you. Is that correct? You have no husband or children?'

A lump formed in her throat. 'That is correct.'

'And there is, of course, the land. Fifteen acres, most of it covered in the vines that were planted nearly a hundred years ago when it became one of the most thriving vineyards in Mendoza. Perhaps . . . perhaps it will thrive again, now that you are home.'

They said nothing else after that cryptic comment, as they passed through the beautiful valley closer and closer to the Andes.

'Here we are,' Santi said finally. 'The start of the property.'

Victoria sat up in her seat as they turned down a long drive, or more accurately, a long dirt road that went on for nearly a mile. She had expected to feel excited. She had expected to feel anxious and apprehensive. She thought she'd prepared for every feeling. But instead, the one that overcame her more than anything else was an overwhelming sense of coming home. A peace. Like the land was hers and she was its and they belonged to each other. Her fingers tingled, numbed at the tips, but in a pleasant way. She rolled the window down and reached her hand out to the vines, aching to touch them.

She did not see the vines reaching back.

~

'Mama!' Pia called, looking through the window. 'She's here.'

'Don't pull the curtain aside, Pia!' Marilena reprimanded.

They both looked from behind the curtain as Santi's car lifted the dirt on the road and sped to the house. Marilena concentrated on her breathing, but she was without air. Las Viñas, her dream all these many years, gone. It hurt to swallow, like there was something there she couldn't quite keep down.

She couldn't help the surge of dislike that hit her when the young woman got out of the car. She looked to be a few years younger than Marilena, with long dark curling hair and olive skin that did liken her to an Anyas de Alveras. Very few Argentinians still carried the blood of the native Inca tribes, but theirs seemed to pass down from daughter to daughter, as if the man involved was simply a conduit for their blood to flow through them, and a name to keep.

But it simply *couldn't* be true. Luce was the last of the line. That was why Pia saw a bud, an actual bud, on La Abuela. Marilena had seen it herself. She had been so certain the curse was lifting. It was impossible – unthinkable – that there could be another Anyas de Alveras.

But Santi, knowing Marilena was going to put a bid on the hacienda as soon as it went up for sale, told her the news. Victoria Bishop was definitely the granddaughter of Luce Anyas de Alveras. *DNA*, he said, not unkindly, *did not lie*.

'Be kind to her when she arrives. Welcome her to the house, show her your love for it. When she goes to sell in a few months, you won't even need to let her put it on the market,' Santi had suggested.

'She's selling?' she'd asked, the first glint of hope. 'You're sure?'

'One can never be certain, but she said that she would come down on her sabbatical from work and assess the property, that she had a lawyer friend who was going to help her with the formalities. Her entire life is in Los Angeles,' he'd said. 'Why on earth would an American woman who probably doesn't even speak Spanish want to live in a big house alone in Mendoza? On a cursed vineyard no less?'

And that was the part, she thought now, that she didn't understand. Marilena remembered it so clearly:

And the curse will be lifted with the last of the Anyas de Alveras blood, and suddenly, a bud will bloom.

When Marilena was a little girl, she had secretly dreamed of being an Anyas de Alveras, of the land being in her blood so she could break the curse. It was so romantic, so ingrained in the story of their small village, Las Viñas. *She* wanted to be the one to break the curse. Marilena wanted to be special. She had told her grandmother that once and ended up getting pepper in her mouth as punishment for sounding ungrateful. Marilena had thought it was unfair – but she never brought it up again. Sometimes she saw her grandmother staring over to Las Viñas, and Marilena wondered what she was thinking.

While Luce Anyas de Alveras had not lived at Las Viñas for many years, Marilena would occasionally see her when she came to visit, often catching the older woman standing alone in the vineyard, seeming to talk to herself.

Marilena had only spoken to her once. She hadn't seen that Luce had come home, so she was out in the vineyard, talking to the vines, daring to dream that she could wake them up.

'I've seen you,' a voice had said, startling Marilena. She saw Luce and jumped up, smoothing her skirt.

'You're the girl that lives next door. Imogen's girl.'

Marilena had nodded.

'I wouldn't let your grandmother see you over here trying to wake the vineyard.'

'She put pepper in my mouth when I told her I wanted to,' Marilena had said, scowling. 'You and my Nonna, you know each other?'

But Luce had not answered, she'd simply looked at the house and back to Marilena. 'Have you tried blowing on the vines?'

Marilena sighed. 'Yes, I've tried everything. I don't suppose you have a secret you could share?'

Luce stared at her for a long moment, then sighed. 'Child, you can't know what it means to have your blood as part of the land,' she'd said gently. 'This land is me and I am it. These vines are part of me, cause true pain. A pain in my soul.'

Marilena had come home from the older woman's house and lain in bed, touching her chest, trying to feel a pain in her soul. She'd daydreamed that she was actually Luce's long-lost granddaughter.

From that moment, when she was only thirteen years old, Marilena dedicated her life to one day owning Las Viñas. She told her parents that she was going to resurrect the land herself.

'Good lord!' her mama had scoffed. 'Why on earth would you want *that* vineyard? It doesn't have any grapes!'

Her papa had been more understanding. 'You never know with curses,' he said, winking at Marilena. 'But it takes more than hope to be a winemaker – it takes skill and learning. You want to buy the land when you're a grown-up, you go for it.

But I suggest you get out there and study and work and make yourself a damned fine winemaker or vineyard manager.'

So Marilena started doing harvest work when she was sixteen. The pay was nothing, and the hours gruelling, but she felt she was paying her dues. When she finished school, she went to the Wine Institute Formacíon Vitivinícola and got a degree in winemaking. She learned the science, the chemistry. She was the only woman in her class that year. She did internships, tried to work her way up. But the wine industry grew, and she could not. They would not allow her to be head winemaker anywhere she worked. And she was married then and had Pia, but her dream was as strong as always. One day, Las Viñas would be hers.

'Ugh,' Pia said, lifting the lid on the pot Marilena had been cooking. 'You've made her locro? What are you trying to do, get her to hop right back on the airplane?'

Marilena snapped back to the present.

'Pia, locro is a traditional, well-loved dish here in our region and for someone new, it's a perfect welcome dish,' Marilena answered, stirring the stew for the last time, and hiding the disgusted look on her own face.

When she turned back to Pia, who had her eyebrows raised and her arms crossed, she knew she hadn't fooled her fifteen-year-old at all. Pia grabbed a bottle of wine and opened the door.

'Let's go welcome her then, Mama,' Pia said with sugary sweetness. 'You can give her your locro, and I will let her wash it down with something pleasant. After all, she's our new neighbour, right?'

Marilena swallowed the bitterness in the back of her throat and forced a smile, following her daughter to the hacienda on Las Viñas.

~

'So, Victoria, what do you think? Do you like your family home?'

Victoria was overwhelmed at how vast it was. After so many years of living in the city, she couldn't even wrap her mind around this amount of land – and apparently her property was small.

The hacienda was built from rose sandstone, and was much larger than the house she and Michael had bought in Santa Monica – five bedrooms and four baths, in the shape of an L. The short part of the L consisted of the kitchen and spacious living and dining areas. The long part of the L housed five bedrooms, three with en suites and two smaller near the shared bathroom. Within the L was a garden courtyard covered by a slated roof so you could walk the length of the house outside and always be in the shade. In the middle was a large outdoor barbeque pit and a pagoda with chairs underneath.

It was beautiful. It was so beautiful it hurt her to be inside it. And yet in some ways she no longer felt infinitesimal, but like she belonged here. Suddenly all the impossible dreaming she'd done with her friends at Pousada Luz felt like a possibility.

Not that it could ever really be a possibility. She'd only be here long enough to sell or rent the place.

The house was old, and it was run down. Though it had obviously been cleaned recently to keep it free of dust and spiderwebs, the furniture was tired, the paint peeling, and it had that musty smell of damp. One of the first things she was going to do was light the multiple fireplaces, she decided, and try to dry the place out.

'It is very beautiful. And very large,' she admitted. 'And it needs a lot of work.'

Santi nodded. 'It does, yes. Thankfully you have a small financial inheritance and the life insurance from Luce that your lawyer is hopefully sorting for you this week. It will help substantially with any renovations you want to do before you sell, which I suspect is your plan?'

When she didn't answer, he continued. 'It is actually small by Mendoza standards these days. Well, for a traditional hacienda. Most of them would have been turned into luxury hotels by now.'

'Is the tourism industry really that busy that the homesteads are now all hotels?' she asked.

'Fully booked months in advance. The pandemic was a nightmare, naturally, but the post-pandemic world wanted more luxury experiences. The smaller guesthouses are suffering in the recession, while the homestead winery hotels are booked solid,' he answered.

Now that gave her pause. If she really took some initiative, she could sell this place to a hotel group, which would set her up financially for a while. She made a mental note to contact her friend Jory, whose husband did that kind of thing for a living.

'Your grandmother visited occasionally but no one has lived in the home since the early seventies, shortly after it was cursed. The building on the outer edge of the property as we were coming in would have been the winery. Made of stone, ideal for keeping the temperature stable. There may even be an underground area – you should explore and see what you find. It will be quite an adventure.'

There was a knock on the front door, surprising Victoria. She looked at her watch. It was only 5 pm, but it felt much later. It was so quiet out here.

'Ah, that will be Marilena!' Santi said, happily. 'Marilena Martinez is your closest neighbour, and I've asked her to come down for a welcome drink. She is the Silvas neighbour I told you about and has lived next door to Las Viñas since she was born, so I'm sure you'll be fast friends.'

Santi opened the door to a tall, skinny girl of about fifteen.

'Are you Victoria Anyas de Alveras?' the girl asked in a bright, welcoming voice, which she then dropped suddenly. 'Welcome to Las Viñas Malditas.' She put out her hands like a zombie in a horror film to match the now-spooky voice.

'The cursed vineyard, I know,' Victoria replied with a laugh, reaching out her hand and introducing herself in Spanish. 'I'm Victoria Bishop.'

'Ah, you speak Spanish! I'm Pia Martinez,' the girl said, shaking Victoria's hand. 'And this is my mama, Marilena.'

The woman who followed Pia was only a few years older than Victoria, so she must have had Pia quite young. She was extremely pretty, with her rich, mahogany hair tied into a messy bun, and thick curtain bangs that framed her face. Marilena was smiling, but something about it felt off, and when Victoria met her eyes, she was quite certain she saw bitterness in their depths, despite the smile. Victoria had a feeling this woman was not at all happy to meet her, though she couldn't imagine why.

'Yes, yes,' Santi said cheerfully, taking a seemingly heavy casserole dish from Marilena and placing it on the stove. He opened the lid and shook suddenly, closing it quickly. 'Ah, locro. How . . . lovely.'

Pia giggled.

'Yes, well as I was saying to Victoria, you two girls are her new neighbours and will welcome her kindly!' Santi enthused. 'Both the house and the land were maintained over the years between the seventies and today. A cleaning service maintained the house each month, and a horticulture company took care of the land. When your grandmother passed some months ago, the service of the house stopped. Marilena here started coming a couple of months ago to keep it tidy at least.'

Victoria turned to Marilena, who still hadn't said a word.

'Thank you,' Victoria said genuinely. 'I can't believe there is no dust or cobwebs, no scary little rodents or spiders that I can see.'

'I've been earning an allowance coming in and cleaning the place once a week, Victoria,' Pia said with a grin. 'Happy to keep helping if you'd like. Big ole place like this, cleaning it yourself . . .'

Victoria chuckled at her gumption. Pia was a breath of fresh air.

'What was it you said about someone maintaining the land?' Victoria asked. She could almost feel Marilena stiffen across the room.

Santi, too, glanced at Marilena, but when she didn't reply, he shrugged and answered, 'I'll follow up on that tomorrow for you, Victoria.'

'But I don't understand why my grandmother would have kept someone on to maintain the land anyway,' she said, confused. 'Didn't you say it's a cursed vineyard or something?'

Pia scoffed and rolled her eyes. 'This town and their curse, honestly,' she said. '*The blood of the last of the line will remove the curse* . . .' she said in the same voice from earlier. 'So why on earth would I have seen a . . .'

But Marilena finally seemed to come to life and grabbed Pia's arm. 'Pia!'

The last of the line. She didn't know what Pia was going to say. All she heard was 'last of the line'. When Santi had mentioned the curse and the last of the line earlier today, she'd thought it was a joke, but now, she didn't know. Could that be her?

Pia looked at her mother again for a long moment. Finally, she turned to Victoria with an apologetic smile.

'We stocked up your refrigerator with a few basics, and the bathroom as well. Mama made you a locro,' Pia said, pointing to the casserole dish Santi had put on the stove. 'It is a traditional Argentinian dish you will only find in a family home, and it is a native dish to the Andean Argentinians from which your family has come.' She stumbled upon a few words and looked down to her hand, where Victoria could see she'd written her lines like a speech.

Victoria took the lid off the dish. It had a savoury sweet smell she couldn't quite make out. Pia, she noticed, made a face as if disgusted, and finally said, 'ugh'.

'Pia!' Marilena admonished again. Finally Marilena looked up, directly at Victoria. 'I apologise for my daughter. Now you apologise, bebe.'

'Lo siento, Mama. Mi disculpe,' Pia said, rolling her eyes and whispering, 'as if *I'm* being rude.' Then, in a louder voice, 'My apologies, Victoria, but I hate locro. It's squash stew. Squash! And sausage. All the teenagers are eating keto anyway now, Mama.'

'My dears, my dears, goodbye and goodnight. Victoria, you can call me anytime,' Santi said quickly, waving and closing the door behind him.

'See, he runs from the locro,' Pia said, grinning at Victoria.

'Pia, enough!' Marilena hissed, and Pia stopped laughing. 'Ms Anyas de Alveras . . .'

'It's Bishop, actually, as I said earlier,' Victoria repeated.

'Ms Bishop—' Marilena amended, starting to say something, but Pia interrupted.

'Victoria, which room did you choose?'

'Room?' Victoria asked, confused. 'What do you mean?

'You speak Spanish, so you will have noticed a common theme on all the doors of the rooms?' Pia asked excitedly.

'Yes, they are named after the colours the rooms were painted in. I've chosen La Rosada, the Rose Room,' she answered. 'I'm planning to renovate while I'm down here, of course, but I want to keep the rooms the same I think, at least the names.'

'Yes, we were going to do the same! La Rosada is definitely the master suite,' Pia said, opening the door and glancing over the room. 'That was going to be Mama and Papa's room. I chose the one on the end, furthest away of course – the Blue Room! La Azul.'

Marilena groaned softly, putting her head in her hands.

Now Victoria knew why Marilena was acting so strangely. Victoria taken away her dream of having Las Viñas by simply existing. Though Victoria didn't appreciate the rudeness, she was sympathetic.

'I must apologise again for my daughter. She is at a particular age,' Marilena said. 'You have no family of your own?'

Victoria stiffened. 'My parents will come to visit as soon as they can. But I am an only child and recently separated, without children.'

Marilena looked as if she wasn't surprised, which irritated Victoria.

'Well, we mustn't keep you any longer. Pia, come, time to go home.'

'Here,' Pia said, pulling a bottle of wine from her bag. 'To wash down the locro.' Pia made a gagging noise again.

Victoria looked at the bottle of Malbec. 'Is this a local wine, from here in Mendoza?' she asked, going to the cupboards and opening them one by one until she found some wine glasses. They were clean, she supposed from Pia's monthly chores for cash. 'Anyone know if there is a wine knife around here?'

Marilena was suddenly beside her, opening the drawer and pulling out a corkscrew with a smile that looked forced, as if she'd just remembered she was meant to be playing nice.

'I worked last harvest at one of the wineries that still uses corks,' she said. 'Most have moved to screw top, but I like the classic cork.'

'Me too,' Victoria said with a smile, taking the peace offering. She poured them two small glasses and took a sip of her own. 'Oh wow, this is spectacular!'

Pia glowed and looked at her mother, who was blushing.

'That's Mama's wine!' Pia said.

'It's not my wine,' Marilena corrected. 'I interned as the assistant winemaker at a Bodega closer to Mendoza last season. They are a small producer, but the grapes were incredibly good.'

'No one can understand why she isn't head winemaker somewhere,' Pia said. 'But then, we were supposed to buy Las Viñas . . .'

'*Pia*!' Marilena cried, putting her head in her hands. 'Please accept my apologies again for my daughter.'

She turned to Pia. 'Home. Now.'

'Bye Victoria!' Pia called as Marilena gently pushed her out the door.

Marilena turned and looked around the house once in longing, and then met Victoria's eyes.

'Welcome home, Ms Anyas de Alveras,' she said, pushing through the door.

Victoria gaped at the swinging door for a minute before her indignation came out fully.

'It's *Bishop*!' she called after them, finishing the rest of her wine in one gulp and mock-saluting them as they disappeared into the vines.

CHAPTER EIGHT

Just before sunrise, Victoria gave up any attempt at sleeping and got out of bed. She dressed warmly, walking to the kitchen from La Rosada. It was to have been the master suite, Pia had said, which made sense, as it was the room closest to the short part of the L-shaped house, directly next door to the kitchen.

She put on a pot of coffee. It was strange to be in the southern hemisphere where the seasons were switched – to be in early October and have it be spring was an oddity, though in this cold it felt more like a North American autumn.

She looked out the large window in the kitchen that faced the rising sun in the east. It was 6.31 am, and according to her iPhone, sunrise was at 6.47am. She knew nothing about wine or growing grapes, but it seemed crazy to her that this healthy-looking vineyard was cursed. What had happened out there? It looked so vital and alive. Her fingers were tingling again, and suddenly, sipping her coffee, she needed to touch the vines. She pulled her fluffy slippers off and pulled her hiking boots on.

Michael had a fondness for the outdoors and used to insist on weekend hiking and camping trips, so he'd bought her all the best gear. She waited for that longing to come where she missed Michael, but instead, looking down at her hiking boots, she felt irritated. She didn't even *like* hiking and camping. She didn't mind it. She loved beautiful scenery and loved to walk. But the hiking and camping thing, that was his. She had followed willingly. Now that they weren't together, she had no desire to do those things on her own. Had she done them only for him? What else had she done only for him? And what had she lost of herself along the way?

She found herself wondering what she'd be doing now if she'd never met Michael. What would her hobbies be? Would she have stayed in her job without Michael? Would she have stayed in Los Angeles?

Don't think about that now, a voice called to her. *Come, come to the vines.*

She brought her coffee cup with her and walked out the door. Perhaps it was because she hadn't slept at all, but she felt she could hear the land calling to her. She could hear it sighing as she drew nearer, and she could have sworn that one of the vines reached out to her as she passed by. She quickly turned back, but the vine was still. Too still, as if it was pretending, trying to convince her she'd imagined it all. Yet somehow she knew she hadn't.

She followed the whispers that called to her on the wind, taking a path through the vines that seemed to guide her towards the highest point of the vineyard. The whispers got louder and louder until she finally arrived at a single old vine atop the hill, overlooking the rest of the vineyard, and the sounds stopped. There were no other vines for a few feet on either side of this single one. And even though Victoria knew it was impossible for it to be so, she could almost feel the vine looking at her, waiting for her, assessing her.

'Hello,' she said softly. 'I'm Victoria . . . Anyas de Alveras.'

The sun came out just at that moment and the vine seemed to stretch, reach, and lift. Like she was . . . introducing herself?

Suddenly the ground started to shake. Victoria dropped to one knee and braced herself for the earthquake, but it lasted only seconds and then was still again. But something *had* changed. The ground beneath the vine was different – something had emerged.

Victoria couldn't immediately see what it was. A piece of clothing? Something leather? As she pulled it from the dirt, she realised it was a little bit of both. An old piece of fabric was wrapped around a leather book that appeared to have most of the pages pulled out. Despite the fact that it had been buried in the earth, it was in remarkably good shape.

Once she removed the fabric, she gently brushed the dirt from the leather cover and opened it to the first page.

The Secret Diary of Luce Anyas de Alveras

'Holy shit.'

Still standing, Victoria turned the page and began to read voraciously.

Spring equinox, 1962

'I cannot believe your mama is letting us come with you tonight.'

It is Caro who says this. It is the night of spring equinox of my twelfth year and one of the most important nights in my life, according to Mama. Tonight, I become initiated into the vineyard. I don't know what happens, but it is very important and it is because I am now a woman that I can have this birthright.

I was the first of us to make the leap into womanhood. Eugenia has since, but Caro and Sylvia are still girls. I should introduce my best friends. Eugenia has been my neighbour basically since we were born. She has hair as black as mine but hers is long and straight and her skin is much fairer. We have known each other so long we sometimes finish each other's sentences.

Since I'm writing in my secret diary, and in your diary you are supposed to only say truths, I will confess that when we were younger we used to practise doing this so that people would comment on it. We also would plan what we were wearing the next day so we would match, and people would think it was just that we were so inseparable in our brains we did it naturally! I think we both wished we weren't only children, so we made a pact when we were young, a blood oath, that no matter what happened we would always be sisters, sworn to one another – we would be one another's greatest loves, more than anyone else, no matter what.

As Las Viñas grew, so too did the land around it, and now we have four working houses around Las Viñas. Gen, or my Eugenia, was the first to move in, before even my time, but since then, we've gotten new neighbours.

Sylvia moved in a few years ago. Her family breeds horses and trains them, so we often get to ride the countryside together. Sylvia is blonde and very beautiful, and we are all jealous, but she doesn't care at all about how she looks. She only cares about the horses, and us of course.

Caro is the funniest person anyone has ever met, and her larger-than-life personality diminishes the fact that everything else about Caro is very small. Her height, her small teeth, her tiny nose, her haircut. We call her our little imp.

Caro, to be honest, is the one of us that is poor. She lives in a neighbouring town instead of on the land and village properties of Las Viñas like the rest of us do. She and her annoying older brother Pedro bike more than an hour every day to get to school. These days, she spends a lot of time floating between my house, Eugenia's and Sylvia's. The annoying Pedro works on our vineyard, so we see him a lot, too, unfortunately.

Then there's me, Luce Anyas de Alveras. I am the darkest of all of us, my skin olive, my hair black and curling, my black eyes slanted slightly over large cheekbones and a wide mouth. My mother's ancestor, my great-great-grandmother who started Las Viñas, was of Inca blood. And tonight, we get to learn its history and become part of it.

Victoria closed the book, her heart racing, pressing the diary into her pocket. It seemed to have its own pulse. She took a sip of her coffee and realised it was cold, so she dumped it on the ground and made her way back to the house to put on another pot. As she waited for the water to boil, she continued to read.

It was nearly midnight when Mama knocked on the door and opened it. We followed her swiftly through the vineyard towards La Madre, the first vine planted, the mother, as she was called, of all the other vines.

'Señora Anyas de Alveras, we've been wondering why you allowed us to come tonight. Is it so that we can be an alibi for Luce when you perform your human sacrifice?' Caro asked. Only Caro would dare to joke with my mother, who is a formidable woman.

Mama turned and pulled the lantern in front of our faces, looking at each of us in turn before she sighed and shook her head sadly. 'Why does it always require a sacrifice of three?' She turned and continued walking.

'I think your mama just made a joke. But I'm just not sure,' Caro could barely get her words out.

'She was joking, wasn't she?' Eugenia whispered, taking my hand.

We were all surprised when we got to La Madre to see that there were many people there, all women, gathered near a fire. A young woman came over and handed us all small glasses of wine – even though we are too young to drink. Argentinians usually share watered-down wine from when they are small children, especially those who grow up on a vineyard. The woman was very small – she had to be under five feet – and definitely native to the Andes like my great-great-grandmother was. She didn't speak Spanish, but we could tell by her smiling gesture we were to wait to drink the wine.

Finally, Mama called everyone around La Madre.

'I feel very honoured to have so many great women here tonight to welcome my daughter as the conduit of the land. Thank you for being here for her induction ceremony, and thank you to Sylvia, Eugenia and Carolina for joining us. Carolina asked me why I allowed them to come.'

The women laughed.

'Are we going to be sacrificed?' Caro asked, and they laughed again.

'We laugh because you are still so young and don't realise the bond you have, the bond we *have, between women. This is our power.*

'Luce Anyas de Alveras, step forward,' Mama said, and I met her at the fire at the vine. 'You are named after my grandmother, Luce Anyas, the daughter of Anyas and Alejandro Alveras, who were the first of us. Alejandro travelled the great road from Santiago over the Andes mountains to Mendoza. He was separated from his expedition by a storm and was left to die in the snow, until a young woman found him and carried him back to her town. She was the last of her line, of Inca blood, a woman of great strength and skill. She was the healer of her people and grew the land. Some called her a witch, but few ever knew her.

Alejandro married Anyas in the mountains as he healed, and she followed him to Mendoza, where she planted a single vine he'd brought from Spain, the only thing that didn't die in the Andes. Anyas blessed this vine with her blood, with our blood. The gift is passed through each generation of Anyas, and once you become a woman you must bless the land with your blood, your honour, to uphold it, the mother vine. She is you and you are it. And your friends are part of the circle that holds together and creates la vid que vive.'

'The vine that lives,' we all translated together.

It was my mother who spoke, but she said later that the words had come through her.

'Luce, Eugenia, Carolina, and Syliva – place your hands before us.'

Two women pressed a knife into my palms until the blood came. It hurt, but I masked my pain, and passed the knife to Gen, who closed her eyes tightly and gasped. Carolina and Syliva followed suit.

'Now, take hands, and then Luce, you place your palms into the dirt at the roots of La Madre. If a bud forms, you have been given the gift.'

'What if it doesn't?' I whispered, terribly afraid. I wanted so badly to have this gift. To be special.

'Your blood will still satiate the land, and it will continue on.' It was one of the other women who spoke, and not in Spanish but in an old dialect, Quechua, perhaps, but I understood her words, though I didn't speak the language. When

Mama realised this, she beamed. She was certain of me. I was still so nervous.

The blood was pooling in my palms and just as the moon peeked over the skyline the women pressed my palms into the dirt at the base of La Madre, saying something I couldn't hear. My ears were buzzing, and I have never felt something so strong. I knew I was part of the land, and it was part of me. And finally, there was a burning so great I called out and pulled my hands from the dirt, and La Madre shook – a single bud had formed on her vine.

My friends ran over to me and Mama rocked me, laughing and chanting.

'Luce Anyas de Alveras. You are now the keeper of Las Viñas. From your blood, through mine, and my mother's and her mother's before me, and to your daughter and your daughter's daughter. Do you swear a blood oath to protect the vineyards with your very life?'

'I swear,' I said.

'And do you women here tonight also swear to honour the land that you are now a part of?'

'We swear,' everyone said at the same time, Caro being the loudest. She looked embarrassed at her own fervour, but Mama gave her a small smile.

And then Marie, one of our workers, pulled out a small guitar and began to play and sing quietly, in a language I did not know and yet I did, for it called to me, and to Mama, too, and all the others from the mountains who followed the first Anyas here.

Eugenia and I started dancing to the music first, then Caro and Sylvia joined us as we held hands and skipped in a circle around the fire until the sun came up the next morning. We walked home together, me and my friends linked arm in arm.

Today I am not only a woman, but an Anyas de Alveras woman, and I am the keeper of Las Viñas. Through me the vines will thrive. And I will protect them with my life.

Victoria closed the diary. There were obviously pages missing, and while this disappointed her, she somehow knew that this was the beginning of learning about her family and where she came from. It was exactly the way she'd felt when she got to La Abuela, or La Madre, today. For the first time in her life, she was a person of history. Her adoptive parents were the best people on earth, but they didn't share her blood type, her medical history, her lineage at all. Victoria wanted to think those things had never mattered to her, and in a way they hadn't. But now that they *did* matter, it seemed like they had always mattered.

What if it explained what happened between her and Michael? What if it explained . . . her hand went instinctively to her stomach. What if it explained why she couldn't carry children? Why *she* was cursed.

That night, when Victoria slept, she had dreams of her and Michael swimming in a river she'd never known, and her bleeding into the land of Las Viñas, as she lost her child as a sacrifice.

CHAPTER NINE

Victoria spent the next few days getting to know her house. She explored every room, nook and cranny – and then every nook and cranny within the nooks and crannies, desperately looking for the missing pages of her grandmother's diary, but to no avail. It was as if the land had gifted it to her as a welcome, but had remained silent since. So, too, had the vineyard. No more earthquakes, no more moments where she was almost certain a vine was aware of her.

Now, it was just what it was – a beautiful vineyard that did not flower. She didn't know anything about the growth cycle of a vineyard or why that might happen, but Santi had been in touch with the local horticulturalists that had been pruning and taking care of the land for her grandmother, and they had agreed to continue their tasks, with Victoria soon to have access to the financial inheritance. She was looking forward to meeting them the following week and had started taking notes, in one of the little pocket journals she'd brought with her, of anything interesting or significant she saw in the vineyard. Not that she knew anything about it, but she was observant.

After she'd exhausted her time looking for more of the diary, Victoria explored the house itself, beginning to understand its many flaws, and even more possibilities.

The five bedrooms had each been named after a colour and were painted and decorated as such. Her room, *La Rosada*, was the Rose Room. Then there was *La Verde*, the Green Room; *La Amarilla*, the Yellow Room; *La Azul*, the Blue Room – Pia's favourite; and *La Lavanda*, the Lavender room.

She couldn't help but see Monique in La Lavanda. Lavender, she always said, was her signature colour. And Victoria's parents would love La Amarilla – her mom loved bright happy colours.

Stop picturing your family and friends here, she said to herself, too many times that day. *This is* not *your home.*

She hadn't been able to stop thinking about what Santi Ceres had said about the traditional haciendas of Mendoza being turned into boutique hotels and bed & breakfasts. The prospect excited her, but she had to be pragmatic about her approach. The house needed work, which meant money. She didn't know yet how much she was going to inherit from her grandmother's estate and insurance, so for now she was simply taking notes.

She had to check the beds and furniture for rot. It had been a very long time since the house was inhabited, but whoever had originally done the decor had done so with tasteful elegance. Everything needed painting and, she reckoned, brightening up with white trim in most rooms.

Victoria couldn't help but start to decorate in her head. There was a beautiful white desk in La Verde that would look so much better in La Lavanda. And if the pine armoire in La Rosada went to La Azul, it would be a match made in heaven. In La Amarilla there was a beautiful old set of drawers that was once some shade of green, but the paint was chipping off. She thought if she could add yellow to the green and still make it look old and chipped, it would suit beautifully.

What is the technique where you make paint look scraped off? she googled on her phone.

Scraffito was the short answer, but when she clicked 'images', hundreds of them came up, so she started a Pinterest board, too. She stayed up half that night taking photos and putting together an email of questions for Ange.

It was getting lighter outside when Victoria woke, groggy from strange dreams and lack of sleep. She'd been in Argentina for two weeks now and it wasn't jet lag disturbing her sleep, but the lack of a routine to her days and nights. She would fall asleep and then wake up thinking it was morning, when it was still the middle of the night.

She looked at the clock and saw that it was the latest she'd slept since she arrived. She reached for her phone and saw she had a reply from Ange in LA, four hours behind.

Hi Vic,

Wow, what a gem you've found. We can't wait to come visit and see it for ourselves! Will look through the photos later and give a more detailed reply, but to answer your question in bold first – ***'what would it take to turn this into a hotel?'***

The answer is and always will be – way more than you can imagine. You'll be involving councils in a country you don't know, building regulations, and permits you can't even begin to think of yet.

My initial suggestion is dream big but start small. You'd do far better in a short sale to have something that is renovated nicely that can go either way – and let the buyers with the big bucks decide which way that is. Save yourself the hassle. Just make it pretty.

Ange

Victoria nodded and almost sighed with relief. It was what she'd expected, and to have it confirmed meant she could move forward with a solid plan – which she'd titled in her head The Mendoza Project.

Feeling enthusiastic and ready to get started, she quickly jumped in the shower then dressed in her jeans and cowboy boots, with a cream fluffy sweater over her tank top. She'd learned that the weather in October, which was the start of spring in the southern hemisphere, was remarkably different in the mornings and evenings compared to mid-afternoon. Now, this early, it was cold – around fifty degrees Fahrenheit. She couldn't see her breath this morning, but yesterday she could. But by midday, it could reach nearly eighty degrees.

She tied her damp, long black hair into a bun, and turned on a Spotify playlist of popular Argentinian bands she'd been listening to each morning. She was trying to immerse herself in the culture as best she could. She turned the music up and started to dance as she waited for the pot of coffee to boil.

The music was interrupted by an incoming FaceTime call. Startled, Victoria turned the volume down, but smiled, seeing that it was her parents. She turned on the video call.

'Bicky, can you see me?' her mom was yelling loudly into the camera. 'I can't see you. Why can't I see you? Frank!'

'Mom, I'm here!' she called, stifling her smile like she always did. 'I can see you, just give it a sec.'

'But where are you? I can't see you, this stupid thing doesn't work,' her mom muttered, before her face lit up. 'There you are!'

'Here I am,' Victoria said with a laugh. 'Hi, Dad,' she said and waved when Frank came onto the screen behind Joyce.

'Hey, Bicky honey,' he said, moving so close to the camera she could see his nose hairs. 'Can you see me okay?'

'Hey, I know we've talked about this before, but you see that little screen at the bottom of your iPad where you can see yourselves?' she asked.

They looked around for a while.

'Oh, yup!' Joyce said, and Frank nodded.

'That's what I see. So, just focus on me, but if you worry about how I see you, look down at that screen, okay?'

'Uh, sure, honey,' Joyce said. She looked at Frank and they shrugged at one another as if what Victoria had said was another language. 'So, we just wanted to check in and see how it's all going down there in Algeria?'

Frank rolled his eyes. 'Argentina, honey. South America. You know this.'

'That's what I said!' Joyce said with frustration, shaking her head and smiling to Victoria on the camera, looking down at herself and checking the image like a mirror, rubbing her teeth.

'What are you guys doing up so early anyway?' Victoria asked with a chuckle, her coffee pot finishing. She poured herself a cup and took in the scent. Just the smell of coffee made her feel more awake and invigorated.

'We always get up around this time,' Joyce said. 'It's 7 am here. What time is it there?'

'Eight,' she answered. 'So just an hour apart.'

'Take us for a tour of the house!' Joyce cried.

Victoria took them around, pointing things out here and there. The service wasn't great through some parts of the house, so there was a lot of freezing, waiting and repeating. Joyce made comments every few seconds, but Frank stayed mostly quiet. Victoria knew he was taking notes. When she got back to the kitchen and put her phone back on the docking station, she poured another cup of coffee.

'Hey, Mom, gimme a second with Dad, okay?' she asked.

'Of course, honey,' she said, giving the camera a kiss. 'So proud of you, and we love you!'

Victoria smiled. 'I love you, too, Mom.'

'I'll go make breakfast, Frank,' she said, walking off camera.

'Hang on a sec, Bicky, let me just wash your mom's lipstick off this thing. Ugh, it's really sticky,' he said, and all she saw was the sleeve of his shirt wiping the camera. 'Alright, now it's just you and me, kiddo. What have you got?'

'Dad,' she said, leaning in, 'remember when you renovated the house?'

'You mean except this vile kitchen I never got around to, stuck in 1970?' he asked.

'I always wondered about that,' she mused.

'Never wonder about anything unfinished – it's called el-runouto-de-money,' he said. 'That how you say it in Spanish?'

She laughed. 'I can't believe you guys made me learn Spanish from such a young age and never bothered to learn it yourselves.'

'Believe me, we regret that now. But we have very few regrets, so I think that being a big one is saying something,' he said. 'Now, hit me, kiddo.'

'I've been talking to that Santi Ceres guy, and the area down here is just thriving with boutique vineyard hotels. My friend Ange, you know, the lawyer at LGM, Levi's wife? She says the paperwork for that kind of thing would be a nightmare so I should just put the money from the insurance into simple renovations to make the house a great sell. I'm thinking I can do a lot of them myself,' she explained.

'Well, that all sounds good, honey, but don't you live on a fifteen-acre property that's a vineyard? Shouldn't you be more focused on that?' he asked.

'Well, here's the thing about that. You see, Dad, the land is vast and beautiful. It's a gorgeous vineyard! But . . . well, you see, it doesn't produce any flowers. Which is kind of a big thing.'

'How big?'

'Like, um . . . like that means it doesn't produce any fruit,' she said.

'But aren't grapes fruit?' he asked, confused.

She nodded.

'And isn't wine made from grapes?' he asked again.

She nodded again.

'So you live on a fifteen-acre winery that doesn't make wine?' he asked.

'Uh, yup.'

There was a moment of silence. 'Okay, so let's have a look back at that yellow room first,' he said, and Victoria smiled warmly, nodding and turning the camera around again. 'I've got a good spreadsheet for renovations. I'll send it to you.'

~

Victoria had checked on the little Peugeot in the garage a few days earlier. She had an inkling that perhaps it had been months, possibly years, since the old car had been driven and it likely had a dead battery.

She was right. She'd called Santi, who dropped in the following day with cables and jump-started the car. She'd run it every day since for ten minutes so that when the day came, she could drive into Mendoza with no fear of breaking down.

Today was that day, and the Peugeot started without issue, though getting a new battery was on her list of things to do while she was in the city.

She followed Google Maps on her phone until she got to the main road through the valley, then followed the road signs instead and enjoyed the drive. The miles and miles of healthy, thriving vines made her feel a deep longing and a sadness that hers were not the same. At this time of the year, they didn't look much different from her own. There were no flowers or grapes yet. She still didn't know anything about winemaking or running a vineyard, and yet according to Luce's diary, it was something that ran in their blood. Was that why she felt this connection to the land? Was her blood a part of Las Viñas? And it a part of her?

She paid more attention now to the larger estates along the way. Santi had been right, hers was small compared to some of them. But hers was also older, more authentic, more beautiful. *Hers.* She felt a rush of pride, of excitement.

We can do this, Victoria. One project at a time.

Maybe it was all myth and legend with her vineyard. Perhaps it was not cursed, but simply dead. Filled with rot or a disease or something. She mentally put on her list to hire someone to do some tests, even if they'd been done before. But the vineyard was beyond her control, at least for now. What *was* in her control was the hacienda. The rooms, the house. This was where she would start.

Santi had given her the valuation report for her property. It wasn't nothing, but it certainly wasn't something. Though the property had never gone on the market, there was one prospective buyer. Marilena Martinez. Having seen the valuation report, Victoria did some research into the value of other properties in the region, and they were all worth considerably more than Las Viñas. She had work to do.

After dropping her car at the mechanic for her new battery, she walked down one of the wide leafy streets and stopped at a restaurant she'd heard had the best brunches in Mendoza. Brunch wasn't a typically Argentinian meal but Desayuno Todo El Dia restaurant, translated to 'breakfast all day', was so popular that even the locals spent hours there, especially on the weekends.

Victoria ordered a cappuccino and a tortilla de papas, which was the chef's special that day. The tortilla, arriving on the table in a small baking dish that was still hot, was like an omelette baked with potatoes, eggs, spinach, onion and sun-dried tomato. The delicious food improved her mood, and she was back on her mission, forging ahead with a smile on her face now.

She made a few stops in the city after brunch. She found a local pharmacy where she spent nearly an hour. Victoria always loved an excuse to peruse pharmacies in new countries, finding new products to try, like cosmetics and skincare she'd never seen back home. She'd only brought the basics with her, so she stocked up on medicine and toiletries, indulging in new bath pearls in lavender and berry scents. There was another shop on one of the main streets, where she purchased a new shower curtain and bathmat, and found a bathtub table with waterproof electric candles that sent her into peals of glee. Victoria loved having long baths and reading.

A bookshop caught her eye on the way back to the car. She bought a book which seemed to provide a basic overview of the wine industry, and a magazine that explored country living and travel in Argentina and seemed to be filled with brilliant design ideas. She also got a rom-com in English for some escapism, and a beautiful cookbook filled with famous Argentinian dishes.

She'd tried to forget her last 'chicken in a bag' cooking disaster – just one of dozens of stories of her inability to cook over the years. But she loved food so very much, and it was a life goal of hers to be able to cook something. Really, how hard could it be? And she was in Argentina, with none of her friends around to tease her, though she knew they did it out of love. But she had no one to disappoint now. She flicked through the recipe book and felt inspired, and ran her credit card for the lot of books.

She could have found everything on her list in the city, but then she remembered the town near Las Viñas that Santi had pointed out, San Alejandro, with its plaza and selection of boutiques. She decided to head there instead.

~

As she pulled into a park near the plaza, she smiled and waved at the faces peering at her – she assumed they were curious to see who was driving her grandmother's car. People whispered but did not stop to say hello.

Her first stop was BeBi's, where she could buy bedding and decor for the bedrooms. The shop was tiny inside, so only the patterns were out on display. She watched a couple of local women select their preferences and then find a salesperson to go into the back, or up a small ladder, to gather the goods. After browsing for a while, she found the perfect set of sheets and duvets for both La Rosada and La Amarilla, so she waited patiently for a salesperson to come to her next.

The shop wasn't busy, but it seemed every time she tried to get the attention of a salesperson, they found someone else to help or disappeared into the back. Eventually she made her way to the counter to ask someone to come to the aisle to help her, but everyone was suddenly gone. It was as if she was in the store by herself.

Feeling confused and frustrated, she went to the aisle and got on the ladder herself, climbing past the shelves until she found the sizes she wanted, then coming down carefully. When she came to pay, a lady appeared behind the counter and took her credit card, but refused to look at her.

At the shop next door, Reno's, she found cream bamboo blinds and fixtures for the windows, with cream linen curtains to pull over. In that same shop, she found tape, paint, and brushes and rollers. She didn't even ask for help, but when she went to pay, the older man behind the counter said, 'Dos siento cuatro.'

She didn't like being put on the spot, but she added the amount up on her phone calculator. She shook her head and showed him the phone. He shook his head and put his number in, twice the price.

Victoria's nostrils flared as she took a deep breath and smiled, tight-lipped. She picked up each item and pointed to the price on the ticket then typed it on his calculator. He didn't even look down, just glared. When the final price on the calculator came to the same as hers, she raised an eyebrow. 'Cien siento cuatro, si?'

He shrugged and Victoria handed him the cash for the right amount, bagging her own items in a huff. What the hell was wrong with these people?

Deflated and upset, she began the drive back home before she realised she'd been so upset she forgot to stop by the market to stock her kitchen. She'd go back to Mendoza tomorrow – the people in the city were much nicer to deal with. She wondered if the locals had discovered who she was, but if that was the case, why didn't they approve of her? Was her grandmother not well-liked? Were the locals hoping for Las Viñas to be sold to Marilena and for the Anyas de Alveras family to be dead and gone, once and for all? Or was she overthinking the whole situation?

She turned the car back towards the charming market and deli Santi had pointed out, where he'd said even the city folk come to buy food from Adriana.

The market was filled with locally cured meats and cheeses, a small but magnificent wine selection, and thankfully a section of refrigerated food. She grabbed some essentials to get her through the next few days, and a bottle of red wine, a bag of tortellini and a premade sauce for dinner that night.

Waiting in line to pay, she suddenly felt that the whole room was looking at her. When she turned around, she was right – they were.

'Hello,' Victoria said automatically in English when she got to the counter. The woman behind it was beautiful, with bronzed skin and highlighted hair. She glared at Victoria.

'No hablo inglés,' the woman said, ringing up Victoria's products.

Not again, she thought.

'Disculpe,' she said in Spanish. 'Me gusta tu tienda.'

The woman put her things into a bag and shoved them into her hand. 'No hablo inglés.'

Victoria forced a smile and left as quickly as she could, fighting back tears as she drove back to her lonely hacienda, wondering what the hell she was doing there.

CHAPTER TEN

Marilena sat at the kitchen window drinking a coffee, peeking from behind the closed curtain to stare over at the hacienda. She was waiting for her sabotage mission to work and for Victoria to come out of the house, defeated and broken, turning around and going right back home to the US, telling Santi to sell the damned property.

She'd talked to her friends at Reno's, BeBi's and Adriana's and asked them to make Victoria feel unwelcome. Not in so many words, but the message was clear, as was the result. Marilena had spied Victoria lugging bag after bag into the house yesterday afternoon, looking dejected and miserable. Marilena had felt guilt rising in her stomach but squelched it.

Today, however, Victoria was going in and out of the house whistling, a skip in her step, bringing out bags of rubbish and what looked like old household belongings for donation or the rubbish pile, covered in paint, looking happy. Looking determined.

'Damn you!' Marilena hissed, closing the curtain.

'Too late,' a deep voice said from behind Marilena, startling her. 'Mama says I've been damned to the devil since I was about nine.'

'Dev!' Marilena squealed and ran to the man, kissing both his cheeks before he pulled her in for a massive bear hug. 'When did you get back? And you'd better say yesterday, or I'll never speak to you again.'

'Yesterday, then,' he grinned. Marilena lifted her chin, taking in the face of her husband Diego's best friend. Diego was currently working in the mines up north, and she hadn't talked to him since Victoria moved in next door. Having Dev home now was almost like having part of Diego back.

'How was New Zealand? Did you find a pretty Kiwi girl and fall in love?'

'Just one?' he said, winking. 'New Zealand was wonderful. I worked on a vineyard in Marlborough, and they taught me everything about vineyard management, organics, whole bunch pressing – all the stuff you are interested in, but hands-on. You'd have loved it, Mari. They even asked me to stay on – offered me a job,' he said, almost shyly, which was unlike him.

'That's amazing! What on earth are you doing back here then?' she asked, taking his hand and pulling him to the table, where she poured him a coffee.

'I said I needed to come home first, as I had an opportunity here, and then would get back to them,' he said, biting into a medialuna. 'Thanks, I'm starving.'

He opened the curtains. 'So who were you damning, by the way? Because you know that opportunity I was talking about was with you at Las Viñas, and yet here you are staring at the house like you want to burn it down instead of happily moving in as I thought you would be. What happened, Mari?'

At his words, she heaved a sigh and her shoulders slumped. She looked up at him, reluctant to burst his bubble. 'There is another Anyas de Alveras. Camila's daughter they didn't know about until recently. She has come home to Las Viñas,' she choked. The words were hard to get out, and her throat was tight.

'Oh, Mari,' he said, sitting beside her. 'Shit, I am sorry, honey. But hey, you can find another vineyard. A better one. One that's . . . I don't know . . . maybe not "cursed"?' he said, rolling his eyes.

Dev had never believed in the magic of Las Viñas, which was refreshing, since it was so encompassing to her.

'When does Diego get home?'

'Not for another three months. He is on a lithium hunt in the mines up closer to Salta. It is the future of our country, apparently. God, he hates it!' she cried, putting her head in her hands. 'He had such hopes for us, with Las Viñas. I haven't had the heart to tell him.'

'Come here,' he said, putting his arm around her. 'I know it was your childhood dream, Marilena. You've loved this land your whole life. And dreamed of actually being an Anyas de Alveras . . .'

'That's not true!' she said, blushing deep red. Had everyone known?

He squeezed her. 'Of course it is. This place is swathed in so much history, so many stories and so much mystery as well. We all felt it, Mari, don't be embarrassed. But at the end of the day, it is just a piece of land. And it belongs to someone else. We have to let it go and move on. We'll start looking at land for sale tomorrow, okay?'

She nodded, even though she knew that would be impossible. Las Viñas was not only her dream, but the only viable dream. It was the only piece of land they could ever afford around here. Still, trying to swallow around the lump in her throat, she did feel better, now that Dev was home.

'So, who moved in then?' he asked, peering through the window.

'Her name is Victoria Bishop. She looks just like Luce.'

Dev turned his face to hide the smile in hearing the bitter jealousy in her voice. 'And?'

'Pia was not pleased with my greeting to Victoria, and she is most adamant that I apologise and we become friends. But I can't,' she said. 'I am mourning the loss of my dreams. Even though I'm sure she is a perfectly nice person, this Victoria Bishop has taken them away from me. It may not be logical, but I cannot help it. We can never be friends.'

'That's fair enough, Mari. But you know what they say. Keep your friends close and your enemies closer,' he said, standing and opening the door.

'What are you going to do?' she asked.

'Go meet the enemy,' he said with a grin.

~

Victoria checked the primer in the Green Room and saw it was ready. She'd chosen La Verde to start with because it was the smallest room. Still, it was going to take at least two coats of the mint green paint she'd bought to fully replace the old colour, which was a slightly dated, mossy green.

She had covered all the antique furniture she was planning on keeping and had moved a few pieces that didn't suit her vision. The mattress on the bed looked old, so she decided she should turn it and give it a good clean. It was a double-sized mattress but very heavy, and she struggled to turn it. She'd have to stand it up straight first and then throw it over to the other side. Standing on the solid oak bed frame, she turned the mattress and dropped it heavily back onto the frame. Something crawled over her foot, and she saw dozens of large spiders running across her feet and the room.

It was like a scene from a nightmare. Victoria screamed and, feeling spiders all over her, tore off her shirt and ran out the front door in only her bra and sweats. She shook out her hair and landed in the arms of a man she'd never seen before.

'Whoa, hey!'

'Spiders!' she cried, shaking her arms and legs.

'Shh, you're okay,' he said, as she took deep breaths and calmed the adrenaline coursing through her. She'd always been afraid of spiders.

'Where are they?' he asked.

Suddenly aware she was virtually topless in a stranger's arms, she pulled back but shook her hair and pants again.

'Spiders,' she managed. 'In the mattress.'

'I'll go have a look,' he said, shrugging off his jacket and placing it over her shoulders. 'Here, this will cover you.'

'Okay,' she sniffed, wrapping the jacket around her. He was gone about ten minutes, which was just enough time for Victoria to be hit with the full force of her embarrassment. She'd literally jumped into a strange man's arms in her pink silk bra because of a few spiders.

He came out, dragging the mattress behind him.

'I'm afraid to say this mattress is officially Hotel Arachnid and has no chance of returning to the human world. I've checked the mattresses in the other bedrooms just to be sure this wasn't a full takeover, but they were all okay.'

'Uh, thank you,' she said, taking a breath. 'I'll buy a new mattress when I'm finished painting.'

'BeBi's is the place to buy a good mattress,' he said. 'You can't tell from the small shop inside, but they have a warehouse out the back of Reno's with mattresses and frames. Reno and his family own both.'

'Ha!' she replied. 'Reno! That cheeky little man tried to double-charge me thinking I couldn't do math, couldn't speak Spanish, or both. And not a single person at BeBi's would help me.'

He looked genuinely surprised. 'Reno? But he's the most honest man I know! Marilena's uncle would never do that.'

Victoria laughed, understanding. 'Ah, Marilena's uncle, how convenient,' she said. 'And you are?' she asked, realising they hadn't introduced themselves.

'Alas, I am merely a local just returned home. Devan Acosta, but call me Dev.' He reached out his hand and she took it hesitantly, shaking it and looking up to his face. His hair was dark brown and curled slightly, lighter at the ends, perhaps from being in the sun all day. His skin was deeply tanned, and he had light hazel eyes that sparkled mischievously.

'Victoria Bishop,' she answered, pulling her hand away. 'Where did you return from?'

'New Zealand. I've spent the last two seasons there, learning everything I could about their winemaking techniques and management.'

'But you're from Mendoza, couldn't you have learned here?' she asked.

'Of course. I did, and I worked here for many years. But competition for the best jobs is very fierce in Mendoza and many owners like to hire winemakers and vineyard managers that can bring skills from Europe, New Zealand and Australia. I mean, that's the excuse I gave my family,' he said with a wink. 'But I always wanted to travel around New Zealand. Do those epic walks, skydiving, jetboats, the whole thing.'

'And did you?' she asked.

'Every bucket list moment in New Zealand – checked,' he said with a grin. 'Your turn.'

'I'm Victoria Bishop, raised in Cleveland. Recently discovered I'm an Anyas de Alveras and was introduced to . . .' she waved her arm over the whole vineyard, '. . . this.'

'Heavy,' he said, nodding, and she laughed. He was the only person she'd met so far that didn't seem to be taking this so seriously. 'It's good your job was able to let you come down for a while. What do you do back home?'

'I live in Los Angeles and I'm a talent manager. Long story very, very short, I'm on a six-month sabbatical from work,' she said. His interest made part of her feel eager to share, the other part – the part that was feeling like she was unwelcome in this town – was hesitant to say too much.

'And how is it so far?' he asked. 'Besides the spiders, of course.'

'It's . . . fine,' she finished. He raised an eyebrow, and Victoria couldn't help but notice how attractive he was. 'It is difficult,' she continued. 'But it's also . . . this land . . . just being here makes me feel like I'm part of something that I recognise and that recognises me, something that I belong to. I just haven't figured out how or why yet.'

'You are an Anyas de Alveras and this *is* your land. You belong to it, and it to you.' He looked around. 'It is good to be home,' he said finally, turning back to her. 'And it is very good to meet you, Victoria Bishop. I'll pick up my jacket soon, maybe take that ole mattress to Reno's and get a replacement for you. He'll come around.'

Victoria huffed.

He smiled. 'Don't worry, you will find friends here. There are quite a few characters around these parts I reckon you'll be quite fond of, and I know they'll be fond of you in time. Good day, Victoria.'

She watched his strong form walk away and felt something stir inside her she hadn't felt for a long time.

'Don't. Even. Think about it,' she whispered to herself, closing the door behind him.

CHAPTER ELEVEN

The following morning, Victoria looked across to where Santi had pointed out the old winery building. She could see the vines parted around a walkway, which she entered with a feeling of familiarity. When she sighed, the vines sighed with her, revealing the path before her as the stone building came into view. She opened the large door and stepped inside. The temperature was different in there. Cool, dry. Lined along the walls were dozens of oak barrels on their sides, stacked atop one another. There were a few larger ones as well, standing upright.

She inhaled the scent of red wine-soaked oak, and her soul seemed to expand. Fingers tingling, she followed the smell, touching everything in her path. This took her to the end of the barn, where she found a little door she never would have otherwise seen.

She opened the door and a staircase dropped down into a cellar. It was black down there, but she noted a lantern and matches just beside the door. She lit it and made her way down the small staircase, like an attic in reverse. At the bottom of the six stairs there was a candle to light other lanterns, and within moments the small space was lit up with a soft glow, showcasing bottle upon bottle of wine that had been aged for at least forty years.

As Victoria glided through the room, she pulled bottles out. Some were simple labels from as far back as 1954 that simply said *Bodegas Anyas de Alveras*. Finally, at the end of the rows, she stopped. She knew why she was here. It had *called* her here.

Bodegas Anyas de Alveras, 1963. Luce.

And with it, the next part of the diary.

Diary of Luce Anyas de Alveras, 1966

The 1963 vintage of Bodegas Anyas de Alveras Malbec is the first bottle that is mine. Not only since I came of age and gave my blood to the land, but the wine that I then picked, crushed, pressed, stomped on with my feet and tasted every step of the way.

Mama didn't tell me when I married the land, which is how she says it, that I would feel it so deeply, that it would be my life blood, the air I breathe, needing it to sustain me more than food, more than water. I began to rise with the sun, following the call of the vines during bud burst. Sometimes I could feel them turning towards me as if I was the sun instead. I knew the taste of the earth, the smell of each block. I knew every grape, and even though we had many workers on the vineyard, Mama and I were part of every process of the winemaking. We had a winemaker, too. Javier, from Spain. But Mama and I were involved at every step.

And the 1963 vintage is the first vintage of mine, so on the label it says 'Bodegas Anyas de Alveras, 1963, Luce'.

Mama and Papa talk constantly of politics and the economy, in hushed whispers. Papa has announced that we are taking our Luce vintage to an international wine show in Buenos Aires to gain interest for Mendoza again, in the wines that people can no longer afford because of the low employment rate.

I don't really know what they are talking about, but that does not in any way dim the absolute excitement of going to Buenos Aires, to the big city. We've never had an international wine show come to our country, so everyone in Mendoza is going if they can.

I heard Mama hissing at Papa that 'the girls are being pranced around like show ponies, and I won't have it.'

Papa has never hit Mama, but he raised his arm and hissed back to her, 'Unless you and your Inca magic can start creating money during our financial crisis, we have no choice. Everything is dependent on Luce.'

Remembering what Papa said, I asked Sylvia if she and her family were coming with their horses.

'Yes, of course. I suppose what your papa said is accurate. But the horses aren't the ones being shown,' she grinned at me. 'They are carrying around the colourful prize.'

'What is that?' I asked, intrigued.

Sylvia laughed in a way only she can. 'You!'

'Me?' I cried, trying to sound embarrassed, but my friends knew me too well. My voice came out thrilled instead. I wanted *to be the most beautiful, popular girl in that show. I wanted to take my wine into the world and be famous. I didn't know how being a winemaker could make you famous, but I was certain I could figure it out. I began putting together my outfit in my head.*

'You *are the show pony, Luce,' Eugenia said. 'For men. For* marriage. *Keep that in your mind while you start dressing yourself in your head.'*

I scowled at Eugenia. Sometimes knowing someone your whole life is annoying, even if they are your best friend ever.

The fact that she could see exactly what I was thinking – well, I knew a few things, too.

'Are you coming?' I asked her.

Eugenia rolled her eyes. 'Yes. You, your highness, are not the only one on show that day.'

I batted my eyelashes at her.

'But, Gen, what if they find you a husband when you already know who you are going to marry?' I asked sweetly.

Eugenia sat up quickly and glared at me. I shut my mouth. While the four of us have been best friends for years, nobody but me knows that Eugenia is secretly in love with Pedro. I was sworn to secrecy, and I wasn't actually going to say anything. I would never do that to Gen. Plus, Caro would be really angry, we both agreed. Her older brother was an annoying pest we'd all been irritated by for years.

I used to loathe Pedro. He either ignored us completely or picked on us or stole our ice cream before we could have it. But he's been so helpful in teaching me in my first year in the vineyard. We've spent a lot of time together lately, something I've not told Eugenia.

Or Caro.

Or Sylvia for that matter.

'Caro,' I said, changing the subject as I was feeling quite guilty, 'you will come as my guest, then we'll all four be together in Buenos Aires!'

Eugenia relaxed and Sylvia winked, making me wonder if she knew more than she let on. She usually did. But Caro let out a groan and fell on the bed.

'Ugh, I'd rather marry the pony than go to the show,' she said.

'Not sure that's legal in this country, Caro,' Sylvia joked, and Caro threw a shoe at her.

'What's the point anyway?' Caro asked, sulking.

It was very rare to see Caro anything other than witty and on form.

'What's wrong Caro?' I asked.

'It's obvious, isn't it?' she cried. 'There's Eugenia with her beautiful fair skin and long black hair so shiny I can see my damn reflection in it. Sylvia – good lord. Blonde, tall, beautiful. And of course there is you, Luce. The Princess of Mendoza. The gem of the vineyards. And then, there is me. ME.'

'Caro, you're the best of us,' Sylvia said. I was so glad it was Sylvia that said it because even though I wanted to say the same thing it only sounds factual when Sylvia says things.

'I know that,' Caro said, and we all laughed. 'But I'm not beautiful. And while you all go out show-ponying around, I'll be the sow. Not even the sow, the gilt.'

'Caro, you are not a wild pig,' Eugenia said.

An idea suddenly came to me.

'I've got it! Caro, we'll give you a makeover! Make you the show pony of all ponies. And the best part is, it's the city and nobody will know who you are or where you come from, so we can make up wild stories and go out on the town. And it doesn't matter anyway. The only thing that matters is that you are amazing and we'll draw all attention onto you.'

'Yes!' Eugenia agreed, her voice wild and excited.

Sylvia crossed her arms. 'You should feel as beautiful as you are without having gross old men ogle you.'

'Says the most beautiful girl in Argentina,' Caro muttered.

Sylvia looked offended. It was unfortunate for Sylvia that it was true. She truly was quite possibly the most beautiful girl in Argentina, and the one who cared the least about it. She only cared about the horses.

'I didn't mean to upset you,' Sylvia said quietly.

'You didn't, sorry Syl,' Caro said, hugging her. 'Let's just go to the city and see as much and do as much as we can!'

~

'Wow,' Victoria said, holding the pages close.

Suddenly she heard a loud bang as the trap door blew shut, most of the lanterns blowing out simultaneously. Victoria pulled out her phone and turned on the torch, climbing the steps and pushing the door she'd come through. It seemed locked. She pushed again, trying a few different angles to open the door, but it was well shut.

The torch went out on her phone.

'What the heck?' she muttered, looking down. Her phone had gone into low battery mode suddenly. 'How is that possible? It was just on full charge!'

She thought she heard something above, so she banged on the door with her fists.

'Is someone up there?! Please help! Help!'

Panic began to creep in, and she found herself somehow saying a sort of prayer she'd never learned, in a language she didn't speak.

The door opened and Pia was there, looking down at Victoria. 'Ah, dios mio! Mierda! Señora Victoria! I saw the open door to the winery but couldn't find you. Thank goodness I heard you knock. Are you okay?'

'I am now,' Victoria said, climbing the stairs, her body shaking. 'I don't know what happened. The door just . . . closed.'

Pia nodded sombrely. 'The house does that sometimes when it wants to show you something. Did it?'

'Did it what?'

'Show you something?' Pia asked.

Victoria nodded and, as she pulled out one of the bottles of wine to show Pia, realised her hand was still shaking. She didn't show her the diary.

Pia's eyes widened. 'That's an original wine from Las Viñas – 1963 – wow! Cool! Here, are you hungry? I brought you desayuno,' Pia said, producing a small brown bag from a bakery and handing it to her as they came into the light.

'Bolas de fraile,' Victoria said, taking one of the small dulce de leche filled donuts. 'Thank you.'

'Oh, you know them. I'll give you the address of Auntie Adriana's bakery – she's not really my auntie, but Mama's closest friend.'

Victoria didn't have the heart to tell Pia that she knew exactly who her lovely auntie was and that she was part of a mission to drive her out of town.

'That's weird,' Pia said, turning to the winery entrance. 'I just walked through this way, and it was clear.'

Victoria looked up. It was the same path she, too, had walked, but suddenly it was thick with vines.

'Dios mío!' Pia cried.

'Is that . . . I mean is it . . . ?' Victoria whispered, her breath short.

Pia nodded. 'Yes. A *bud*.'

They both looked around. The entire row of vines from the winery to the house was suddenly covered with tiny green buds.

CHAPTER TWELVE

After the cool welcome she'd had in the village, it was both a surprise and a pleasure to receive a handwritten note in her mailbox from one of her neighbours, extending an invitation to stop in for a visit and a cup of tea.

Dear Victoria,

Welcome to Las Viñas! My husband and I would be honoured if you would join us for a cup of tea at your convenience. I will alert the other neighbours, as the fastest way down to ours is through Soto property. Everyone is looking forward to meeting you!

Walter and Romina Munoz

They'd given their address and phone number, and Victoria called Romina to confirm she'd come down that day, with a stop along the way to visit her Soto neighbours first.

The vines that had bloomed between the house and her winery, and the bottles of the 1963 vintage, gave her a sense of confidence in her place here, something that allowed her to feel that she was a person worthy of joining this community. Even if she was only going to be here for a short while, something was happening in the vineyard, and she was pretty certain that with each diary entry she uncovered and every bud that bloomed, Las Viñas was telling her its secrets.

Google Maps had shown her that there were four houses in walking distance of her own. The Soto property was just to the south, and past that was Romina and Walter's. There was another unknown house to the west of theirs, which linked to the last house, the closest to hers, which was that of Marilena and Pia. She would finish there, despite her dread of seeing Marilena again.

The day was so perfect it was like a painting. The air, so close to the mountains, was thinner, dry, the land vast and flat, expanding endlessly until the suddenness of the impenetrable wall of the Andes. The sky was an almost surreal shade of blue, the lines between objects so distinct and clear it looked like a photo that had been sharpened and clarified with every single Instagram filter.

It took her forty-five minutes to get to the first house, the Soto property. It was a classic rancher of the same era as her own home, she reckoned, with endless hectares of land stretched out in front, not in vines, like hers, but in paddocks. She saw at least three horses grazing, including a curious white one that walked towards her at the fence line.

Victoria's breath caught as she reached her hand out to the approaching horse. 'And she cared about nothing more than the horses . . .' she whispered.

'Good lord, you look like Luce,' a woman said from behind, her voice deep and strong. She wore a button-down top tucked into high-waisted pants with tall boots up to her knees. Her body was slim and lithe, and appeared much younger than her face, which was tanned and lined everywhere it could be, her white hair in a long braid down her back. She was old, and yet timeless. Beautiful, classic. She leaned against the door, shaking her head and smiling.

'It is said the Anyas de Alveras women come from the same blood of the original girl from the Andes. That it is like the genes are only passed through them. I always thought it was codswallop until seeing you today. Luce looked like her Mama but not in the same way you look like Luce. It's uncanny, really.'

'You . . . you're Sylvia, aren't you?' Victoria asked. 'From her diary?'

Sylvia looked stunned. 'Diary? What diary?'

'Las Viñas,' Victoria said, 'is sharing her secrets with me, I believe. I found pages from my grandmother's diary. Two entries so far. It is a very vivid read. I recognised your land before I even saw you.'

Sylvia's expression was unreadable. 'Why's that?'

Victoria smiled. 'The horses. The first entry was the night of her initiation into the vineyard when she was twelve. She took you, and Caro and Eugenia as well,' she said. 'She said you took her riding through the land when you were younger.'

'Horses were always my passion. Your grandmother and I used to go riding on my family's horses late at night after our curfew. She was a terrible rider,' she chuckled. 'Come in, let's have a yerba mate, and you can tell me what Luce has to say in that diary of hers.'

'Yerba mate?' Victoria asked as they ambled to the rancher. 'Is that the same as just "mate"?

'Yes. It's a very caffeinated herbal tea you sip – it is quite the social experience here in Argentina. Have you had any yet?'

'No – nobody around here except Las Viñas has decided to be very social with me yet,' she said.

Sylvia chuckled and opened the door.

Victoria was always taught to offer to take her shoes off when she entered someone's home, but she knew she wouldn't have to ask Sylvia as she followed her into the kitchen, Sylvia's own muddy boots leaving marks on the linoleum floor. It reminded

Victoria of her parent's kitchen in Ohio – left behind in another era that should have moved on decades ago. Still, Sylvia seemed comfortable. Which made sense. According to the diary, Sylvia had been living here most of her life.

Sylvia put a hunk of tea leaves into a strange-looking cup, wooden with metal fittings, and round, like a miniature oak barrel.

'This is the gourd,' she said, pouring cold then hot water down the metal straw coming out the side. 'We'll let it steep. Very Argentinian tradition. I feel honoured to be the first to share it with you.'

Sylvia sat across from Victoria and put the gourd in front of her. 'I wish you would have had the chance to know your grandmother Luce. She was a true force of nature,' she said fondly, looking towards the hacienda.

'The last passage I received was when you were all preparing to go to Buenos Aires as "show ponies".'

Sylvia cackled. 'Oh my, what I wouldn't give to relive that time of our lives. We were so young. Whole world in front of us. No idea that life . . . well . . .'

'That life what?' Victoria asked.

'Doesn't always end up how you think it might,' Sylvia said, picking up the gourd and handing it to Victoria. 'Go on, sip the mate now.'

Victoria took a sip through the straw. It was a bitter concoction, but at the same time herbal and fragrant.

'Do you like it?' Sylvia asked.

Victoria nodded. 'Sylvia, can you tell me anything about my mother? Or why my grandmother left? Or why the vineyard is cursed? Do you know anything about my father, or my grandfather even?'

'I'm afraid I can't tell you much that you want to know. I knew Luce when we were girls, and then we all left in the seventies and went our separate ways in life as we grew older, as you do,' she said. 'Your grandfather's name was Felipe Ortega. He was from Spain – Andalucia, I believe. He talked about bullfighting, I remember.'

'I hate bullfighting,' Victoria said with a shudder. During their backpacking trip in Europe, she and her girlfriends had gone to a fight in Sevilla in Spain, and walked out of Plaza de Toros de la Real Maestranza within the first five minutes.

'So did your grandmother,' Sylvia said, and then stopped, pressing her lips together as if she'd let something slip. But then she smiled and gestured to Victoria to take another sip. 'You pass it back and forth,' she instructed.

'Oh, sorry,' she said, taking a sip and handing it to Sylvia, listening intently to her.

'Barbaric business, bullfighting. But it was – still is, I hear – very big in Spain. Felipe was older than us, a man when we were practically girls. Very rich, very handsome. An excellent match for the family.' She looked thoughtful. 'Of course, we were young romantics, so we didn't think much about the political situation and the economic situation at the time. But looking back at the problems in Argentina then, which only got worse, I can see that it was an advantageous match.'

'But not a love match?' Victoria asked, and Sylvia forced a laugh, her jaw tight.

'There were not many of them in this region in the 1960s. But Felipe's life was mostly in Spain, so he spent much of his time there and only came back for visits. Then one day he just didn't come back. He had a mistress in Spain or another family – I can't remember really,' she said with a breezy laugh. 'It was so long ago. And then Las Viñas stopped growing. So Luce left with Camila when Camila was still young, and made a new home for them. I was already in university then. We all lost touch around that time. I did occasionally get a letter from Luce. She and Camila had a falling out after Camila went to a school in America – high school or university? I can't remember,' she said with an apologetic look. 'I'm old.'

'Didn't you know? Seventies are the new fifties,' Victoria said.

Sylvia smiled, but it was tight.

'You really don't remember anything else?' Victoria asked, leaning in, her eyes pleading.

'Camila fell in with the wrong crowd, apparently. I'm not sure what crowd that was, but she stopped talking to your grandmother. Luce found out that Camila died in a car accident five years later. She was devastated. When she found out you existed, she could die happy, she said.' Sylvia looked out towards Las Viñas again. 'Even after we lost regular contact, we remained the most loyal of friends. There are some things time and life do not change.'

Sylvia's gaze never wavered from Las Viñas, and Victoria heard a trace of something deep and meaningful in her words, but she said no more. After a few moments, Victoria thought Sylvia was lost in a reverie too far away from now, so she changed the subject.

'I see you still keep horses here,' Victoria said.

Sylvia seemed to come out of her trance and looked at her, her face brightening. 'Do you ride?'

'Likely as badly if not worse than my grandmother,' she answered. 'I've gone on a couple of little trail rides. But I wouldn't say I know how to ride, just how to sit on top and hopefully not fall – off if the horse is well trained.'

'Come,' she said, leading Victoria to the barn. 'I was just going to take Fuego out for a run. He is my prize champion. But we can run later. Gorda needs to move her ass, the lazy girl, so you can ride her. She is very slow, but she'll get you down to Walter and Romina's. They are most excited to meet you.'

Was that it? Was that literally everything Sylvia was going to say about her family? She felt there was so much Sylvia could share with her, so many memories that could make her history come alive. Perhaps Sylvia and Luce had had a falling out as well, and Sylvia didn't want to upset her with it? Victoria didn't want to push.

'Yes, I'm looking forward to meeting them, and I have brought them a gift. And one for you, too,' Victoria said, reaching into her bag and pulling out one of the 1963 Luce wines.

It was impossible to read Sylvia's face as she stared at the bottle.

'Come, let's get to Walter and Romina's. Walter will adore you, I can tell,' Sylvia said finally, putting the wine bottle down before walking them down to the horses. Victoria noticed her hand was shaking as she did.

Gorda, Spanish for 'fat,' was a short and quite literally 'fat' horse who wanted to graze on everything. This didn't bother Victoria, who was more than happy to take it slow. She'd never really trusted horses after a nasty fall as a child. Michael had made her do a few small rides, for which she was grateful now. She didn't particularly enjoy sitting on Gorda, but she wasn't utterly terrified. She sighed. She wasn't ready to think kindly about Michael yet.

They arrived at a small cottage about twenty minutes later. An old man was sitting outside on a rocking chair. He looked to be well into his eighties, but his eyes sparkled and he grinned when they arrived.

'Sylvia! Romina said you were coming around with a special guest today. This her?'

Sylvia gracefully dismounted Fuego and tied him loosely to a post, before helping Victoria down from Gorda.

'Victoria, meet Walter Munoz, one of your new neighbours. Walter—'

He whistled long and low. 'Well now, aren't you the spitting image of Luce Anyas de Alveras? You must be a relation.'

Victoria smiled. 'I am the granddaughter, apparently. Though I didn't know my mother or my grandmother while they were alive, sadly. I have recently been introduced to my family home, though, and Romina was kind enough to extend an invitation. I brought a gift,' she said, handing him the bottle of wine.

'Whew!' he whistled again as he looked at the label. 'Now you sit down and let me tell you the story about the time I had to rescue Luce from quicksand when she was just a young one,' he said, settling into his rocking chair as Victoria sat beside him. 'Not staying, Sylvia?'

She shook her head.

'Have to get this one off for a long ride or he'll cop an attitude,' she said, nodding to Fuego. She smiled at Victoria and pulled her in for a hug. 'So happy to have you here, my girl,' she whispered softly, brushing the hair from Victoria's forehead the way her mom did, looking at her face almost in awe. 'Spitting image indeed.' She shook her head and walked away.

'Walter, bring Gorda home later for me, okay?' Sylvia said, hopping back on Fuego.

'Sure, sure,' he said, turning back to Victoria. 'Have you ever been in quicksand, little lady?'

'Um, no, I don't think I have,' she answered distractedly, watching Sylvia ride into the woods, with an uncomfortable feeling in her belly that Sylvia was hiding something.

'The thing about quicksand is that the more you struggle, the faster you sink. Ever hear that?'

She turned back to Walter. That's exactly how she felt at the moment, but he didn't seem to notice that he'd said something more profound than he'd intended.

'It sounds familiar, but I don't think we have quicksand where I grew up.'

'Well, we have it here alright, so you listen to old Walter. Luce was just a girl when she was drowning in the quicksand out there. And I was a bit older than her, so I knew better. I said to her, "you hold still now, little lady," just like I'm saying to you now. I ran and ran so fast that I wore holes in the bottom of my shoes and got burns on the bottom of my feet from the little fires they created. Just when I thought I couldn't go any further, I found a wild horse grazing in the meadow,' he said, leaning in.

'A wild horse?' she asked, intrigued. 'What did you do?'

'The only thing I could do – I jumped on that horse bareback and tugged his mane to take him to the rescue. But he refused. Wild horses, you see, they don't like being told what to do. So, I took off my shirt and wrapped it around his eyes, blinding him, so he had to follow me. I became the boss then, and we got back just when Luce was buried up to her shoulders, her eyes huge and scared. I tried to reach over and pull her out, but to no avail. Finally, I heard the horse whinny, and I knew! I tied myself to the horse, and a long branch to me, and when Luce finally grabbed on, I said, "giddy-up"! And the horse took off, pulling Luce out of the sand. When she was safe, I jumped off the wild horse and took my shirt off his eyes. He galloped off into the sunset, and I picked up Luce and walked her home in my arms.'

Victoria's jaw dropped. 'Wow, I don't know what to say. That was . . .'

'Absolute bullshit,' a female voice came from the porch door, the speaker opening it with her hip as she was carrying a tray of empanadas. 'Walter, you tell the tallest tales,' she said with a laugh. 'Hi, Victoria honey, I'm Romina, we talked on the phone?'

Victoria nodded.

'And this here is my husband, Walter, the biggest storyteller in all of Argentina. Here, have an empanada. They are filled with shredded chicken and onion. My mother's recipe.'

'Thank you,' Victoria said, taking one. The juice from the empanada burnt her mouth and she sucked in her breath.

'Hot, dear, be careful.'

'Delicious,' she said, though it was still too hot in her mouth. 'I just bought a new cookbook in town and I'm going to try empanadas.'

'Butter and lard, my dear. You think the recipe is wrong because it's impossible for there to be that much butter and lard in a dish so light and flaky. Follow it anyway.'

Walter took one as well, grinning at his wife and winking.

Victoria nodded and took another small bite.

'So that wasn't a true story, Walter?'

'Of course it was!' Walter scoffed, eating his empanada. 'Oh, hot.'

Romina shrugged. 'Well, Walter, I didn't know you then, so I can't say for sure, but you have to admit, it sounds like a bit of a whopper.'

'I agree, it would sound like a bit of a whopper if it wasn't from me. Because you know I always tell the truth.'

'Now that's not true at all. The truth is you never *completely* lie. There's a big difference,' Romina amended, daintily nibbling her own empanada. 'Victoria, tell us a little bit about yourself, since nobody here knew you even existed until recently. Must be hard to arrive in a place like this, steeped in history and legend and way too much drama. I mean, really, who inherits a cursed vineyard?'

Victoria laughed, feeling lighter.

'I remember the stories I used to hear when we moved here,' Romina continued. 'That the Anyas women were sacrificed to the land or to the wine gods or something. Poor Luce. She was so young when her handsome husband left her here with their daughter Camila and went back to Spain. Never came back.'

'Ah, but he did come back, they say. One night, he found Luce . . . well, rumour has it he wasn't happy, and he was never seen or heard of again,' Walter said.

Victoria's jaw dropped.

'Walter! You leave Victoria and anyone else out of those tall tales of yours!' Romina reprimanded. 'Walter grew up in one of the neighbouring towns but moved to Santa Fe with his family back in the sixties. That's where he met me. We didn't move back here until the eighties, so whatever silly rumours this ole storyteller has are just that . . . rumours.'

'Tell us about yourself, Victoria,' Walter said, taking another empanada, pulling it apart this time before biting in. It was still steaming. He handed her half.

'They really are delicious,' she said, and Romina glowed.

Victoria stayed for the next hour or so chatting with Walter and Romina, and no more mention came up of Las Viñas or its curse, or the uncomfortable rumours that Walter had raised.

Instead, they seemed genuinely interested in Victoria as a person, and Walter was the funniest storyteller she'd ever met. Romina would either confirm or deny his tales, or answer again with 'Well, I didn't know you then, Walter, but . . .'

Victoria laughed and laughed, and felt like she'd made genuine new friends. She said as much when she stood to leave.

'Where are you headed next, honey?' Romina asked.

Victoria pulled up Google Maps and pointed to the next house on her list.

'Oh, that one's empty at the moment,' Walter said.

Romina looked at the map and nodded. 'The Ramirez family still own it, but they moved to a little condo down in Bariloche now that the kids are all out of the house. Never seen two parents happier to get rid of the last of their kids. Ski bunnies,' she added. 'They're renting it out though, if you know anyone looking. It's similar to this, small, but tidy.'

'I hear Dev Acosta just got back into town,' Walter said. 'Have you met him yet, Victoria?'

She found herself blushing, remembering the exact state in which she'd met Dev Acosta. A state of undress. 'I met him a few days ago. He said he'd just returned from New Zealand.'

Romina shook her head, winking at her. 'I'll bet he had eyes for you, pretty thing. A man with those looks was born to flirt. Tried to keep my daughters away from him for years, but they all crushed on him.' She laughed. 'Still, good man. Great viticulturalist. I'll give him a call and let him know the cottage is for rent. He'll be wanting to get out of his mama's house as soon as possible with all those nieces and nephews there every day. He adores them, but a bachelor needs a place of his own.'

'Especially a bachelor like Devan. He's quite the ladies' man, just like I was back in the day,' Walter started. 'Victoria, next time you come, if my wife isn't here, I'll tell you about the time Brigitte Bardot came to Buenos Aires and asked me to whisk her away. We were so close, if the National Gendarmerie hadn't stopped us in the helicopter . . .'

'Oh, Walter!' Romina huffed, rolling her eyes.

Victoria laughed. 'That sounds like one I won't want to miss. I'll be back, I promise. And since the other cottage is empty, I'll leave you another bottle of wine and lighten my load. Now just one left, so I'd better head to Marilena's now,' she said, making a face.

Romina patted her shoulder. 'Mari's a good woman, with a big heart. I feel for her. Don't actually know anyone who loves Las Viñas the way she does. It's that love that will make her come around, I promise. But until then, don't you let her or her friends bully you. Las Viñas is yours, you hear, honey? You and the vines belong together. You're an Anyas de Alveras. You'll see.'

Victoria hugged her, taking an extra squeeze. She'd needed to hear that today.

'Do you need a lift? It's a couple miles in either direction but a short ride,' Romina continued.

'Thanks, but I think I'll walk,' Victoria said. 'Google Maps say it will take me about thirty-five minutes, which will be just the right amount of time to get my legs working like normal again. Gorda might not have moved quickly, but she sure is wide. I feel like I've done the splits.'

'Speaking of,' Romina said loudly to Walter, 'get off your lazy bum and walk or ride Gorda back to Sylvia, why don't you?'

'Fine, fine,' he said, standing and dusting off his pants, putting his hat on. 'Might just be another adventure, Romi. You never know what stories I might come back with!' he laughed, untying Gorda and setting off.

Romina rolled her eyes fondly and turned back to Victoria. 'You'll shave a few minutes off if you cut down this path to the empty Ramirez cottage, then you'll find the road, instead of having to go round our property. It's very straightforward. Ah, and I'd better give Dev a call. It was a pleasure to meet you, Victoria.'

~

By the time Victoria arrived at Marilena's doorstep, she had an entire speech planned. Well, she had about six different speeches planned. In some she was strong and firm in her intolerance of Marilena's behaviour. Others where she played on her sympathies. Some where she came out with 'what impression are you making on your daughter?' – which even she thought was below the belt.

She hadn't yet decided which she was going to use as she pounded on Marilena's door. Pound wasn't entirely accurate. That would have been rude. But she did knock. Then knocked louder, and slightly louder, until she did pound, at least a little bit.

Still, the door remained closed. Not knowing if the feeling inside her was more irritated or deflated, Victoria turned to leave, when she tripped and the last bottle of Luce's 1963 fell out of her bag, rolling down the hill.

'No!' she cried, reaching out and managing to catch the bottle just before it hit a rock. 'Thank god!' she cried, dusting herself off and putting the bottle back in her bag, which immediately broke at the bottom, so the bottle rolled out again.

She caught it and huffed. She knew it was completely impossible, but she had the very distinct impression that this would keep happening if she didn't leave the bottle with Marilena.

'It would be a lot easier if she opened the door!' she hissed to . . . who was she hissing to?

She looked around once more but seemed quite alone. Victoria slowly walked back to the porch of Marilena's house and left the wine bottle by the door.

'I'm leaving it! See?'

She was nearly on her own property when she heard a slight creak. Looking back, she saw that Marilena had opened the porch door and found the bottle. Her joy, sadness and love of the wine was palpable, even from so far away. When Marilena hugged the bottle to her, Victoria could feel it in her very soul.

CHAPTER THIRTEEN

The following evening, Victoria was sitting in her kitchen when she heard a knock on her window.

'Housekeeping,' a small voice called, and Victoria was brought out of her reverie, looking up.

'Jesus!' she said, jumping when she saw a face in the window.

'Sorry Victoria! It's me, Pia.'

Victoria took a deep breath and held her chest. 'Jesus,' she whispered again, opening the door.

Pia was standing there with another girl her age, who looked at Victoria with big eyes.

'Hi, girls. What are you up to tonight?' she asked, looking at her phone. The sun had only just gone down but it was 8 pm.

'Victoria! This is my best friend, Gabi. She's staying the night, and we wanted to come over and invite you to come to the Bud Burst Festival with us tonight!' Pia exclaimed.

'You mean you are trying to get a ride to a festival to meet all the cute boys at some party, right?' Victoria guessed.

'It's not a party, Victoria,' Pia said. 'It's the *Bud Burst Festival* – there's a bonfire and events and even a band, which Gabi's boyfriend Julio is in. Honestly, the whole region goes, you'll love it!'

'The whole region goes and your mother doesn't?' Victoria asked, crossing her arms.

'No, Mama isn't going this year,' Pia said with a grim look. 'She's rebelling. Honestly, she's acting like a teenager.'

'Hey, we are teenagers!' Gabi huffed.

'Worse than a teenager then,' Pia amended. 'But she does know we're going; she just won't drive us, and it's too far to walk. Come on, Victoria, you need to get out and meet the locals! Have some fun! Plus, it's tradition.'

Victoria knew that every word out of Pia's mouth was the manipulation of two fifteen-year-old girls who just wanted to go meet boys at a bonfire, but so long as Marilena knew they were out, what harm could it do her to go out and try to have fun? The last few weeks of her life had been an adventure, but not a particularly sociable one. She deserved to have fun, didn't she? She deserved to meet new people.

'Oh, fine,' she agreed finally. 'I'll drive you and stay for an hour, but that's it.'

'Yay!' they squealed together, hugging, and Gabi ran to the car.

Victoria put her hand on Pia's shoulder. 'Pia, wait,' she said quietly. 'I don't want anyone to know about . . . you know . . . what we saw the other day on Las Viñas. Not yet, okay?'

Pia pretended to zip her lips. 'The secrets of Las Viñas are safe with me,' she said, but turned back guiltily. 'I did kind of accidentally mention something to Mama. I'm sorry, Victoria.'

Victoria knew that had been inevitable and smiled, guiding Pia to the car.

'As you should have,' she said. 'Go on, get in the back, girls.'

Victoria glanced in the rear-view mirror as the two girls did one another's make-up in the light from Gabi's iPhone. Pia was just barely fifteen and still slight, with a skinny frame and long dark hair. She was very pretty, but she still looked young, and had an innocence about her. So she looked adorable as she pouted her lips for Gabi to apply a pink lipstick, shrugging off her jacket to reveal a tank-top dress.

Victoria laughed quietly as she saw Pia start shivering.

'Pia, I know it's spring, but it's freezing outside. Why are you wearing a summer dress? Won't you be cold?'

But it was Gabi's eyes who met hers.

'Because we want to look pretty,' she said. 'All the girls wear dresses to the bonfire. It's warm once you get around the fire, because it's massive. But it's never warm enough that you don't need a boy's jacket,' she finished with a cheeky grin.

Gabi was the opposite of Pia. She had honey highlights in her brown hair, and she had a figure like Salma Hayek. If Pia was fifteen going on fifteen-and-a-half, Gabi was fifteen going on twenty. Victoria didn't miss being their age, but she did miss that kind of excitement about every moment, where the whole world was yours to make of it what you could. Where the future was unwritten, and dreams were still possible.

'We weren't lying about this being a family event, Señora Victoria,' Gabi said respectfully. 'I don't know how many exactly, but over a hundred people will come tonight, who have been part of the tradition for ages. It is a celebration of the first buds blooming in the vineyards. It's called bud bloom, or bud burst. The grown-ups drink wine, and the teenagers steal some and hang around the fire. But one of the best parts of the night is when we nominate the Lady of the Buds!'

'What's that?' Victoria asked, easing the car into a park.

'Oh my gosh,' Pia gushed. 'It's the highest honour. They vote the prettiest and most popular and most beloved girl from the villages to be the Lady of the Buds. But even more importantly, we send her to the big Harvest Festival in Mendoza, where they name the Lady of the *Vines* in the whole of the province.'

'It's like a pageant,' Gabi explained. 'Do you watch Miss America? Pia and I watch it every year. We make popcorn and everything.'

Victoria smiled. 'So, are you girls in the running for the Lady of the Buds?'

Gabi sighed dramatically, falling back on her seat. 'Sadly no, we are too young. You have to be of age, which is seventeen here.'

'I think Mama said it was originally fifteen,' Pia said. 'Back when it was a festival to introduce the local girls for marriage. Ugh, could you imagine being married at fifteen?!'

'Gross!' Gabi said, opening the door of the car. 'Victoria, will you come with us to the bonfire?'

Victoria looked around and saw a large bonfire with lights all around, just down from where they were parked. She could hear music playing and laughter in the air. Maybe this *would* be fun.

'Lead the way, girls,' she said, and followed Pia and Gabi towards the lights.

There were definitely over a hundred people there, some of whom she recognised. Walter and Romina waved over to her from a long table where glasses of wine were being poured. She waved back and grinned. She saw Adriana talking to a man in line at a stand with 'Choripán Parilla' hand-painted on a wooden board.

'What's Choripán?' Victoria asked.

Pia followed her gaze and waved at Adriana, whose eyes widened when she saw that Pia was with Victoria. Victoria gave her a small smile and wave, which Adriana ignored, looking down at her phone instead.

'Choripán is the most delicious sausage you will ever have,' Pia said. 'It's considered one of the five best sandwich fillings in the world, did you know that?'

'Nobody knows that except your papa,' Gabi said, turning to Victoria. 'Pia's papa is an excellent asador, and he's completely obsessed with Argentinian grilling.'

'That's what makes him the best,' Pia defended, and Gabi shrugged. 'Did you want to go get one, Victoria?'

She did, but Adriana was looking over at her with a hard glare that she'd rather avoid, so she shook her head and they moved on.

'Look, Victoria, there is Sylvia with Gorda,' Pia pointed to the field. 'She offers rides to the kids at the festivals. Only way she can get Gorda to exercise, the lazy fat horse. But Uncle Dev will definitely be here, so look for him!'

'Dev's going to be here?' Gabi asked, jumping up and shoving off her jacket. 'Why didn't you say?'

'Ew Gabi! He's old, cut it out,' Pia said, making a face and grabbing Gabi's arm. 'Bonfire. Your boyfriend, Julio, remember? Playing the guitar just there,' she said pointing to the band. A teenage boy was smiling at Gabi.

'Wait, Dev?' Victoria asked. 'What do you mean, "Uncle Dev?"'

'He's not really my uncle, just like Auntie Adriana isn't really my aunt. He's my dad's best friend. Devan Acosta. He just got back, and I heard him telling Mama he was going to introduce himself to you. Well, if you are "the enemy", which I think you are,' Pia said, laughing.

'Gabi! Pia!' a boy called from the raging bonfire below.

'That's Alex and Dante – they work on the vineyards with Julio. Can we go join them, Victoria?' Pia asked.

'Yes, but give me your phone number so I can text when it's time to go. One hour!'

'Bye, Victoria!' the girls called together, running towards the fire.

'The enemy?' she hissed to herself, remembering their conversation, remembering her attraction, remembering her being *shirtless*. She stopped in front of a table covered in bottles of wine and some glasses. 'No, I will not be embarrassed. He should be embarrassed. That lying, two-faced piece of—'

'Uh oh, who's the enemy?' a deep voice said close behind her. She turned to see Dev there, an empty glass in his hand, a smile on his face. He reached past her and picked up one of the bottles, smiling.

'Me, apparently!' she yelled. 'So, so . . . *you*!'

Dev's eyes widened as Victoria poked him with her finger, so furious she could barely speak.

'Did you put the spiders in my bed? Did Marilena ask you to? And then to come meet "the enemy"?' she demanded.

'Yes! I mean no – NO! I did not put spiders in your bed – that is a very unfortunate side effect of having a house not properly lived in for multiple decades. Yes, I came to meet the enemy, but it was a joke when I said it,' he tried to explain.

'But I am the enemy of Marilena, and you are her best friend,' she said, matter-of-factly.

Dev opened his mouth to say something but closed it, putting his hands up.

'Yes, you're right. Diego, Mari's husband, has been my best friend since we were kids. Mari is one of the most important people in my life, and I came home to hear that her – our – lifelong dream has been taken away. It's not your fault. But please try to understand that it will take her time to accept this new reality.'

She hesitated, trying not to shout her next reply. If she were in their place, wouldn't she be the enemy? Like Skye was to her. The new person. The usurper. The one who took away other people's dreams. It wasn't her fault. In fact, Skye did nothing wrong – it was Michael who left. But she still resented this new woman in his life, who would replace her, who would have his family and her house . . . so, yes . . . she could understand.

Still, she angrily sipped the wine Dev had poured her, a sip too quick for the vastness of the Malbec, and she started coughing.

Dev patted her back and handed her his water bottle.

When she was better, she handed it back, glancing at him. 'Thanks.'

'I'm sorry, Victoria.'

'Fine, I forgive you,' she said, defeated, leaning against a tree. 'I still wish I had someone other than the enemy to hang out with, seeing as I got conned into coming here like this. No offence.'

'None taken. Pia?' he asked, hiding a smile.

'And her friend Gabi,' she amended.

'Oooh, I've heard she's a master manipulator. You had no choice, really,' he laughed.

'They tricked me?' she asked.

'Nah,' he said, smiling. 'They're good kids. Pia is a perfect little human. Kind and good and funny as they come. Gabi is a firecracker growing up a little faster than she should, but she's loyal and hard-working. My nephew is in love for the first time. With her.'

'Let me guess,' she said. 'Your nephew is the great Julio?'

'Julio put the guilt on me! I had to bring my nephews, especially now that they are working on vineyards. They put on this whole to-do about being a part of the community and reintroducing me since I just got back, but as soon as we got here, I realised they were just chasing girls. Sheesh.'

Victoria laughed. 'Well, we were both duped. I promised the girls an hour, but I'm thinking I made a mistake. Everyone is looking at me, either because they hate me or they want to bombard me with questions about Las Viñas. I feel like an intruder.'

'I have an excellent hiding place if you're keen to escape?' he asked.

She hesitated but eventually nodded. He grinned and grabbed a blanket and backpack from the back of a truck.

'I hope that's yours,' she said.

'I prefer you to think I'm a bit more dangerous,' he said, grinning.

'I prefer not to think of you at all,' she quipped, but her body was responding differently.

'Come on, I thought you said you forgave me,' he said in a low voice. Victoria found herself blushing, not because he embarrassed her, but because she was embarrassed by her sudden intense physical attraction to him.

He led her away from the smoke of the bonfire, looking up occasionally, until finally he seemed satisfied and put the blanket down. He lay on his back, then let out a grunt.

'What's wrong?' she asked.

He drew a full bottle of wine from his backpack.

'Forgot about that,' he said, searching the pack for a corkscrew, which he found. He opened the bottle, pouring a small amount into two plastic glasses he had in his bag.

Victoria took a glass and raised her eyebrows. 'Do you always carry a blanket, a bottle of wine and two glasses in your bag? I mean, Walter and Romina told me you were a ladies' man, but this is exceptional planning.'

Dev threw his head back and laughed. 'Old Walter and Romina! And no, I was coming with my sister, Julio's mom, or so I thought. Then at the last minute she threw all the boys in the back of my truck, ran back inside and locked the door.'

Victoria chuckled.

'It must be nice to have such a big family,' she said.

'Oh, it's great, on holidays. But every day? Thank god Romi called me and told me about the empty cottage . . . I've taken it, by the way. Just a pre-warning in case you decide you want to be friendly with your neighbours,' he teased.

She gave him an exaggerated grimace as her insides melted into her thighs. Thank god it was dark, as she was blushing again. He offered her a top up, which she refused since she was driving, so he corked the bottle and set it on the grass. He lay back and rested his head in the grass beside hers. She could smell his cologne, a subtle, clean smell that, mixed with the earthiness of laying on the ground and the red wine in her hand, made for a heady combination.

'Ever been to the southern hemisphere before now?' he asked.

She thought about that.

'You know, I don't think I have . . . Why?'

'The skies. It wasn't something I ever thought about. But part of what I worked on in the vineyards in New Zealand was biodynamics. It's kind of . . . moon science in the vineyard. I resonated with that, having grown up with "Las Viñas Malditas,"' he said, with air quotes. 'You know, a bit of magic never hurt a vine.'

'Until it cursed one,' she muttered.

Dev huffed and sat up. 'Please don't tell me you've succumbed to all this bullshit about the curse of Las Viñas?'

'You don't believe it?' she asked.

'No!' he scoffed, running his fingers through his hair. 'Look, I'm not dismissing the fact that Las Viñas has not had a growth cycle or produced fruit for over fifty years. That is an undeniable fact. Every year, something keeps that vineyard from bud burst, which is the first step – why we're all here celebrating tonight. It could be a frost, or a nutrient deficiency. A disease. There are many reasons a perfectly healthy vineyard would not flower one year.'

Victoria was confused. 'But it's every year. For over fifty years, like you said.'

Dev conceded with a nod. 'But I don't think it's cursed. I don't believe in curses. Neither should you.'

'So how do you explain it then?' she asked, truly curious. This was the first person she'd spoken to in Argentina who was not wrapped up in the magical curse of her land.

He leaned forward. 'Do you see any other vineyards around Las Viñas?'

She thought about that.

'No,' she said. 'I mean, close, yes, but not within the confines of the township.'

'Exactly. The closest vineyard to Las Viñas is fifteen miles away towards the valley and away from the mountains. No others are planted on that same soil and that close to the ranges. I reckon it is basically the worst spot in Mendoza to plant grapes, but when Alejandro Alveras and Anyas came down after what had to have been a terrible trek through the Andes, that was where they stopped,' Dev said, sitting up. 'The climate would have been different then, and possibly the soil. Plus, there was hardly anything else around. But I will concede that Anyas was supposed to be gifted as a grower, which is a kind of magic I can get behind. And Alejandro Alveras was a winemaker from Spain. I mean, he brought a vine all the way through the Andes to plant here. That is determination.'

'So after all those years of being a successful vineyard and making award-winning wine,' Victoria asked, sitting up as well, 'what happened?'

Dev shrugged. 'Maybe a big change in weather, a bad frost, a fire? Who knows? But the vineyard had a bad year, and then the Anyas de Alveras family left the land, and it just never really recovered. I don't think it's cursed by magic. I think it's cursed by being an abandoned piece of land that hasn't had any love.'

Victoria thought about this. 'Santi said the land has been tended over the years by a company that come in once a month.'

Dev laughed, leaning back. 'Yeah, that's my family's company. It's how I got into the work. They're good people, including my nephews and the boys they hire every season – the boys Pia and Gabi are hanging out with at the bonfire as we speak – but they're not viticulturalists or vineyard managers. They just take really good care of the soil and the land. Probably why the vines are still healthy at the roots.'

'Oh,' she said, feeling disappointed.

'I could come with them on Tuesday, if you want? Work with them, get the lay of the land?'

'You would do that?' she asked, sitting up.

He smiled. 'I would *love* to do that.'

Something about the way he said it sounded like a delicious promise, and when he tilted his face to hers, she realised their faces were so close she could feel his breath. It made warmth pool in her belly and her mouth go dry. She realised quite suddenly that she wanted Dev to kiss her. Not only kiss her. Ravage her mouth, then her neck, her body. She couldn't remember the last time she'd physically wanted a man as badly as she wanted him. What was wrong with her?

'Victoria!' Pia yelled loudly from near the parking lot, not too far from where they'd ended up.

Victoria shot up, feeling suddenly embarrassed.

'I'm sorry! I have to go!' she cried, getting to her feet and hurrying over to Pia.

'What's wrong?' she asked.

Pia looked guiltily at her as Gabi walked up beside her.

'Well, see, Mama did know we were coming to the Festival,' she said, putting her jacket on and zipping it tight. 'She just didn't know we were coming with you. Auntie Adriana must have called her. She demanded we come home right now.'

'Oh crap,' Victoria said, pulling her keys out of her jacket pocket. 'Let's go. Quickly.'

~

It was nearing ten o'clock when Victoria pulled into Marilena's drive, and said woman came out the front door.

'Pia, Gabi, get inside, wipe that make-up off your faces and go to bed. *Now,*' Marilena hissed when she saw them.

'Sí, Mama,' Pia answered, and the girls ran inside.

'Marilena, I apologise. The girls said you knew they were going to the festival.'

'And it did not occur to you to call and ask me if it was okay for them to go with you? Or what their curfew was?'

Victoria swallowed. 'No. I didn't have your phone number, but if you give it to me now,' she said, pulling out her phone, but Marilena crossed her arms. 'I didn't think to question Pia, she is . . .'

'She is a child!' Marilena yelled. 'But of course it didn't matter to you. You don't have children, you don't know.'

It was a slap in the face.

'You're right. I don't know, and I'm truly very sorry.'

But Marilena wasn't accepting her apology.

'Please leave, Victoria.'

She turned and got into her car, berating herself for her stupidity the entire three-minute drive home. She would buy a plane ticket first thing in the morning. She was leaving, giving up on this project, on anything that had anything to do with Las Viñas.

'I quit!' she yelled, stepping out of the car and tripping on something, landing face first on the ground. 'Ow,' she cried, lifting her face and tasting dirt in her mouth. She touched her nose. It was sore but not bleeding. Still, tears pooled in her eyes as she felt sorry for herself. She reached into her bag, only to discover her phone wasn't there. She went back to the car and looked around but couldn't see it.

'Shit,' she said out loud. She must have dropped her phone somewhere between Marilena's door and her car in their driveway. After that confrontation, the last thing she wanted to do was drive her car back there and alert Marilena to her presence. So, Victoria marched all the way down to the street and back up to Marilena's.

She found her phone a few feet from Marilena's front porch, tucked under a rogue bush, like it was hiding somehow. She picked it up with a sigh of relief, when suddenly her alarm went off loudly.

'Shh!' she cried, trying to turn it down or off, but it just kept going. A light flickered on at Marilena's house, and Victoria quickly dove into the bushes between their two properties, hiding, finally finding the button to turn off her phone.

She could see Marilena outside, looking around suspiciously. Finally, the door closed, and Victoria let out a deep breath.

She began to walk but couldn't see much in any direction, until a tiny little light shone in the dirt in front of her. It looked like a lit cigarette, the embers dying. Were Pia and Gabi out here?

She got to the embers, but nobody was there. She bent down to the light and next to it was a pack of cigarettes so old she couldn't read the label. Next to them, a pack of matches.

Alvear Palace Hotel

That was the name on the pack of matches. She lit one and noticed that there was something else along with the matches and cigarettes.

'You've got to be kidding me,' Victoria whispered, pulling pages of the diary out of the dirt.

The cloud cover left then, and the moon was full, lighting up the vineyard around her and the Southern Cross above.

CHAPTER FOURTEEN

Buenos Aires, 1966

The Wine Competition was happening in the Alvear Palace Hotel, the oldest, most historical hotel in Buenos Aires, and we were staying there. We had a suite, so Mama and Papa had the main bedroom and there was a second bedroom with a toilet and kitchenette. It was originally just Caro staying with me, but by the end of the first night it was the four of us on the big king bed, Eugenia and me heads top, Caro and Sylvia heads tail.

We had our plan in place, and everyone was nervous, but I knew it was right. Sylvia, Eugenia and myself, we all had something that Caro did not – we were confident in who we were. She had no awareness of her fairy-like beauty and didn't think that there was much possibility out there for her, because she was poor. We wanted to create a whole new image for her in Buenos Aires so that she could have fun and embrace the amazing woman that she was, without feeling stifled by her poverty like she was back home.

I wasn't too much taller than Caro, but I was fuller. My breasts had filled out and my hips, too. Sylvia and Eugenia were too tall, so I brought a few dresses from when I was thirteen. They were too young and garish for Caro now, but Eugenia was an excellent seamstress who pulled off all the frills and did the hemlines, so that by the time we did her hair and make-up, Caro was officially Carolina el Diablo!

The door opened.

'Ah, Mistress Anyas de Alveras, you and your friends look lovely,' Juste said. 'Shall I call the escorts to take you out?'

Juste was our butler of sorts at the hotel, assigned to arrange anything we wanted.

'Escorts?' Caro asked. We were planning to explore the city on our own.

'Of course, Miss Carolina,' Juste said. 'We insist ladies be escorted through the city by a man.'

'Mierda,' I said, making my friends gasp. Juste's eyes widened.

I cleared my throat and put on my most authoritative voice. 'My sincere apologies, Juste, but I've just remembered something that, I . . . I forgot. We'll ring shortly.'

I turned dismissively, and Juste closed the door behind him as my friends gasped.

'What?' I asked. 'If there was ever an appropriate time to swear, it would be now.'

'We need an escort? But then we can't explore,' Caro said glumly, sitting down.

'They won't let us do anything. And Luce might be recognisable if we bump into anyone from the wine show,' Sylvia huffed.

'Well, I guess we'll just have to see the city the way they want us to see it, and Caro will just be Caro. Who is perfect already,' Eugenia said, pulling Caro in for a one-armed hug.

But I had an idea just then, the craziest idea I'd ever had in all my life.

~

'Quickly, follow me down the hallway. And remember, call me Señor,' I reminded my friends.

Catching a glimpse of myself in the mirror, I could barely recognise my face. I was wearing a man's tie and jacket that I stole from Pedro's room, and Eugenia had drawn a fake little pencil moustache above my lip that I kept accidentally licking off. I have a deep voice already, but it is hard to try to sound like a boy, so despite my practise, the girls kept telling me to keep it guttural.

I could feel my heart pounding in my chest as we snuck down the back stairs of the hotel. When we got to the bottom floor, we peeked through the door to the lobby.

'Dammit,' I muttered.

'Your cursing tonight is atrocious,' Eugenia whispered behind me.

'Yes, but tonight I am a man, so I can say whatever I want,' I said, turning to grin at them.

Caro grinned back but Eugenia looked nervously over my shoulder.

'We'll never get through without anyone seeing us.'

'Not that way,' I agreed. 'Out the back there is the staff entrance to the kitchens – we can go through there.'

'But—!' Eugenia spluttered.

'Excellent,' Caro agreed, and Sylvia shrugged and sneaked down to back corridor to the staff entrance.

'Follow me,' Sylvia said, and pushed open the door to a bustling kitchen full of staff who all turned to stare at us.

Sylvia, despite her apathy about her looks, had the kind of stop-men-in-their-tracks beauty that . . . well, stopped men in their tracks. She always had, and it surprised me tonight, all of us, I think, to know that Sylvia knew this about herself. She'd never acknowledged it before.

Sylvia, dressed in her finest and looking like a Hollywood movie star, glided through and found the biggest, strongest man in the room.

'Oh, sir, thank goodness we found this entrance,' she said in a breathy voice I'd never heard her use before. She even took his strong arm in hers. Eugenia's jaw dropped so distinctly I could actually hear it.

'Ladies and . . . uh . . . sir,' he said, looking at me funny. I tipped my hat down. 'You really shouldn't be here.'

'I know, but you see there is a gentleman downstairs at the party in the lobby where we were trying to pass through, and he simply won't leave us be. It's rather lewd, so I went and got my brother here . . . Lucio . . . and tried to pass again, but he is looking for us! Please, will you let us through this way,' she begged, batting her eyelashes.

If I hadn't been so nervous, I would have laughed. I heard Caro snort indelicately, so I had to elbow her in the ribs. Sylvia had never batted her lashes in her life, and the effect was like she had something stuck in her eye.

Neither the big man nor the rest of the surrounding men seemed to notice though. Instead they puffed up and looked angry.

'Which one is he?' the big one asked.

Uh oh, *I thought. We certainly didn't want to get some poor man removed from the premises.*

'Ah, peacock coat,' I said gruffly. There wasn't really anyone with a peacock coat out there, was there?

'Don't worry, gentlemen, there is no need to intervene. He's simply much too old, and we are trying to enjoy our night in the city with my brother as our escort,' Sylvia lied easily. 'Can we pass, please?'

He looked at me. 'Well, you're in a safe part of the city, which is good, 'cause, no offence, but your brother ain't going to scare off nobody.'

I tried to look grim, but the collar around my neck was too tight and bothering me, and instead I was pulling it from my neck when they glanced over at me.

'He's tougher than he looks,' Sylvia replied, smirking at me.

'Go on through,' he said, pointing to the back door to the street. 'Stick to this neighbourhood, and if you see big crowds, turn around. Lots of university students uprising at the moment, can get too ugly for ladies so lovely as you all.'

He told us his name was Marco, and taught us a special knock to alert him when we returned later.

'Thank you,' Sylvia said, her relief palpable. 'Lucio, come lead the way.'

'Sylvia!' Caro said, breathless from laughter and from running down the streets as soon as we were free from the hotel. 'I didn't think you had it in you!'

We were all laughing then, even Sylvia, though hers was shaky.

'I was so nervous,' she admitted.

'Well, you should give up the horses and get to Hollywood now, pretty lady,' I said, 'because that was quite the performance. You seemed so cool and collected. I was so hot and bothered I almost started stripping off my shirt with nervousness.'

Even Eugenia was enjoying herself now that we were out in the city and receiving admiring looks from everyone we passed.

'When we were visiting the Recoleta Cemetery earlier, I heard someone say there would be a celebration there tonight,' Caro said. 'It's just a block away.'

'A party in a cemetery?' Eugenia scoffed. 'Why?'

'It's very famous apparently, and there are going to be musicians and dancing outside. Perhaps we can have a stroll through and then find a nice place to have a drink and some food?' she suggested.

'I'm all for checking out the family-friendly street entertainment, but wouldn't it be great to find a not-nice place to go for drinks? Where the university kids hang out, and the music is loud, and we can bum cigarettes and drink whiskey?' I asked longingly.

'Sounds like a dream,' Sylvia said, nodding. 'But not all of us are dressed up like you, Lucio.'

'Let's let Carolina el Diablo decide,' I said, 'seeing as she's all dressed up for a night of being the star, and we are finally free! Caro?'

Caro laughed, looking down at her dress and twirling.

'Let's do all of it!' she said. 'Cemetery, somewhere nice, and somewhere dodgy!'

And we did. We watched tango in the streets around Recoleta Cemetery, and Eugenia was even picked to dance with the lead man – she was so graceful! When we got to the 'nice' bar, I bought us all a glass of wine and Caro shone, her wit and humour making her a favourite. She danced with three men! Sylvia declined to dance, though she was asked many times. I did notice that she befriended Calista, a lovely woman a bit older than her, and leaned into her in a way that made me wonder. Not that I would ever voice that, but this is my diary and it's private. Now, when I think about it again, I am more certain that Sylvia looked at Calista the way Eugenia looked at Pedro. And I wonder how I feel about that. I've decided that I feel okay about it, and it changes nothing for me.

But we did *finish the night my way, in a rowdy university bar, drinking whiskey, smoking cigarettes and dancing to raucous music until the sun nearly came up. I couldn't dance because I didn't know the man's parts, so I got to play billiards and darts instead. When the bar closed, we went back to the hotel through the staff entrance. We used Marco's special knock, and when he opened the door, he gave us a relieved shake of his head and let us through to the guest floors.*

In my room, we all took turns in the washroom. One by one, we crawled into the big king bed together, the sun coming up outside.

'That was the best night of my life,' Caro said, yawning. 'I've decided that I am going to move to Buenos Aires when I'm old enough, and work for a newspaper. Report all the amazing things I see in the streets, like tonight.'

'I want to stay with my horses. But maybe I can move away for a little while, and learn more, maybe go to veterinary school. And maybe, you know, live . . . a little,' Sylvia said. I wondered if she was thinking about Calista.

'I want to have the great kind of love that lasts forever. And have a family, the most beautiful children . . .' Eugenia began, dozing off.

My friends were all asleep by the time I had changed out of my boys' clothes.

But now I can finish this entry and safely say that tonight was the best night of my life so far.

~

We never did get caught, though I could see Pedro confusedly sniffing the jacket I'd stolen from his room during the award ceremony the next day, which put Caro, Sylvia and me into fits of giggles. Eugenia refused to make eye contact with Pedro and tapped her foot, swallowing guiltily. She had it so bad.

What was even more funny were the looks the kitchen staff gave me when they came out and noticed Sylvia with her two friends but no brother in sight, and with one young lady they definitely hadn't seen the night before, who looked remarkably like Lucio. To be fair, they didn't say a word. But Marco had it figured out, I was certain, as he came over to hand me a glass of champagne and whispered, 'Watch out for the man in the peacock feathers . . .' which nearly made me spit out my drink, but lo and behold, there actually was a man in a peacock hat, not a coat like we'd said. Still, it was close enough, and he happened to be talking to my parents on the other side of the room. I elbowed Caro, whose mouth dropped open. She whispered it along to the others.

'I hope the kitchen boys weren't too hard on him,' Caro said, her face in a panic.

'He doesn't have any bruises,' I said, looking at him through the crowd. 'Maybe they just spit in his food or something.'

'Ugh, vile, Luce,' Eugenia hissed. 'Oh! Turn away, quickly! He's seen us staring!'

We all turned away quickly, but I couldn't help glancing back. He was staring at me. Staring hard, not even pretending he wasn't. I couldn't tell if he was happy or unhappy with what he saw.

'He's staring at you like the men who come to buy horses from my father,' Sylvia said.

'Show pony,' Eugenia and I whispered together, shivering.

I didn't like the way he was looking at me, and though he was very handsome, he was far too old for me, and his stare was cold and hard.

I turned to my friends. 'I'm going to the restroom. Guard me so no one follows.'

They milled around so I could run out to the large, ornate restrooms in the lobby hallway. It felt good to be on my own in there for a moment, and I put cold water on my neck. We'd had very little sleep and too much to drink the night before, and the champagne was flowing today.

When I stepped out, a hand took my elbow. Someone whispered, 'I know your secret,' in my ear.

I jumped and nearly screamed, but it was Pedro, laughing with that grin of his I'd gotten to know well.

'You scared me!' I said, punching his arm. He laughed and pulled me around the corner so we couldn't be seen.

'Good. You need a little fear in you – you and my sister both. I know you stole my clothes last night and snuck out,' he said, leaning against the wall. I couldn't help but notice the way his veins snaked through the muscles on his forearms as he pulled up his sleeves. My swallow got caught in my throat.

'I don't know what you're talking about,' I said, barely getting it out.

Pedro raised his eyebrows and pulled himself up, taking a step towards me and putting his arms on the wall on either side of my shoulders, his face so close to mine I could smell the clove cigarette on his breath. Trying not to let him intimidate me, I met his eyes.

We'd been spending a lot of time together on the vineyard, and I knew that he'd grown up, that the girls got excited when he got to work. I hadn't thought much about it . . . well, a little, if I can be honest, but not too much. But it was impossible to be this close and not notice his soft caramel skin; his eyes, not brown but sort of a shimmery gold, with thick eyelashes; and the stubble of a soft beard newly growing. I could see the light hair on his chest just at the collar of his shirt and it did something funny to my insides, knowing that he was a man now, and I was a woman, and I could feel the heat radiating from him to me and me to him. I didn't know what I was feeling, but it was so strong that when he leaned in and whispered in my ear, 'I can smell you on me,' my knees buckled and he had to catch me and stand me up, but not before I saw the self-satisfied smile on his face, which I suddenly wanted to slap.

I gathered myself and leaned in, smelling him. 'You're right, you do smell like a woman. So perhaps grow a pair,' I said, pushing past him to walk back to the party, hearing his laughter behind me. The sound was nice.

We had a lovely day. Caro was in her dress from the previous night and people were noticing her left and right, which made Pedro glare from across the room when I accidentally met his eyes, time and time again. Not that I was looking for him. I wasn't. But Eugenia was. She always was, and I felt guilty immediately, even though there were no feelings in me for Pedro. Or so I kept telling myself.

My wine won the big award for Best Malbec and my parents were so proud, they took me around and I drank a lot of wine. I think maybe I was a little drunk when Mama and Papa introduced me to the peacock man from earlier. He was from Spain, and he talked of bullfighting, which I hate, and money, and he touched me in a way that made me feel violated even though it was only a handshake. I snatched my hand from his, and his gaze made me feel cold. He was the only part of the day I didn't like, but I could feel my mother's glare from across the room, telling me not to be rude. So I smiled as best as I could until I was given permission to leave and go back to my friends, but I felt him staring at me long into the day.

But then I looked up and saw someone else staring at me. Pedro. And suddenly I felt warm all over.

CHAPTER FIFTEEN

Victoria was not as cold as she'd expected, she thought, as she woke to the first light in the sky. It was probably 1 am when she fell asleep after reading the new diary entry, right here in the vineyard. She tried repeatedly to pick up the diary and take it back to the house, but every time she did, she dropped something she couldn't find, or the light of her phone went out. In her desperation she gave up and read the passage in the vineyard, where she'd eventually fallen asleep quite unexpectedly. She was tired, but in a good way. A way she didn't feel back in her normal LA life, where waking up started morning anxiety that wouldn't go away until she got up and had too many coffees and started multitasking her way through the day. She would make herself so busy she never had a chance to stay still for long. Product of her generation, she knew, and though that life had excited her for a long time, she was changing. She felt different. She wanted to slow down. To look around her more. To be more present. To *notice* if something wasn't right. God, she hadn't even *noticed* when things with Michael fell apart.

Victoria surmised it was just after 6:30 am, for the sky was starting to lighten with the rising sun. Even though her back hurt a little from sleeping on the cold dirt instead of a mattress, she still felt revived.

Victoria gave her back a crack and stood, then she noticed something. First, it was a smell. She didn't know the smell just yet. It was new to her. Sort of young and yet old. Musty, dirty, and yet herbal and fresh. It made her feel . . . grounded.

And that was when Victoria looked around and realised that her vineyard was filled with little green buds. Thousands of them.

~

It took her half an hour to run back to her house and change into her jeans, boots and sweater to be presentable enough to see someone. Could this really be happening? If so, who should she call? Marilena? Marilena hated her. What about Dev? Her heart jolted at the thought. Which meant no, not yet.

She needed to find out what this all meant. She wanted to see Sylvia, her grandmother's friend. She had a feeling Sylvia knew more than she let on.

~

'Victoria! To what do I owe the pleasure at this early hour?' Sylvia said as Victoria rushed into her paddock. The sun was up but it was still cool. Sylvia was brushing Gorda while she kept trying to steal the hay Fuego was eating. 'Is everything okay up at the hacienda?'

'I'm sorry to bother you so early,' Victoria said, putting her hand out to Gorda, who sniffed it, then ignored her and went back to looking for food. 'Yes, I'm fine. I just . . . Something has happened on my land, and I hoped you could help me. I wasn't sure who else to talk to.'

'You're being quite cryptic, Victoria. Are you sure you're okay?' Sylvia asked.

Victoria breathed, and a tear escaped.

'Yes. More than okay. The vines. They are budding. Thousands of them.'

Sylvia stopped and stared at her, mouth ajar.

'But that's impossible. The vineyard is cursed. Has been since Luce left.'

'I know that,' Victoria said. 'But it's waking up. I think . . . I know this sounds crazy, but I think it's trying to tell me something. To rid itself of a secret and grow again.'

Sylvia swallowed and then shook her head. 'You are more like Luce than I thought,' she said, her voice strong. 'She believed that nonsense her mother told her about her people. Even went into the Andes one year on a trek to see if she could find them. With me and my horses, of course,' she laughed.

'And did she?'

'No, we didn't,' Sylvia sighed. 'I think we all wanted to believe in magic back then. But unfortunately, life is not filled with magic,' she said sadly.

'I just finished my latest gift from the vineyard – another diary entry,' Victoria said, watching Sylvia closely.

Sylvia seemed to straighten. 'And?' she said, with a tight smile. 'Did you find a great secret or a magic spell?'

Victoria believed Sylvia knew more than she was letting on. Why was she hiding it from her?

'No, you girls were in Buenos Aires together when Luce dressed as a boy and took you out.'

Sylvia's tension faded and she let out a laugh.

'Gorda, stop trying to eat all the time, and leave Fuego alone.' She turned back to Victoria. 'That was one of the greatest weekends of my life,' she said, leading the way. 'All of ours,

I think, though perhaps not Eugenia. She was a rather serious girl. Marilena reminds me a bit of her grandmother.'

Victoria stopped suddenly. 'Eugenia is *Marilena's* grandmother? My grandmother's oldest and closest friend?'

'One and the same,' Sylvia confirmed. 'They were very different, but still, they loved one another like sisters.'

Victoria was quiet, thinking of the last entry about Pedro. She decided not to say anything to Sylvia about that yet. Sylvia seemed guarded, on edge. Victoria had no idea if there were more diary entries, if she would find anything, if there even was a secret, or if, for the same unexpected reason Las Viñas had *stopped* its growth cycle, it had unexpectedly *started* again. But she knew after seeing the bud burst that morning that she wanted nothing more than to see her land flourish. Whatever that meant about her future, she knew she had to see this through.

'Come, sit,' Sylvia said as they went into the kitchen. 'I always make a fresh pot before I go to the horses so I can have it when I get back.'

Victoria sat at the table, and Sylvia poured them both coffee.

'Has the vineyard been empty ever since Luce left with Camila?' Victoria asked, sipping her coffee.

This time Sylvia's expression was very clear. 'No. Just after Luce left, her husband's family came from Spain and moved onto the land, hoping to make good on the investment they made. They stayed a couple of years and the vineyard gave them nothing, so they left. Luce came back annually after that, though she never moved back in permanently.'

Victoria asked the question that had been plaguing her since she started the diary. 'Why did Luce leave with Camila in the first place? Did something terrible happen that coincided with the "curse"?'

Sylvia stared into the distance for a long time, and Victoria could hear her whisper to herself. 'Why then? Why now?'

'Sylvia?' she asked. 'What do you mean, "why now"?'

Sylvia turned back, laughing. 'I'm old, I'm sorry, and get easily distracted. Victoria, here is what an old woman can say quite genuinely,' she leaned forward and grasped Victoria's hand, and looked at her with intent. With purpose. Victoria was sure. 'Follow the bud burst. Tu eres el madre de las viñas.'

You are the mother of the vines.

They looked at one another for a long moment before Sylvia shook herself free.

'When Felipe did not come home to see his wife and daughter, Luce was heartbroken. She was young and in love and a new mother. We think her heartbreak is what caused the vineyard to die,' Sylvia finished, but she did not meet Victoria's eyes.

She was lying. Sylvia was lying. There was something that happened on Las Viñas that she knew about, that happened a long, long time ago. Something Sylvia was not going to share.

'Thank you, Sylvia, you've been very helpful.' Victoria stood.

'Where are you going?' Sylvia asked as Victoria quickly started back to the hacienda.

'I've got a phone call to make.'

~

Victoria felt her heart flutter in anxiousness and excitement as she dialled Dev's number. He was a vineyard manager. This was what he did for a living. He picked up on the first ring.

'Victoria?' he asked as he answered with a yawn.

'Yes, it's me,' she said quietly. 'So, you know how you were going to accompany the boys on Tuesday to assess Las Viñas?'

'Yes . . .' he replied, but she could tell he was alert now.

'Can you maybe come over now?'

'Are you okay?' he asked. She could almost feel him stand up on the other end of the phone.

'Yes, I'm fine. It's just that something has happened on my land, and I hoped you could come around and have a look.' She paused. 'It can't wait until Tuesday.'

He was quiet for a moment. 'I'll be right there.'

~

'I can't believe this,' he said for the hundredth time. 'I just can't believe this. How?!'

Victoria shook her head. 'I don't know. You're the one who doesn't believe in some sort of magical curse, so talk to me realistically. You're a vineyard manager. You know the land. Is this . . . real? Will it last? Will more grapes grow? Can you tell if they will live? And if so, what does it mean?' She sighed. 'I am afraid this is too good to be true. Too much to hope for.'

He looked at her curiously. 'Is this what you hope for? This land, these vines, to grow? To see Las Viñas awaken?'

She nodded.

'I don't know what I want to do with my life and my time here, but I do know that from the moment I arrived, I felt this incredible pull to the land,' she said. 'I just . . .' she began, trying to figure out how to explain. 'These buds, I need to see them grow. I don't know why but just seeing the life there, I need to see them grow,' she repeated, her voice stronger. 'Does that make sense?'

Dev nodded. 'More than you know. Come, let's walk through the vines. I'll assess it as I would any other new vineyard, though this is anything but.'

She followed his lead, slowly walking through a row. He reached down occasionally to touch or smell a bud shaking his head.

'I can't believe they budded in a frost,' he murmured. 'It's impossible.'

'What's impossible?' she asked.

'Last night was a frost. Other vineyards had to protect their buds. Sometimes they light fires and use big fans to keep them warm. It is early enough in the season that we expect frost and the danger wasn't high. Baby buds are vibrant, resilient. They are new,' he said lovingly, bending to touch some of the vines they'd stopped in front of. 'They just want to live.'

The way he spoke about the vines, like the children she couldn't have, gripped her. Suddenly Victoria found herself welling up, tears overwhelming her.

'Are you okay?' he asked, standing back up, touching her shoulder. Seeing the tears in her eyes, he pulled her in and held her close.

She nodded, swallowing the aching pit of grief in her throat, burying her head into his neck. He still smelled as wonderful as the night of the bonfire, but at this moment it just made her feel comforted and safe.

'Come,' she said, wiping her eyes, 'let's walk to La Madre.'

'La Madre?' he asked, following her. 'You mean La Abuela? You think she is at the centre of the growth?'

She nodded. 'It would make sense. You know, if you were talking about some weird magical land with a mother vine and a fifty-year-old curse.'

Dev nodded and chuckled.

'Well, isn't that the truth. Alright, I'll do an assessment,' he said, pulling a notepad from his back pocket. 'Walk me through what happened. Where did the first vine bud? What time of day was it? What was the weather like? Did something in particular happen?'

Victoria stopped. 'What do you mean? Why do you need to know all of those things? I mean, it just . . . you know, budded.'

He raised one eyebrow. 'If you don't want to tell me, that's fine. But there is only so much I can assess without the information, Victoria.'

She strolled ahead of him, listening to him make observations, thinking about what she should say. She felt incredibly protective of her land and didn't want to involve anyone else in the secrets the vineyard was trying to tell her. And yet she couldn't do this part alone.

'The first row budded a few days ago,' she said, finally. 'That one.' She pointed to the vines between the house and the winery. 'But I have reason to believe that La Madre, or La Abuela, was the first.'

Dev took notes and looked at her, waiting for more.

'And then this morning, there were more. All of this,' she said, her arm out.

'And do you know why this happened? Was there any particular reason for it?'

Victoria thought about how to answer. She could have sworn she saw one of the vines duck down towards Dev, almost like it was sniffing him. But that couldn't be – her lack of sleep must be catching up with her, she thought. She started picturing the vine dancing around Dev's head, like one of those dashboard dancing toys, and pressed her lips together when she started to laugh.

Dev, confused, glanced behind him. 'Victoria?'

'Sorry, I didn't sleep well, I think I'm seeing things,' she said honestly. 'The thing is, I don't know why . . . yet. But I feel like if we focus on what *is*, on the vineyard itself, it will all make sense in the end.'

After a moment, he put his hands up in surrender. 'Okay, the bud burst is beautiful. It's rich and vibrant – kind of magical and unexpected, sure. Which is the part that worries me.'

'You're worried?' she asked, following him now as he touched each vine. 'Do you think it will die again?'

'Well look, I haven't worked with many cursed vineyards, so all I can do is treat this as I would any other vineyard if I was the manager.'

'What would that entail?' she asked.

'What do you know about the stages of growth for a vineyard?' he asked.

'A week ago?' she asked. 'Nothing. But I bought a wine book in Mendoza when I first arrived and have been reading it since the first bud appeared. So I know that in the southern hemisphere, specifically here in Mendoza, the bud burst, also called bud bloom, happens between mid-September and October, right? And we're in October now, so on any other vineyard, what is happening now would be normal.'

Dev nodded appreciatively. 'Exactly. The new bloom is drawing upon an internal supply from the grapevine. That means water. Vines need water, like all things that bloom. I imagine that La Abuela – or La Madre, as you call her – I imagine her block has a lot of moisture. It's probably why it sits where it does. It could cause internal competition for resources and limit moisture supply. What I want is for the entire vineyard to bloom, if it's possible, though we'll focus the heart on the block that is in bloom now.'

'How would you do that?'

'Growth balance is essential. At this stage you need someone out there all the time, making sure the leaves are separating properly during bud burst. Over the next two months during shoot development, they need nutrients and water to grow and separate to about sixteen leaves before they start flowering. That's usually in December here. When the cap-fall is complete . . .'

Victoria shook her head with a laugh. 'One step at a time! Just because I read all of that doesn't mean I can wrap my brain around it yet.'

Dev ran his hand through his hair and chuckled. 'Fair enough. I can't wrap my brain around all this yet either. So for a start, as we go through bud bloom, I need to be here, monitoring. And I may need to find ways of fertilising the land to make it rich with minerals . . .'

'Did you just say "I" – as in, you?' she asked quietly. 'Dev, you just got back from your time in New Zealand to get a prime job. You could do anything.'

'Victoria, I had a dozen job offers in New Zealand. I came back because it was Marilena's dream to buy Las Viñas. Instead, you are here, and things are different, they are changing. I don't believe in the curse. I don't believe that there is anything other than science at work here, but this is your land and you are the last Anyas de Alveras, so it's up to you to tell me what you want. Because if the curse was true, and now you're here and the vines are waking up, it doesn't make sense.'

'What doesn't make sense?' she asked.

'You're alive. A woman,' he said pointedly. 'You can't be the last of the line. So why did she wake up? See, no curse.'

And it all came into place for Victoria. That feeling when she found out she couldn't have children, that she was cursed. She was. She was part of a fifty-year-old curse on Las Viñas, and that was now proven tenfold. She had to be the last of her line, or Las Viñas wouldn't be growing. It was as if her hopes had died all over again. And yet . . . she looked out to the vines. She would never be able to have a child, but she was still a mother. The mother of the vines. *She* was La Madre now.

Victoria knew there was more to learn, a journey ahead. She turned to Dev, but stopped, deciding not to tell him. Not yet. It was too personal, and she didn't yet know what was happening between them. Except that he wanted to be here, on Las Viñas.

'Give me two months,' Dev said. 'I can oversee this vineyard to the best of my abilities, and in two months, if the vineyard flowers, I reckon we will know what it is capable of.'

'I'll have my grandmother's money to pay you and your team, so don't worry about that. I can provide a meal for you all, each day,' she said, getting excited.

She could practise cooking. Surely it was something she could learn to do while she renovated the house and got it ready for sale.

'For the time you're here, I will provide my vineyard manager and his team the most amazing food while he tells me what's happening with my cursed vineyard!'

He laughed. 'That sounds a treat. I didn't know you were a cook.'

'Oh,' she said, blushing. 'I . . . um . . . well truthfully, I'm the most abominable cook on the planet. But I mean, how hard can it really be?'

Dev raised an eyebrow. 'Okay then. Normally we Argentinians have a light breakfast and coffee, a very late lunch, a siesta and an even later dinner. But seeing as how most people in the vineyards can't get an afternoon siesta in the first crucial weeks, we go to what we call "American time". Breakfast at 5 am, lunch at noon, dinner early, and asleep when the rest of our family is dining,' he said with a laugh. 'As I'm on my own at the cottage, I'm happy with that. No other schedules to interrupt.'

'Well then, I will see you tomorrow for lunch at noon,' she said, beaming. 'Thank you, Dev. Thank you for everything.'

~

'Victoria, you will take this recipe and you will go to Adriana's. You will act like a grown-up. You will be persistent. You will not let her bully you again.'

She nodded to herself and went to open her front door, but hesitated.

'No, you will not chicken out. Get out that door!'

Victoria finally decided she had to stop thinking and just go, despite the dread at going back to the local shop owned by Adriana Lomos, who was Marilena's closest friend. She hadn't been out in San Alejandro town since the day everyone was so rude to her.

But things were different today. Today, she was the mother of Las Viñas. Today, Dev and his team would be eating her food.

Finally getting her courage together, Victoria drove to Adriana's. She parked and took a deep breath, pulling out the cookbook she'd brought with her with a page marked. She did a roar in her mirror and jumped out, heading into the store and directly to where Adriana stood behind the counter, her eyes wide as Victoria headed straight to her, aggressively. She opened her mouth to speak, but Victoria spoke first.

'I need everything for this recipe,' she said boldly in Spanish, handing her the book open to the page she'd marked, 'and I need it now.'

'Oh, um. Humitas en chala,' Adriana read slowly. 'That is a very complicated—'

'Everything is complicated for me. I have no cooking skills, no friends, and I am in a foreign country. This recipe has "easy" on it. So that's what I'm starting with. I have a vineyard manager starting on Las Viñas today, and I have promised him lunch. And no matter what Marilena has said to you, I highly doubt she'd want me to accidentally poison Dev and his workers.'

For just a moment, Adriana was stunned into silence. Then she spoke, sputtering, 'Dev? You mean Devan Acosta? He's your . . . your *vineyard* manager?'

'That's correct,' Victoria said coolly.

'But you are . . . you're at Las Viñas. The Cursed Vineyard,' Adriana struggled.

'Also correct.'

'But that would mean . . .' and suddenly Adriana inhaled deeply, her mouth opening and closing without a sound.

'Yes, it would. So I would appreciate it if you could gather everything on that list, please. I have a phone call to make, so I'll just wait outside,' she finished.

Outside in the fresh air, Victoria pretended to make a phone call, but she really took a breath and forced herself to keep from punching the air in victory.

'You can do this, Victoria,' she whispered.

She paced back and forth, looking down at her phone. It was already 9.30 am, and she'd promised Dev lunch at noon. She wanted to do this right. She was turning to go back inside when the door opened and Adriana came out with two shopping bags.

'This is an okay recipe, but I've added some tips that will make it tastier if you really want to try to do it like an Argentinian,' Adriana said, all business now. 'I have made notes and added the ingredients you will need.' She looked at her watch. 'The prep takes the longest; the steaming of the husks and the filling just minutes. I shall put this on your account.'

'But I don't have an account.'

'The Anyas de Alveras family have had an account here since my parents opened this store seventy-five years ago. You have an account.'

Adriana placed the two bags into the Peugeot and closed the door, tapping it fondly. 'Good to see Mierdita back on the road,' she said with a half-smile.

'But doesn't that mean . . . ?'

'*Little shit*, yes. Luce bought her from my father thirty years ago and named her then. She's a good car, though. Mierdita or no.'

Victoria wondered if she meant more than just the car.

~

'Okay Victoria, how hard can this be?' she said to herself, reading the altered recipe Adriana had given her. 'Fry onion, pepper and garlic. Got it.'

She realised she didn't have measuring spoons or cups, so just guessed at the amounts. She fried them for one minute as the recipe called for, but they sizzled and started to burn.

'Dammit! I forgot butter! Who uses oil and butter at the same time anyway?'

So she started step two at the same time, throwing the butter in with the tomatoes, paprika, oregano and salt and pepper, but it didn't look the same as in the pictures. Perhaps she should have measured with something other than a coffee spoon.

'Hey Siri, set timer for fifteen minutes,' she called desperately to her phone.

'Okay. Fifteen minutes,' Siri answered.

But after just two minutes, things weren't smelling quite right. 'Hey Siri, please become a human and cook my lunch for me!' she cried.

'There's nothing called 'lunch' on your calendar,' Siri answered.

'What the hell is that supposed to mean?! I didn't actually want you to cook my lunch. You're a bloody phone,' she muttered. 'Okay, I can do this. I'll just take it off the heat and go to the next step.'

She read the next step.

'Add the corn, milk, cheese and sugar mixture?' she said, confused. 'What mixture? Where's the mixture?'

It was then she realised she'd missed the entire preparation portion of the recipe.

'Shit!'

She quickly ran around trying to find a grater for the corn. Finally she did, but it was old and rusted. Victoria gave it a quick clean but noticed the sauté was still sizzling and cooking, burning the garlic, onion, tomatoes and seasoning even more.

'No! Stop!'

She went to toss the corn into the mixture to stop it, not even caring that she hadn't measured any milk or cheese, when she saw that all of the corn was dusted in rust from the grater. Leaning over in a panic, she tried to pick out little bits of rust. But it was really starting to smell bad. Really bad, like burnt.

'AHHHHH!' she cried, as she saw the ends of her hair burning where they'd caught on the gas fire of the stove. As she pulled her head away to stop the embers, the entire cast-iron skillet was pulled down, dropping on her big toe so painfully she thought she may have broken it. She cried out. And then the remnants burnt her bare ankle, and the entire disaster was left on the floor of her kitchen for her to clean up.

Hobbling and desperate, Victoria quickly turned off the stovetop and sunk to the floor, crying into her burnt hair.

~

Adriana was just pulling the door to her shop closed to go on her lunch break when she saw Mierdita pull back up. She looked quizzically at the car, which remained closed for a few minutes, before finally she saw Victoria's left foot come out slowly, looking red and burnt at the ankle, her toe slightly blue. The rest of Victoria followed, as she hobbled towards Adriana. The rest of her didn't look much better, Adriana thought. Her eyes were red-rimmed, and it looked as though she'd cut her hair but just on one side and very badly.

'Victoria, what happened?'

Victoria couldn't meet her eyes. 'The recipe didn't go so well.'

'I swear that was a fantastic recipe! I would not have sabotaged you like that!' Adriana cried.

Victoria raised one eyebrow at her.

'Okay, I would, but I wouldn't do that to Dev, and I didn't today. I swear.'

Victoria sighed. 'I know. It just didn't work out that well for me. But I . . . I promised Dev lunch,' she managed.

Adriana felt herself filled with pity for this woman she was determined not to like. Marilena was her best friend, and she was devastated that her dream had been taken from her. But it wasn't Victoria's fault she existed. A woman who grew up with an adoptive family, never knowing where she came from, and now she was here, on a cursed vineyard in a town that wasn't being very nice to her. The guilt made Adriana open the door.

'I'll put together a lunch for you to take back to Dev. Is he bringing a couple of the local boys with him to help?' she asked.

Victoria sniffed and nodded.

'Okay, come on inside. We've got this covered,' Adriana said softly, and Victoria managed a very small smile.

CHAPTER SIXTEEN

Las Viñas stopped spilling her secrets to Victoria as Dev and the boys began assessing the vines, probably because there was so much hustle and bustle all the time, but Victoria could almost feel her vines hum happily as they were pruned and admired.

'Show off,' she whispered one day to one of the vines that had separated its shoot tip into five separate leaves. Alex, one of the local boys working with them, turned around.

'Sorry, Ms Anyas – uh – Bishop? Did you say something?' Alex asked.

She nodded to the vine, and he turned.

'*Dios mío! Impossible*! Dev!' Alex turned suddenly and ran down the row.

Victoria smiled fondly and walked back to the house to start lunch. She felt as if she was followed by the vines quite regularly now as she walked through. They sometimes even bloomed here and there, like this one just had. It was strange the way they did, in some ways, feel like her children.

Victoria was intensely focused on the new cooking aspect of her Mendoza Project, as well as renovating the house. This helped distract her from thinking too much about the past or the future. And if she was honest with herself, it stopped her from thinking too much about Devan Acosta. She loved walking through the vineyard with him every morning, loved their banter over lunch, the way he grazed her arm here, touched her back or neck there.

'Victoria, what are you thinking about?' Pia asked one day as she helped with the dishes after lunch. 'You're spacey again.'

'Oh, the uh, new mattress. Did you girls get all the new sheets on alright?' she asked, fanning her cheek. She'd been thinking about Dev. Again.

She'd managed to get a new mattress delivered by Reno himself and was not overcharged again when she purchased different coloured paints for the other four bedrooms, so she assumed Adriana had quietly passed the word around. This must have riled Marilena, who Victoria could often see looking through the window before and after she came home from work.

Victoria could practically feel the longing from her and wished things were different between them.

The boys Dev had chosen to work with him those couple of weeks were Dante, Alex and his nephew, Julio. Dante was a good-looking kid from Paraguay who was seventeen and staying with his grandparents over the summer to learn the trade. Alex was a classmate of Julio's, and Julio was Gabi's boyfriend – which meant that Gabi and Pia were also at Victoria's most hours they weren't in school.

'You need a pool, Victoria,' Gabi said, as they sat on the front porch in bikinis pretending to get suntans while really trying to impress the boys.

'Gabi,' Victoria said, '*you* have a pool. At your own house. Why don't you girls hang out there?'

'Oh, please don't make us leave, Victoria!' Pia cried. 'We'll make ourselves useful, we promise.'

'We do?' Gabi said.

'We *do*,' Pia said, teeth clenched, looking at Gabi with wide eyes.

Victoria knew that look – that was a look of two best friends silently sharing an entire conversation which usually translated to, 'because of that boy I like'. It didn't take Victoria longer than an afternoon to realise that boy was Dante, and she wondered how Marilena would feel about Pia crushing on a boy of seventeen, and from another country no less. She reckoned she'd better keep them so busy as to not earn more of Marilena's scorn.

'Fine, if you want to hang out here and not relax getting tans at your own lovely pool this summer, then you'll have to work. You girls can start with your room, Pia, La Azul.'

Pia was enthusiastic and hugged her. Whether it was because she could stay or because Victoria always called it 'her room', Victoria wasn't sure. Gabi pulled her button-down top back up over her red bikini and moaned, but followed Pia nonetheless.

'Cover all the furniture and give the room a good clean and let me know when it's ready for paint!' she called after them, laughing. 'I'll call you when it's time for lunch.'

Gabi's shoulders popped back up and she turned with a smile. 'We get to have lunch with everyone?'

'Every day you work, we can all have lunch together. I've got a whole list of recipes I'm so excited to try out,' Victoria said.

Gabi deflated again and met Pia's pained look. 'Um, Victoria, are you sure you wouldn't rather us help you in the kitchen, perhaps?'

Victoria gave them a scowl and shooed them away as she went to the kitchen to prepare today's dish: Empanadas.

Adriana had shaken her head when Victoria had brought her the recipe and asked her to help her gather the ingredients.

'Victoria, I put some little notes in your cookbook of lunch dishes I think you should try, didn't you see them?' Adriana had asked.

Victoria had rolled her eyes. 'Fig and mozzarella salad? Pears and Ibérico ham? Endives, sun-dried tomatoes and olives? They are salads!'

'They are delicious!' Adriana had insisted. 'And *easy*.'

'Translation: Even you can't mess *these* up, Victoria?' she'd asked.

Adriana had given her a long stare, reminiscent of her less-friendly days. 'Victoria, there is no dish you couldn't mess up, in that I have full faith.'

'Ha. Ha. Ha. I'm making empanadas, and they are going to be brilliant. I reckon I'm getting better,' Victoria had said.

She wasn't, as everyone knew, so Adriana always packed up some handmade sandwiches and pastries for her, just in case. It had only been three days, but she'd served the sandwiches every time.

'Here,' she'd said, handing Victoria the bags a few minutes later, with the cookbook in one. 'I've made some notes again. Do *not* try to change the dough recipe.'

'I remember Romina saying something about empanada dough, too,' Victoria had said thoughtfully. 'What was it?'

'Probably, "yes, it really is that much, don't change it."'

'Okay, thanks,' Victoria had said, smiling and piling the bags into Mierdita.

She'd turned and Adriana had handed her a platter of sandwiches. She'd tilted her head. 'I won't need them, I won't mess this up!'

'Just take it. On me today.'

'We've got quite the party happening over at Las Viñas now, with Dev and the boys, and now Pia and Gabi helping me renovate the house,' she'd said. 'You should come by and join us for lunch this week on your break. See what's happening up at Las Viñas Malditas.'

Adriana had looked surprised. 'You—you're inviting me?'

'Sure,' Victoria had said with a smile. 'Maybe one of these days Marilena will find it in her heart to join us as well.'

'I doubt that,' Adriana had said under her breath. Victoria had heard her. 'Sorry, it's just . . .'

Victoria had sighed. 'I know. Stolen her dream and all that by existing. Anyway, have a think about coming up.'

'Let me know how the empanadas go,' Adriana had said as Victoria closed the door to the car.

'They'll be perfect! I have a feeling!'

'You always have a feeling! And it always goes wrong!' Adriana had called after the little car, watching Victoria wave out the window. She'd laughed when Victoria's wave turned into a good-natured middle finger.

~

'I've got it, I've got it, I've got it!' Victoria cried excitedly, as the filling of her empanadas came together quite nicely. The onions and capsicum sautéed perfectly with the sunflower oil Adriana had stuck in her bag with a note saying, *use this for the filling!* The mincemeat browned nicely, and once she returned the veggies to the pan and added the spices and flavours, her kitchen actually smelled beautiful. She reckoned it was the music she had on in the background. She'd read online that opera music was a soothing sound for cooking, so she tried it. She did get a *little* over-excited when *La Traviata* from *Pretty Woman* came on, but managed to reign herself in.

She looked down at Adriana's notes as she put the mixture aside. *Victoria, you forgot to read that this mixture should marinate for at least 24 hours before you make the empanadas.*

'Dammit!' Victoria yelled, then picked up the next note.

Give it a whirl anyway, I'm sure it will be fine. Go ahead, make the dough now.

Victoria laughed. She was beginning to like Adriana.

But when she got to the recipe for the dough, she was

absolutely certain it wasn't right. As she mixed both lard and butter into the bowl, the dough grew larger than the bowl itself.

Don't change the recipe.

'I know they're messing with me – this recipe is way wrong,' Victoria mumbled, cutting the butter by a third and the lard by half. It still made her cringe at how much was in there. 'This will be *much* better.'

~

'These sandwiches are delicious, Victoria!' Pia said.

They all agreed enthusiastically as Victoria smiled wanly, and they all ignored the burnt mound of ruined dough outside.

~

'You know what you need here, Victoria?' Adriana said a few days later when she came to Las Viñas and they made lunch together.

'A winemaker?' Victoria said, her chin resting on her hand, looking out the window towards Marilena's house as she had been all week. Victoria didn't know why they were connected, but she knew they were, somehow.

She felt Marilena's longing for Las Viñas within her, a subtle longing, which made her look out to Marilena's as she knew Marilena was looking out to Las Viñas.

Adriana chuckled and patted her back. 'The two of you, I swear. But no, on this particular occasion I meant you need a parilla here. It would be perfect.'

'What's that?'

'A parilla! You don't know it?' Adriana asked, surprise in her voice. 'An asador. An Argentinian grill.'

Victoria nodded. 'Yes, sorry, I know that term now. Asado. A big grill-up, right? But on a particularly famous type of grill?'

'Exactly. That would be perfect for Las Viñas, especially if it ever opened as a hacienda hotel stay. You could put one in without needing any sort of council approval because it's all outdoors, but it would add immense value. I stayed on an estancia once in Las Pampas, just outside Buenos Aires. They are hacienda-style homes like yours but instead of having a vineyard, they are working cattle or horse farms. I stayed at this one where we learned to play polo all day and had a big barbecue on the parilla every evening. Heaps of red wine. I reckon that would suit Las Viñas. Here, look.'

Victoria looked at photos on Adriana's phone, taking it and scrolling through. She nodded. 'This would be amazing here, if I . . . I mean . . . if it ever . . .'

'Exactly,' Adriana said, packing up a takeaway of lamb loin. 'I'm taking this to Mari. She's really hating me at the moment, but I'm hoping to convince her it's time. I mean . . . look at this,' Adriana said, pointing to Las Viñas.

It had been two weeks, and she was thriving. No, she was more than thriving. She was growing.

'Good luck,' Victoria said sarcastically, taking the beautiful dishes into the middle of her table outside. 'You sure you won't stay? You made all of this!'

Adriana stood at the table beside her and looked out at Las Viñas.

'And you're making all of *that*.'

~

'So,' Marilena said sadly as she heard her door open the next morning, 'you, Adriana, the boys, even my own daughter – you are all working on Las Viñas now. For *her*.'

'Mari,' Dev said, walking to her forlorn form sagging in the window. She turned and punched him.

'Ouch! That hurt!' Dev yelled, blocking his face from her next swing.

'It's just . . . how? Why?' Marilena said softly, still staring out the window.

'Mari, I don't understand.'

'Las Viñas! Why is it awake now? I don't understand. Why is the curse lifting? I went back to all my old journals and talked to the locals, and we didn't get it wrong. *The curse will be lifted with the last of the Anyas de Alveras blood.*'

'Mari, this is enough! There is no curse! Curses do not exist. I know that it was a part of our village, our land, our growing up. This great magical entity in the midst of us. But it was never real. All it was was a sick vineyard that hadn't grown – and now it is! Probably because it's being looked after, not because some girl with Anyas de Alveras blood has come to somehow lift a curse!'

Marilena's jaw dropped. 'How can you say that? It's Las Viñas! It is cursed. And now the curse is lifting. What, you think that all that,' she hissed, pointing to the flowering vineyard, 'is because of your greatness as a vineyard manager?'

Dev shook his head, and she sighed. 'I'm sorry, I didn't mean anything against you.'

'Funny, it sure sounded that way,' he said, but he wasn't angry with her. She felt her shoulders sag with relief.

'Mari,' he said gently, 'I'm sorry that your dream has not come true and your heart is hurting. But if you let go of your personal pain, and you remember your love for Las Viñas, for the land, for the grapes, you would feel complete joy to see what I have seen. To see it *live*. And to see it needs a winemaker.'

CHAPTER SEVENTEEN

The season was changing. As they moved into November and then early December, an even greater miracle than the bud bursts happened on Las Viñas – the buds had grown, and now, they were ready to flower.

'The leaves are separated to about sixteen leaves, and the flower caps are loosening,' Dev said, with joy in his eyes, one evening in early December. 'It is happening, Victoria.'

They hugged tightly, and Victoria had the same warm sensation she did every time they touched. But this time, he kissed her, fully, on the mouth.

It wasn't romantic. Not in that way. But it was intimate. It was their shared passion for their shared love, Las Viñas.

When Victoria wrapped her arms around his neck and pulled him closer during that kiss, it started to turn into something more. It turned into moans, a softening of lips, a hardness of their bodies. They both slowed down and desperately drew each other closer, until they heard the truck start and a collection of wolf whistles.

They pulled apart quickly and Dev glared at the truck, where Dante, Alex and Julio were grinning broadly.

'Little assholes,' Dev muttered, shooing them off, running his fingers through his hair and glancing abashedly at Victoria.

She chuckled and turned back to the vineyard, waving to him over her shoulder with a sensual smile. God, she really was acting like a teenager.

After everyone left that day, Victoria found herself strolling through the blooming Las Viñas as the sun was setting. Victoria had been dying to find out what happened after Buenos Aires and was certain there were more pages of her grandmother's diary that Las Viñas was going to give to her. But she didn't know when, or how.

Until that night. That night she could feel it, the call from one of the dark parts of the vineyard. That was what they called the plots that hadn't had bud burst, that still were 'under the curse'.

That night it was calling to her, whispering. She followed the whisper, the call, and in the darkest place she found glittering fake diamonds that had summoned her, long-buried but come out of the earth. A tiara. And tied within it was the next part of the diary.

~

Bud Burst Festival, 1967

I have a secret. A beautiful, terrible secret I can tell no one, not my friends, not even my best friend. Especially not her. I am just home now after the most wonderful night of my life, my hands shaking as I write this. I can even see my usually neat penmanship is not how it should be. I should start from the beginning of the night.

Yesterday was the Bud Burst Festival, my favourite day of the year. We've made it through the harsh winter and the vineyard has come to life, which is why we celebrate every year. Not all the vineyards did this year. But Las Viñas thrives as always.

The four of us are seventeen now and nearly grown-up. We are growing apart, I can feel it, knowing our lives might change when we turn eighteen. What will each of us do? Who will each of us be? Will we stay friends forever? Sometimes we still talk about it, but other times we stay silent, ignoring the fear of the unknown and pretending today is all there is. I have kept such a big secret from them, and I wonder if they have kept theirs from me, too.

Today we were just us again, in my room, getting ready for the festival, fixing each other's hair and make-up in our shifts before we put on our dresses.

'I miss Maddi,' Eugenia said, looking in the mirror as she brushed her hair. 'She's so much better at this than we are. I wouldn't even know how to start curling it the way she does.'

Maddi has worked at Las Viñas since I was young. She cleans and does some cooking, as Mama is not an overly ambitious chef. Maddi is a vivacious young woman, and she adores sitting with the four of us, doing our hair and make-up. She says she wants to move somewhere like Hollywood or New York and be a stylist or make-up artist, so she practises on us. She's become one of my closest confidantes, especially now.

'Where is Maddi, Luce?' Caro asked.

'She's visiting family somewhere for the weekend. Maybe she'll find out more about moving to America to be a stylist.'

The truth is that I've heard my parents arguing that we don't have any money. The economy is terrible and despite how good our wine is, Mendoza is growing a reputation for making cheap and bad table wine, and people aren't buying. Not even people from overseas, because they don't trust the product despite our well-known name. So I'm pretty sure Maddi is visiting family to find another job because we can't pay her anymore. But I hope she'll come back first.

'I'll do your hair, Eugenia,' I said, going over to her with the curling wand.

She smiled at me, and the guilt writhed inside. I love Eugenia. She's my best friend in the world, more like a sister. I didn't know how I could be doing what I was doing.

'Have you decided yet if you are going to go to university, Sylvia?' Eugenia asked as I wrapped her luxurious hair around the wand.

Sylvia pulled her own blonde hair into an elegant twist that seemed effortless and looked stunning. 'No. My parents want me to consider all options, but I just want to be on the farm with the horses. Mama thinks I should at least look into going to Córdoba for a couple of years, even if I study veterinary science or something completely useless. I don't know though. I can't imagine leaving here.'

'I can't wait to leave,' Caro said suddenly, pulling on the dress she'd borrowed from me. 'I'm on that bus the moment I've got enough cash.'

'Still Buenos Aires, Caro?' I asked. 'Have you heard back from any of the newspapers yet?'

'Not yet, but I will.'

'I love your big dreams!' I said, hugging her. 'I can't wait to come visit you in Buenos Aires when you're famous.'

She blushed. 'I don't expect to be famous, but I have been taking night classes after school for typing and secretarial work.

I've got top grades, and it's a place to start at a newspaper. I figure I can just spy on whatever is going on while I do boring shit like bring coffee and typeset some man's stupid article. And at night, I'll go out to these rallies for women's rights that are happening, and drink coffee and smoke cigarettes, and then write about it and, one day, change the world.'

'Of course you will!' Sylvia cheered, sliding onto the bed next to her. 'I'm going to come visit, and we'll picket together. And maybe I'll even meet someone special . . .' she murmured, then stopped as Eugenia turned her head.

Though Sylvia had never come out and said it, we all knew now that she was a girl who liked other girls, the way other girls liked boys. All of us were fine with it, except for Eugenia, who always blushed and changed the subject quickly.

'What about you, Luce?' Eugenia said too loudly. 'Still planning to stay on the vineyard?'

'I can't leave this – it is my birthright, my home. I feel like if I was away from the land too long, I'd die. Does that make sense?'

Sylvia nodded. 'How I feel about my horses.'

Caro shook her head adamantly. 'I know it's how you feel, and I respect that, but no, I don't understand it. I don't have magic Inca blood or something. What about you, Gen?'

We all looked at Eugenia. She put on red lipstick and looked back at us in the mirror.

'I don't want to leave. I only want one thing, have only ever wanted one thing, and he is here, in Mendoza. Pedro.'

We all gasped. In all the years she'd been in love with Pedro and we all knew about it, she'd never said it out loud.

That was all she said, and we went back to talking about the night to come and which boys we might dance with, even Sylvia, because she still loved to dance and boys were fun to dance with. We talked about whether I'd be Lady of the Buds or not, and even though we all knew I would, it was still fun to talk about it.

Once we were dressed and ready, we went to the festival and had the best time. I did win the Lady of the Buds, and my friends cheered a little too raucously because we'd all had too much to drink when our families weren't looking. My parents looked happy I'd won, and relaxed a little, which hopefully meant I wouldn't wake up to them yelling at each other, which had been the pattern for the past few years.

And the whole time, I pretended that there was no one that had my attention more than anyone else, though I could feel him everywhere on the night, wherever he was.

And this is my big secret.

I am in love with Pedro. The same Pedro that my best friend, Eugenia, has been in love with for years. Even worse, Pedro is in love with me too. I am the worst person on the planet, and I have no idea what to do about it.

It started when he was teaching me about the vines, about how they live and breathe as plants, and I was trying to teach him how they lived and breathed as my children.

It escalated in Buenos Aires when he confronted me in the bathroom.

In the year since we've been back, it has escalated into a full-blown love affair.

Our first kiss was the best moment of my entire life, after the night I became one with the vineyard. Nothing will ever be greater than my love of the land.

I sleep in the vineyard sometimes. Whatever the temperature or the time of year, when the vineyard calls to me, I go to it.

I woke up at 3.23 in the morning after the festival, and it was calling for me. My friends were still asleep. I pulled a coat on over my nightgown, put on some woollen socks with farm boots over top and wrapped a blanket around myself. I went out to the vines. The moon was so full, so beautiful, I wanted to lie there staring at it forever. I fell asleep but woke up a few hours later, freezing.

The temperature had dropped significantly while I slept. For a moment, I panicked, wondering if there was a frost, so I tried to sit up, but I was frozen. I couldn't feel my fingers or toes. I could see the faintest hint of light in the sky, but it was still hours before the morning staff would arrive. Suddenly I was terrified.

'Dios mío,' I heard a voice say. The blanket was ripped from me and arms wrapped around me then. They were cold, and when I still couldn't stop shaking, I felt my nightgown pulled up and I wanted to say no but I couldn't speak, my lips were numb. Suddenly there was a warm, shirtless chest pressed against my back and the blanket was over us, and soon my body warmed up and I could speak again.

'Th-th-th-thank you . . .'

The heat from his body calmed me. My breathing rested. My body stopped shaking. Wrecked, I fell asleep.

When I woke, I was hot. Overly hot. Pedro's body was burning me. I wanted to push him away, and yet I needed him closer. I turned, instinctively. Suddenly his mouth was on mine, the way it had been in my dreams. Previously we'd had sneaky kisses in the vineyard, but nothing like the burning passion that enveloped us now. My body responded like the seventeen-year-old I am. I yearned for him.

'Amor,' he whispered, and his lips were back on mine, his tongue probing my lips, opening mine, and my tongue tentatively exploring his. It was so wonderful – I felt warm and amazing all over. My passion and desire overwhelmed me, and we clumsily took off the rest of our clothes, intertwined in a new way.

It felt very strange, having my body invaded that way. But I needed him so much I kept drawing him closer, and the more his warmth covered me, and his mouth embraced mine, and my love for him grew as his for me grew, I knew it was right.

When we finished our lovemaking, we stayed rolled up in the blanket holding each other until sunrise, talking about our dreams for our future together on Las Viñas, and laughing and kissing some more. I have never been so happy in my life and yet so guilty at the same time.

The sun started to rise, and reluctantly Pedro left me. Removing every trace of his presence, he kissed my forehead, and then my lips, and left, erasing his footprints as he went. I began to shiver with the cold of the morning but dressed myself again and kept warm by replaying our love over and over in my head.

I heard footsteps shortly after, and whispers. Mama and the staff were arriving. I decided not to pretend I'd been asleep. I sat up and leaned against the closest vine and I felt something tickle my neck. I turned, to find the mother vine wrapped around my front, at my face. My stomach sank into my guts as the voices drew so close that El Madre whipped herself back into the vine.

When my mother arrived, she stopped suddenly, mouth dropping. The gasps from the women hinted that something had happened. All of the vines had budded, a month early. As if they had grown around me. The women went around smiling, touching each vine, welcoming it to the world, touching my head.

My mother said nothing but never took her eyes off me. And I knew that somehow Mama knew what had happened in the night.

Suddenly the joy was gone, and I was very frightened.

~

Victoria looked down at the tiara in her hand, which ended in more vines blooming.

'What are you trying to tell me?'

Victoria knew that there was something secret that would only be revealed to her as she learned about her grandmother and her friends, about Pedro, about the past. And for some reason she needed Marilena to be part of it. She simply didn't know why yet.

But when Dev told her the next morning that she was going to need a winemaker, she thought that Las Viñas sighed when she whispered Marilena's name.

CHAPTER EIGHTEEN

~~Dear Marilena,~~

Marilena,

It would be my ~~honour~~ to have you . . .

Please would you . . .

'This is impossible!' Victoria finally growled, sending a message to Dev.

Tomorrow, 6 pm. Invite Marilena if you want.

Dev sent her a thumbs up.

~

'Mari agreed to come tonight,' Dev said before he left the vineyard that day. 'You haven't changed your mind?'

'Can I?' she asked. When he raised his eyebrows, she sighed. 'No, it's fine. I mean, she agreed to come, that's a start, right?'

'Exactly,' he said. 'Can we bring anything? You know, like, food?'

She punched him lightly on the shoulder, but when she went to Adriana's that afternoon, there was a bag packed for her, ready to go. For once Victoria was grateful. She didn't feel confident cooking again after the last disaster.

'It's a platter, meant for wine tasting,' Adriana said. 'It will be perfect, I promise.'

Dev turned up at 6 pm exactly in a button-down top and pants with boots, a bottle of wine at his side.

She opened the door and, without thinking, murmured, 'Wow, you look sexy.'

He grinned. 'Thanks.'

She blushed profusely. 'Did I actually say that out loud?'

'I hope so. Otherwise, you'll ruin my best day ever,' he laughed. 'Can I come in?'

'Oh, yes! Of course, I'm sorry. Is Marilena with you?' she asked, looking behind him nervously.

'She said she'd be a few minutes late. Diego, her husband, calls on Saturdays,' Dev said, as she heard a pop behind her. She turned to see him grinning, cork in hand. 'Wine?'

'Please. Sorry, I'm nervous,' Victoria said, taking the glass of white wine from Dev and taking a sip, closing her eyes.

'Are you nervous to talk about Las Viñas or are you nervous to be with me after—'

'I've set us up outside if that's okay,' Victoria interrupted as her face flushed. 'It's such a beautiful night and the days are getting longer and longer. I'm not used to being in the southern hemisphere.'

Dev lifted his glass and opened his mouth to speak but she nervously continued.

'In October back home, the days get shorter and shorter instead. Though LA is relatively mild year-round.'

'I was in Los Angeles once,' Marilena said, appearing quite suddenly in the open doorway. 'That's your home, right?'

Victoria looked up. Marilena was trying to be friendly, but the question surprised her. Los Angeles *was* her home, and yet she'd barely thought of it since she arrived. And she definitely hadn't been thinking about her little IKEA-filled apartment or the dream house that was never meant to be. How interesting.

'Yes,' Victoria finally answered, as Marilena fidgeted, looking as uncomfortable as Victoria had been just moments before. It calmed her, somehow. 'But I grew up in Ohio. Have you always lived here in Mendoza?'

Marilena glanced at Dev, who was fighting a smile. She pulled out another wine bottle and handed it to Dev to open, and he led the way to the porch.

'Yes, I have lived in the house next door all my life. Which must seem very boring to an outsider,' she answered.

Victoria had set out a nice new tablecloth and jugs of water, china plates and cutlery for each of them.

'Quite the opposite, actually,' Victoria said, as they sat around the table. 'I love the idea of having a long history with a place and a family. When I go home to Ohio to visit my parents, it feels like a rock that centres me.'

'Will your parents come to Mendoza to visit you? Christmas is just around the corner,' Dev asked.

'I don't think they'd be up for the long trip, especially around the holidays. My dad loves Christmas. He's one of those Americans who decorates the lawns and nearly every inch of the house and sets it all to music.'

'They really do that?' Marilena exclaimed with a genuine laugh. 'Last year Diego was home for the holidays, and he and Pia and I sat up half the night watching YouTube videos of those houses in America!'

'I reckon my dad has been working on this year's theme since July.' She stood, feeling more relaxed now. 'I'll go get the platter.'

'Will Diego get back for the holidays this year?' Dev asked Marilena.

Victoria could hear Marilena's murmured answer as she went into the kitchen to pull out the beautiful old serving platter she'd spread Adriana's selections on a few hours earlier. She took a deep breath, feeling hopeful. Marilena was being friendly. This could actually be a really nice night. Maybe it was possible for them to be friends, after all.

Marilena was still speaking to Dev. 'They are going down into the mines soon and will be through the holidays. The project ends in February, so he'll be home then.'

'It must be hard to be away from each other for so long at a time,' Victoria said, bumping open the door with her hip while carrying the large platter with both hands. 'Clear the middle if you can, Dev?'

'It is, but Pia keeps me busy enough to not spend too much time thinking about it,' Marilena said with a shake of her head.

Dev chuckled. Victoria placed the large tray in the middle of the table and said a silent thank you to Adriana when Marilena and Dev both leaned in and murmured their appreciation.

'Everything needed for a perfect wine tasting,' Dev exclaimed. 'What do we have?'

'Um, cheese, charcuterie, fruit. I hope you weren't expecting a full dinner. I, um . . . well, I'm not sure if you noticed, Dev, but the cooking aspect of my Mendoza Project hasn't been going too well,' Victoria said, blushing.

'Your Mendoza Project?' Marilena asked.

'Oh, yes,' Victoria said, clearing her throat and glancing at Dev, who gave her an encouraging nod. 'Well, doing renovations to the house, really.' She almost said, 'in order to sell,' but she found she couldn't honestly say that now. Too much was happening. And suddenly Victoria knew, without a shadow of a doubt, that she was going to stay and see this through. Whatever this was. On her land. With her curse. With her heritage.

'Pia and Gabi have been helping,' Victoria continued. 'And I truly appreciate that you have allowed that, so thank you.'

Marilena's eyes widened the smallest amount, but her jaw relaxed, and she nodded her head imperceptibly.

'Pia is a joy to have around,' Victoria said.

Dev poured them each wine as Victoria relaxed a bit.

'Part of my project was cooking for Dev and the boys each day. I am a deplorable cook, but I've been attempting to learn traditional recipes and have been trying them out on Dev and the boys. It hasn't been going very well, but Adriana has helped by always sending me off with prepared sandwiches as well.'

Marilena let out an obviously unintentional laugh. 'Why keep trying then?'

'I have no idea,' she said honestly. 'But don't worry, tonight I made no attempt to burn my hair off again, so please, help yourself to the food.'

Dev and Marilena both made small plates of olives, artichokes, meat and cheese. Food always made people more open to discussion.

'So Marilena, Dev said you had some ideas about making the wine for Las Viñas?'

Marilena gave Dev a withering look but finished chewing the beautiful Ibérico ham Adriana had imported from Spain. Finally, she spoke.

'The French say terroir is the most important thing. Do you know what terroir means?' Marilena asked.

Victoria shook her head.

'Don't worry, even those who do know what it means don't, not really, for terroir is simply *terroir*. There is no synonym, nothing that translates from one language to another. The best translations of the French word hint at 'a sense of place'. Some say it is the region, some the land, others the soil, climate, the vines and how deep they go, their age. But it is just terroir. Both Dev and I believe in terroir, so the wine that will be in the bottle, it starts here, in the vineyard.'

'*Ter-wah*,' Victoria repeated. 'I like it. I like a word that can only mean one thing, and that is what it is.'

'I wanted the wine from Las Viñas to *be* terroir,' Marilena said. 'I wanted the bottle to say "I am Las Viñas" and that be enough. It would be a Malbec that is not only its grape, but its vineyard,' she proclaimed.

'Is it only Malbec on the land?' Victoria asked.

'Sí,' Dev answered, bending down to show her the grapes. 'Look at the size, the colour. Mendoza is planting many grapes now, beautiful Cabernet, Chardonnay, Rosé. Our favourite white is Torrontés, which is mostly grown up north near Salta, though we grow it here now. But Las Viñas has always produced only one grape – Malbec. We can make that grape the best grape, the best wine.'

'And we have options,' Marilena added, her passion growing. 'We could decide to separate the free run juice from the press and age it separately, blending the perfect wine as we go. Or we could make single row wines.'

'That would be bold,' Dev laughed.

'Slow down, mad scientists!' Victoria said, spreading a beautiful Brie cheese over Adriana's homemade sourdough. 'What is free run juice? You're going to need to walk me through this step-by-step – the most I know about wine is how to open a bottle. And that's usually a screw top.'

Dev leaned forward, swirling the Malbec in his glass. 'Okay. Once we pick the grapes, they are pressed. Back in the day, there used to be a harvest festival where the locals would come together and stomp on the grapes in a big vat.'

'Like that *I Love Lucy* episode?' Victoria asked.

Dev looked perplexed, but Marilena grinned and nodded.

'Exactly like that! Actually, I heard that back when it was still producing wines, Las Viñas took one vat every year and did a traditional foot press case. I would long to bring that tradition back.'

They were silent for a moment.

'These days,' Dev continued, winking at Victoria, 'vineyards use a press machine. The first press gives you free run juice. All winemakers agree that is the purest, best juice. As you press and press again, you get more juice, but the tannins and bitterness of the skins and stems, especially in red wine, can start to impart flavours. So having a vineyard that only used free run juice would be an exceptional wine – but not very efficient.'

'Could we just use the free run juice for ourselves and sell the other pressed juice to other vineyards, put a little cash flow in the business?' Victoria asked.

'Hmm,' Dev and Marilena said, looking at one another, impressed.

'The vines are very old, nearly a hundred years,' Marilena continued then, looking more confident. 'Even though they haven't produced a grape in fifty years, that's not because the vines were unhealthy. Still, to be safe, I would want to handpick everything at the perfect time. Even if it means over different days. And I'd love to use the basket press in the cellar, though it may be too small, even though our production is tiny, comparatively.'

'What is the production, Dev? And speak to me in bottles or cases, not in acres,' Victoria interrupted.

'In a successful year with all acres and all plots making grapes? That would equal about 30,000 bottles for the vintage.'

'That seems like a lot,' Victoria said.

'It's not,' Marilena said. 'That's small-scale, boutique actually, which is a winemaker's a dream,' she sighed.

'A medium-sized producer in Mendoza probably produces close to half a million bottles, Victoria,' Dev explained.

'Oh, wow, okay. So, we are boutique-scale. Why is this a dream?' Victoria asked.

'Don't get her started,' Dev said, rolling his eyes. Marilena stuck her tongue out at him. The childish gesture charmed Victoria.

'Boutique-scale wineries give you a little more freedom to be creative. For a winemaker, creativity is so exciting,' Marilena explained.

'We've got the perfect-sized vineyard to actually make a really great wine and showcase it to the world, make a name for ourselves.'

'Is that what you both wanted? For Las Viñas?' Victoria asked them.

They glanced at each other and nodded.

'I've dreamed of making wine at Las Viñas since I was a little girl,' Marilena said quietly. 'Of picking an uncursed grape off a vine each day, rolling it around on my tongue, and the moment it was perfect, picking them, pressing them, watching the free run juice pour into a barrel, and a year or so later, tasting the perfect wine of Las Viñas. I dreamed . . . it would win awards and gain international recognition,' she finished, turning her eyes away.

Dev took Marilena's hand and smiled at Victoria. Victoria took a deep breath and looked around to her land. It also seemed to be holding its breath.

'Then Marilena, will you join us? Will you be the winemaker here at Las Viñas?' Victoria asked.

A world of emotion stirred in Marilena's dark eyes. Victoria could feel the sadness, the longing, the disappointment, the possessiveness, but gaining more and more clarity in them was the love of the land, her desire to make the wine for Las Viñas.

Finally, she nodded. 'Yes. Yes, I will be your winemaker.'

Las Viñas released its breath, and this time Victoria was certain she heard a sigh – when they looked up, she knew that they had heard it as well.

~

'Right!' Dev said the next day as they stood in the winery. 'Let's do a stocktake and see what we've got.'

'The basket press,' Marilena cried, walking over to the old press and leaning to hug it.

'There's a regular press as well,' Dante called out, 'and a sorting table.'

'Vats and plungers are in good stock and good shape,' Julio said from further down the room.

'Whew!' they heard a whistle from the next room. Marilena, Dev and Victoria followed the sound into a large room lined with oak barrels.

'Old oak, mostly French,' Alex said from atop one row. 'And as you can see, plenty. This place is filled with some fancy stuff considering it was never a working vineyard.'

'Oh yes it was,' Marilena corrected, 'and the best in the region, as well.'

'My grandfather, Felipe Ortega, came from Spain and wanted to invest in the land and the vineyard, I was told,' Victoria said. 'Just when the wine industry in the rest of Mendoza was crumbling, ours was about to thrive.'

'And then the curse. What I wouldn't give to find out what happened there,' Marilena said quietly, walking through the vast room, taking a deep inhale of the red wine-stained barrels.

Victoria closed her eyes and took in the smell as well, feeling transported.

'I reckon we have enough to get started, and we can ask around friends in town as things come up. If we last through this vintage, planning a March harvest, then that's twelve to fifteen months in barrel?' Dev asked, glancing at Marilena.

'At least,' she said. 'So that puts our 2025 vintage debuting in 2027. Maybe even in the competitions that year. But what about in the meantime?'

'I wouldn't quit your paying jobs yet!' Victoria said in a panic.

'You already mentioned selling what we don't use to other vineyards. If we have a good yield, that could fund the vineyard until the wine comes out,' Dev said. 'Any other ideas?'

Victoria crossed her arms and looked around, smiling and nodding her head.

'Uh oh, I see a project forming,' Marilena said. 'What do you see?'

Victoria turned. 'We've got a cursed vineyard that just woke up. The hacienda still needs some work, but it will get there soon, with some help. We could open up to tours and tastings.'

'But we don't have any wines to taste,' Marilena said.

Victoria laughed. 'Except for the entire cellar of original wines from Bodegas Anyas de Alveras from the 1960s!'

'But Victoria, that is your heritage,' Dev said softly. 'Are you certain you want to just give it away?'

'I will only have a heritage if I can keep it. Plus, give it away?' she laughed. '*Sell* it. And yes. A wine is not meant to sit in a cellar forever. It is meant to be drunk, with friends. An experience within an experience. I want Las Viñas to *live*. And that means she is remembered, tasted, explored, experienced. Plus, the publicity will add great value to the name and the land. What do you think? Do you guys think it might work?'

Dev and Marilena looked at one another and finally nodded.

'Let's do it,' Marilena said.

'Excellent,' Victoria said with a grin. 'It's time Las Viñas got a chance to show off again. And thankfully, I know exactly who can do the job.'

CHAPTER NINETEEN

'Remember, girls, the film crew is coming down in January just after Christmas break, so we have to be ready by then. Which means, you need to actually work,' Victoria said the next week, as Pia and Gabi sat on the bed in La Amarilla, the Yellow Room, reading a magazine instead of painting.

'Actually, Victoria,' Pia said, jumping off the bed with the magazine, 'we are working. Have a look at this hacienda in La Rioja in Spain.'

Pia opened the magazine to the pages they'd marked with furniture and room ideas.

'We went to the library and raided their old copies of *Condé Nast* to look at different hacienda and winery stays in Europe and here in South America. What do you think?'

Victoria looked up, surprised. 'That's what you girls have been doing?'

Pia rolled her eyes. 'Victoria, Las Viñas is part of all of us. We may be silly teenage girls to you, but it still means something to us to see it thrive, and to be a part of it. Especially since my mama's involved now. Anyway, a lot of places here in Mendoza are going for the really modern look. But we thought that this one,' she said, pointing to the Spanish one again, 'was more Las Viñas style.'

'You're in the Hollywood industry, right?' Gabi interrupted, standing. 'Don't you think that the story of the curse should play on its history? Almost like it was frozen in time? I mean, that's a story that would sell.'

Victoria was momentarily speechless. Then she shook her head with a laugh.

'Remind me to get you girls internships the second you're out of school, okay?'

The girls laughed and met eyes, looking jubilant.

'Gabi's got a cousin about an hour from here who has a big consignment shop with loads of old antiques and stuff. We thought we'd go next weekend.'

'That sounds fantastic, but I can't next weekend. And I know neither of you drive yet, so we'll just have to wait.'

'Dante drives,' Gabi said. 'He's seventeen so he's the only one who can drive on his own, since he has his parents' permission. We could ask him?'

Victoria raised an eyebrow. 'I love your idea, but don't you use me for sneaking out with boys again. Your mother has just started working with me, Pia.'

Pia smirked.

'Uncle Dev!' she yelled across the yard when she saw Dev and Marilena there together. 'Can you take Gabi and me to town on Saturday? It's for the hacienda. We need a truck!'

The three watched him lean towards Marilena then turn back. 'I'm busy, kiddo, but have Dante take you. You can take my truck!'

Pia pressed her lips together to keep from laughing while Gabi grinned unabashedly.

'How wonderfully convenient,' Gabi said.

Victoria laughed. 'Well played, niñas diablitas.'

The girls snickered. They loved it when she called them the little devil girls in Spanish.

'Go! Paint!'

She looked around and saw Marilena and Dev in the vineyard, looking jubilant at the beautiful flowers Las Viñas was starting to produce now that they were into December. The fact that the vineyard was on schedule with the rest of Mendoza and following a healthy growing cycle meant that in some way, their dream was happening. Victoria knew it was time to create her new life and her new dream now, too.

Las Viñas was where she felt at home. It was in her blood, her veins, her soul. She wasn't ready to go back to her old life. Where she wanted to be was here. She wanted to see her vineyard – her children – thrive.

So, too, it turned out, did others. Victoria was moved and surprised to see her local friends show up one morning piled into trucks, including Adriana with the finest products from her shop, with Romina and another woman in tow.

'Victoria,' Adriana introduced her, 'this is Val, my esteemed auntie from El Chaltén, whose recipes you have been completely destroying since you arrived.'

Victoria laughed and took Val's hand. 'An honour,' she said, 'and I do apologise for not representing you properly.'

'Oh hush,' Val said with a laugh. 'Adriana filled me in on what's going on at Las Viñas, now you're here.' She looked around in wonder. 'Never thought I'd see the day the curse would be lifted and Las Viñas would thrive. I had to come. And I hope you've taken some time off today, because we are cooking together. Me, you and Adriana. Consider this your one free cooking class from Auntie Val. I charge ridiculous amounts in US dollars down south.'

'Wow, that sounds amazing. Thank you—'

'Eduardo!' Adriana interrupted, yelling out to the next truck pulling up. 'In the garden, just in the middle I think!' The handsome man with a black moustache nodded and directed the truck. 'Eduardo is a butcher, and he had an old parilla he's going to set up in the garden. Like we talked about?'

'Oh, I . . .' Victoria started, but couldn't finish her sentence. She was overwhelmed as the group set up in and around the hacienda. 'I don't know what to say,' she finally finished.

'This is us bringing Las Viñas back to the world. This is us helping you lift her curse. She built our village, created our world. Now we repay her by bringing her back to us,' Romina said, grabbing a paintbrush.

'Victoria, Adriana, come!' Val called. 'Let's start this meal if we want to feed twenty people by 5 pm!'

They were going to grill a whole picanha steak on the parilla and make a chimichurri on the side.

'The quality of the meat is what makes our asado famous around the world, Victoria. Eduardo's is the best outside Patagonia. Because there is no bone, we'll slather the meat in my homemade chimichurri, which will keep in the heat but also build a heavenly crust.'

Victoria was in charge of making the chimichurri, using a mortar and pestle to grind a paste of garlic, chilli and a massive bundle of green herbs like parsley and oregano, mixed in with olive oil, vinegar and spices.

'Even you can't mess this up, Victoria, so long as you follow the recipe,' Adriana said with a wink.

Halfway through, Victoria squinted at the measurements. 'Are you *sure* there is supposed to be this much—'

'YES!' Adriana and Val said together, laughing, and Victoria said no more, following the recipe to a tee, and making her first perfect concoction – chimichurri.

Val used half the sauce to coat the beef as Eduardo fired up the parilla, and put the other half into a bowl for serving.

'What will we make with it?' Victoria asked.

'I brought everything that just came in from the farms. December is a fantastic month,' Adriana said. 'Spring and summer vegetables combined. I've got peppers of all colours, beans, asparagus, tomatoes and eggplant. We'll just throw them into the oven with some salt and olive oil.'

'And no asado is complete without papas,' Val said, showing her the thinly sliced potatoes marinated in lush, fresh green herbs and olive oil and salt.

Victoria pulled out every chair, every table, every plate and all her cutlery and wine glasses when the workers finished that day. Pia and Gabi had instructed the local townsfolk where to paint. Dev, Marilena and the boys in the vineyard had worked another long day, and when they came in with a clipping of a flowering vine from the vineyard to bless the house with, everyone cheered. Victoria poured the wine and Val and Adriana served the food.

Each day after that, more and more townsfolk gathered until most of the locals were part of the process, laughing and joyful together, enjoying the land, helping with the grapes. It took a week for them to transform Hacienda Bodegas Anyas de Alveras into a place that they could be proud of.

It was as if Las Viñas brought them all together somehow, and because of it, she thrived.

~

Victoria was incredibly nervous when she knocked on Marilena's door a few days later, dinner in hand. Pia answered in her pyjamas, looking very young without Gabi to do her make-up.

'Victoria! Mama said you were having a catch-up,' she said, taking the dish from her. 'Come in. She's still in the shower after a spill in the mud on her way home. Third time this week.'

Victoria wondered if Las Viñas was trying to tell Marilena something, but she couldn't ask without giving too much away.

Pia sniffed the large pot of food, suspiciously. 'It does smell good. And I am starving.'

'You are a little beast.' Victoria laughed. 'Come on, help me turn on your stove so I can reheat it. It's from Val, Adriana's auntie. Her famous risotto.'

'Yes please!' Pia said, turning on the gas oven and watching until the risotto started simmering. 'Don't let it burn, Victoria! I've got to go wait for my dad to call. 6 pm, every Saturday, on the nose,' she beamed, running to her room.

'Don't let it burn!' she called again before slamming her door.

'I'm not actually that bad!' Victoria yelled to the empty house she'd never been in before. It was warm and homey, and there were pictures on the walls of Marilena looking happier than she'd ever seen her look, and Pia with a man who must be her father, Diego. He was very handsome. Suddenly Victoria realised how nervous she was. She needed her opera.

She turned her Spotify onto her favourite opera playlist while she finished the risotto as Val had instructed, doing a mantecatura, which was adding cold butter and cheese at the end.

'Butter and cheese at the end, really?' she muttered to herself, then found another note.

Follow the recipe, Victoria!

'*La Traviata*. My favourite,' a voice said behind her. Marilena was leaning against the door, smiling, eyes closed as she hummed the soprano. 'I remember seeing *Pretty Woman* when I was a girl, and I was obsessed with one day seeing that opera. When I met my husband, Diego, he asked me just after he proposed, "What is the one thing, the big thing, that will make you say yes?" and I said to him, "You've got five years to take me to see *La Traviata* at a proper Opera House or I will leave you."'

Victoria laughed, stirring the last portion of the risotto. 'How old were you?'

'When we married? Twenty-two,' she said, smiling. 'When Pia was born the next year, I thought I'd give up the dream. And then on my thirtieth birthday my then seven-year-old daughter woke me by covering my eyes with a tie, and she and my husband kidnapped me and took me to the airport. Diego directed me to the airplane with the blindfold still on so I couldn't see our destination. I realised then he must have planned it quite meticulously for them to allow me on the plane like that.

'I assumed we'd go to Buenos Aires,' she said with a nostalgic smile, stepping into the kitchen and leaning over the dish, stirring it herself. 'But when we landed, we were in Manaus in the Amazon of Brazil, at the most famous theatre in the world, the Amazonas Theatre. We went to our hotel, just across from the theatre. He'd bought me a red dress, like from *Pretty Woman*, and we got dressed and went to the rooftop bar for cocktails, and then we went to *La Traviata*.' She smiled fondly. 'One of the best nights of my life.'

Victoria smiled widely. 'Whatever could possibly top that?'

Marilena looked sideways, thoughtful.

'Pia. Having my Pia.' Marilena caught Victoria's sad look. 'But only just.'

Marilena's face changed suddenly. 'I'm sorry, what time is it?'

Victoria looked at her watch. '6.14.'

She scrunched her brow. 'He's never late.'

'Your husband?' Victoria asked.

Pia came out of her room, looking confused and holding the phone. 'Mama?'

Marilena smiled and relaxed her brow, but Victoria could see the veins in her temples.

'I'm sure he's just running late, bebe,' she said. 'Remember he was in the mines this week. Come, let's have dinner and chat with Victoria.'

Victoria sat and so did Pia, looking at Marilena worriedly. Marilena winked at her daughter and squeezed her hand. She took a serving spoon from a drawer and served them each a plate. Victoria could see the stress working in her throat.

But they didn't speak. Their catch-up on the progress of the vineyard was on hold, and they ate in silence.

At 6.49 pm, the phone rang. Pia jumped but Marilena reached it first, answering, 'Está bien?'

The room was filled with silence as Marilena's face got more and more pale.

'Mama?' Pia asked.

Finally, Marilena nodded and hung up, and suddenly she was covering her face, sobbing.

'Mama! What happened?!' Pia cried, but Marilena continued to sob.

Pia turned to Victoria. 'Victoria?'

'It's okay,' she said softly, and picked up the phone, calling Dev.

'Please come quickly to Mari's – something has happened, I'm not sure what,' she said, and hung up. 'Pia, honey, your Uncle Dev is on his way. Why don't you go to your room and wait while I help your mama, okay?'

But Marilena looked up and met her eyes. 'I have to pack.'

'Mama?' Pia asked, her voice quavering.

'Pia, help your mama pack?' she asked.

Pia looked to Marilena, then back to Victoria, and nodded, taking Marilena with one hand to her bedroom.

Something was very, very wrong.

~

'Mari, honey, what happened?' Dev called as he ran into the house about ten minutes after Victoria called him. 'Is Diego okay? What's wrong? Mari?!'

'She's packing in her bedroom,' Victoria said, coming out of the kitchen where she'd been cleaning up. 'Pia is with her.'

'Victoria,' Marilena said in a low voice, coming from the other room with a bag in hand. She was pale and distraught. 'Can you please keep Pia with you while I go north?'

'Of course,' Victoria said, still trying to make sense of what was happening.

Pia was crying. 'Mama, please take me with you. I want to be with Papa.'

'No, bebe, you must stay here. Dev,' she said when she saw him, falling into his arms in despair. 'There was an explosion in the mines. They . . . they are still trying to get them out,' she whispered so Pia couldn't hear. 'I must go now. I must be there . . .'

'Oh my god,' he whispered, hugging Marilena tightly.

She whispered something into his ear and pulled out of their embrace, as Pia then threw herself into his arms, crying.

'He'll be okay. He has to be,' Dev said, and looked back to Marilena. 'I can take Pia with me if you want.'

'No,' Marilena said, wiping her eyes. 'Let her stay at Victoria's where she has a room and a lot of space.'

Marilena turned to Victoria and lowered her voice. 'You'll let Gabi come?'

Victoria nodded.

'Make it fun for her. Keep her relaxed. She loves being near you, it will help . . . distract her. Just in case . . .'

'I got this,' Victoria said quietly, squeezing her arm.

Marilena hugged Pia, whispering softly in her ear as Pia cried quietly. She turned to Dev. 'Please can you take me to the airport? I want to get there as quickly as possible.'

Dev shot one glance at Victoria, who nodded, taking Pia into her arms as she cried.

'Of course, let's go. You've booked a flight already?' he asked.

Marilena nodded and tried to stifle the sob in her throat, but she couldn't, so she quickly hugged Pia again and ran out the door, Dev following her.

'Come, bebe,' Victoria said softly, the words feeling natural as she rocked the girl in her arms. 'Let's go watch a movie. How about *Miss Congeniality*? It's the epitome of a pageant movie . . .'

CHAPTER TWENTY

It was an unbearably long forty-eight hours for Pia at Victoria's house, despite how much they did to stay distracted. Gabi came for a sleepover, and Victoria took them shopping in Mendoza, then treated them to lunch in a fancy winery restaurant while they wore their new dresses. The next day, Victoria had them help her make lunch for the boys so they could sit at the table and flirt, but Pia remained distracted. Not even the reminder of her drive with Dante could bring her out of her state of anxiety. So it was a great relief to everyone when Pia's cell phone rang and it was Marilena, assuring her that her father was in the hospital but would be absolutely fine, and not to worry. Pia lit up when the phone was passed to her papa.

'Papa, you're okay! We've been so worried,' she cried through the phone, running out into the garden.

'Are you okay?' Victoria asked Dev gently, putting her hand on his shoulder when he leaned against the wall with his head on his forearm.

He lifted his face, and Victoria could see his eyes were glistening, but he nodded, took a deep breath and managed a smile.

'Diego is like my brother. Don't know what I would have done . . .'

She pulled Dev in for a hug. 'He's okay,' she said, rocking a bit. 'He's okay.'

'Okay, love you, Papa,' Pia said, coming back into the house. 'Yup, here she is.' She handed the phone to Victoria. 'Mama would like to speak to you.'

'Hello?' she said, taking the phone while Pia hugged Dev.

'Victoria, thank you again for taking Pia. She said you've been desperately trying to distract her the last two days. I appreciate that,' Marilena said on the other end of the phone.

Victoria walked outside and closed the door. 'How is he?' she asked quietly.

Marilena took a long pause, and her voice was shaky when she started speaking. She must have put on an incredibly brave tone for Pia.

'They were all very lucky,' she said. 'There were no fatalities, which is a miracle. There was an explosion in the mine, but thankfully it was not too far in. So there wasn't as much debris. Diego has a broken leg, and many very bad burns. They think some may be third-degree, so they must keep him here for a while to watch for infection and to see if they need to do a grafting surgery.'

Her voice broke.

'But he is okay,' Victoria said soothingly. 'He will heal, and you'll be home before you know it. Pia will be fine – we'll be keeping very busy on the vineyard and at the hacienda. And we've got Christmas Day luncheon here that she can help me plan. So you just take all the time you need, okay?'

Victoria could hear Marilena choking back her cries. 'Thank you.'

Dev knocked on the window and Victoria smiled at him. He pointed to the phone.

'Mari, Dev wants to talk to you. Shall I pass you on?' she said.

She heard Marilena chuckle on the other end.

'You called me Mari,' she said.

'Did I now?' Victoria asked, surprised. 'How 'bout that? It's almost as if . . .'

'We're becoming friends?' Marilena replied.

'Nah,' they said at the same time, after a beat.

Victoria smiled and handed the phone to Dev, something warm inside her heart that felt a little bit like friendship.

~

They spent the weeks before Christmas in a frenzy. The vineyard was flowering beautifully, and though no new sections had opened up overnight, they were at about sixty per cent capacity.

'We will still have more than enough for a vintage, even if it's half of what it is capable of. But I wouldn't give up yet.' Smiling, Dev took Victoria's hand. 'The flowering is beautiful. Look at her. Looks like berry formation is set for January.'

Victoria's stomach tingled with butterflies and her face grew warm on their contact. She was terribly attracted to Dev, had started dreaming of him, both when asleep and awake. She thought of kissing those full lips again, the lips that were almost always slyly smiling at her, the first lips since Michael's. She thought of running her hands up his strong forearms, to his chest and broad shoulders. She wondered what he would look like without clothes, what his body would feel like above hers. He was so different from Michael, who'd been slight and lanky. Dev was a *man*. A man with tanned skin from working outside, hands that were calloused, muscles that were strong from labour, dark hair on his arms and chest, and stubble on his face that make him look so earthy, so sexy, that her throat had begun to go dry when she saw him.

You're spending so much time with teenage girls, she thought, *you're starting to act like one.*

Still, she relished the feel of her hand warm in his.

'Is it even possible for there to be any bud burst now, this late into the season? It's nearly Christmas.'

He shrugged. 'Who knows with a cursed vineyard? She's not telling you any secrets, is she?'

Victoria's head snapped up but the grinning look on his face was innocent. She shook her head.

'Actually,' she began, hesitating. 'She had been, for a little while. But there's been nothing lately. I'm not sure if it's that there is so much happening around here. Or if it waits for the opportune moment. I know,' she said when she felt his curious gaze, 'it sounds ridiculous.'

'It sounds magical,' he corrected, and they kept walking with their hands entwined.

Pia seemed back to her usual self once she could talk to her papa, who was getting better every day.

'Thankfully the larger burns are all first- and second-degree,' Marilena said over the phone as they neared the holiday. 'There are a couple of third-degree burns, but they are very small and have not had any infection. He's on antibiotics and healing well, so hopefully we'll be able to come home before New Year.'

'I'll make sure we have quite the party on Christmas, so Pia doesn't feel too sad that she won't be with her family for the holiday,' Victoria said.

~

Three days before Christmas, Victoria started getting anxious about hosting the day. The parilla grill Eduardo had set up outside was ready, but she was panicking she wouldn't be able to use it properly. Dev was going to help, but she spent hours watching YouTube videos and reading up on the importance of cooking a proper asado.

When the doorbell rang, she answered, assuming it was one of the boys to grab afternoon snacks.

'Happy Christmas!'

Her parents stood on her doorstep, her mom dressed in a floppy hat, a flamingo sundress and sandals, as if she were on a tropical holiday instead of in the vineyards of Argentina.

'We hear that's what they say here in Argentina, "Happy", not "Merry". I kind of like that,' Joyce said. 'And Christmas in summer! I thought I'd hate it, but I've never been so happy to be warm in my life. Not that it's that warm, mind you. And look at this! Look at you!'

Victoria choked up and immediately threw herself into their arms.

'Whoa, big hugs, we love those!' Joyce said, looking at Victoria and seeing tears. 'I hope these are happy tears. We wanted to surprise you.'

'Happy tears,' she answered, 'definitely happy tears.'

She pulled back to smile at them. 'Mom, you look ridiculous.'

'I told your mother Argentina wasn't a tropical country, but she was adamant,' Frank said, hugging her. 'Hi, sweetheart.'

'That's because of your stupid crossword the other week! Tropical Caribbean country – Argentina!' she scoffed.

'Except that it was Antigua, because, as per usual, your answer was wrong,' he said patiently.

'Well, how was I to know that?!' she answered.

'Because I told you. Again and again and again as you packed,' he said, picking up their suitcases and following her inside, winking at Victoria, who grinned and laughed.

'Hey, Mom, what's the capital of Argentina?' Victoria called, taking a suitcase from her dad and rolling it across the kitchen.

'Manchu Pinchu,' she called, not only giving the wrong answer but pronouncing it wrong as well. Victoria chuckled.

'Wow, look at this place! Bicky honey, this is beautiful!' Joyce continued.

'Least she got the same continent this time,' Frank said, shrugging, following her. He whistled. 'Sure is spectacular. Where should we park up, kiddo?'

'Here, Mom, Dad. Why don't you leave your bags here and I'll give you a house tour? You can pick your own room! We've been painting and doing some renovations, so most of them are quite pretty now, though Pia, the neighbour's daughter, has some nice ideas for swapping some furniture out. She'll be able to show you over dinner. She's staying here,' Victoria said, when they looked at her quizzically. 'Her dad got into an accident at work so Marilena, her mom and my neighbour, is up north with him until he recovers.'

'Wow, you must have made some good friends pretty quick down here, honey,' Joyce said.

'Oh no, we hate each other,' Victoria said with a laugh. 'Come on.'

She took them through the rooms of the hacienda. 'I kept the names the same from the original build, so all the bedrooms are named after a colour. La Azul is the Blue Room. That is Pia's. Mine is La Rosada, the Rose Room. Which one did you prefer?'

'I like the yellow one,' Joyce said, and Frank nodded amiably.

'You know, when I first moved in, I pictured you guys in that one,' Victoria said. '*Am-ah-ree-yo* is how you say it in Spanish. Just in case that question ever comes up.'

Joyce looked around for a pen, so Victoria gave her a mini notepad with an attached pen she could put in her pocket.

'I have dozens lying around.'

'Your "project books?" honey?' Frank asked.

'You know me too well, Dad,' she said. 'Mom, did you get it?'

'I think so,' she said, writing in the book. 'Seriously, honey, did you just accidentally get nouveau riche or something?'

Victoria laughed. 'More like nouveau in debto,' she said, which made her dad squeeze her shoulder.

'Still, honey, owning property has value.'

'Even a cursed vineyard?'

'A what?' they said at the same time.

'Come on,' Victoria said, leading them outside. I'll take you around Las Viñas and introduce you.'

'To the vines?' Joyce asked. 'You're going to introduce us to the vines?'

Laughing, she nodded. 'I have so much to tell you guys.'

~

'That was delicious, honey,' Frank said, patting his stomach after they finished eating a few hours later.

'Was that traditional Antiguan?' Joyce asked, and Pia looked quizzically at Victoria, who winked at her.

'Argentinian, Mom,' she corrected. 'And sort of. I've been trying to learn to cook . . .'

'She's really made some terribly appalling dishes,' Pia said. 'Thank god you weren't here a couple of weeks ago – she'd have her hair all burnt off and we'd be having Uber Eats.'

Frank chortled. He already adored Pia.

'Oh jeez, thanks, Pia,' Victoria said, poking her tongue out at her. 'Though to be fair, she's right. There's a local here named Adriana who has been helping me—'

'After she tried to sabotage you,' Pia interrupted.

'Well, there was that, yes. But then between Adriana and Pia—'

'My mama is a terrible cook as well so Papa bought her a slow cooker years ago, when he went off to the mines, so that I wouldn't starve to death. Auntie Adriana had to show Mama how to use it, too, Victoria, if it makes you feel any better,' Pia finished.

'It really does, actually, thank you,' she said, brightening. 'Anyway, when Pia moved in here for a couple of weeks, she brought her slow cooker from home, and between her instructions—'

'—and Auntie Adriana's fully prepared "throw everything in and turn the dial to 360"—'

Victoria looked at Pia.

'Sorry,' she said, standing and collecting dirty plates.

'We've had a few small wins,' Victoria said, smiling. 'You don't have to do that, Pia.'

'That's okay, Victoria, I'll do the dishes so you can have time with your parents,' Pia said, very grown-up. 'I know I'd want the same if mine were here.'

Pia disappeared through the door of the dining room to the kitchen.

'Well, well,' Joyce said, looking between the door and Victoria. 'Who'd have thought?'

'Thought what, Mom?'

'You've found yourself a little family here, honey. I'm so pleased,' she said, wiping her eyes at the corners.

'Mom, I'm only just on the verge of maybe winning over a few locals. Most people are just tolerating me here, not knowing what to do with me or this cursed vineyard that's waking up.'

'Family comes in many forms, Victoria. Like me and your mom who raised you,' Frank said in his low cadence. 'Like your blood family here – that includes a cursed vineyard and getting to know your grandmother as a young girl through the diaries. And the townsfolk here who are helping you see your dreams through, and these women next door, Marilena and her Pia, who, no matter how much you think are your enemies, are connected to you. We don't always choose our families. But once they are a part of us, we hold them close in everything we are and do. You are a part of something bigger than yourself, Victoria. We all are. Don't fight it.'

CHAPTER TWENTY-ONE

Dev arrived on Christmas Day at 11 am, as promised. Her parents had already warmed to him when they met that first day.

He took Frank over to the newly installed parilla and walked him through how it was built, winking at Victoria. Joyce caught the look.

'So, what's going on with you and Dev?' she asked in a sing-song voice. 'He's gorgeous. And much more your style than Michael.'

'Mom!' she said, turning. 'We don't talk about Michael, remember?'

'Oh, come on, Victoria. You think about Michael, and you know it's true. He was a sweet boy, at first. But he was weak – actors usually are, you know. I know what happened was shocking and unexpected – not being able to have a child, your life's dream, and then losing your fiancé and your home, then your career.'

Victoria let out a breathy laugh. 'Jeez, even I didn't know it was so bad, Mom, thanks.'

'Oh, hush,' she said, swatting Victoria playfully and then bringing her in for a hug. 'You know what I mean. Because Victoria, I think if you let yourself think about Michael right now, you will find that you aren't still heartbroken or lost. I think you will find yourself doing just fine.' She glanced out to where Dev and Frank were standing. 'Maybe even better than fine. So maybe you should feel okay about moving on.'

Victoria realised quite quickly that when there was a pit of fire and hunks of meat, men seemed to go back to their caveman roots. Dev lit the fire and began explaining to Frank how it worked. Victoria brought the meat out: the steaks, choripán, the chicken and pork. By the time she got back with the rest, Dev and Frank had been joined by Walter and the boys; Julio, Alex and Dante, and they were seasoning the meat and arguing over who was the best asador and which was the best way to cook each dish. They would slip into Spanish occasionally, and Dev would translate for Frank. Finally, Victoria gave up trying to help and relinquished the parilla to Dev, who shrugged and put his hands in his pockets with an uncustomary bashful smile.

'Did I ever tell you boys about the time I was hunting wild boar in the Andes, and I was rescued from the cold by a herd of red stag that took me in and kept me warm during the storm?' Walter asked.

'Hey, I haven't heard that one,' Victoria said, leaning into Dev, who put his arm around her.

'Oh, man, it's definitely one of his best,' Dev said. 'Hey, Walter, save that one for the dinner table, eh? Victoria and her parents haven't heard it, and it's a goodie.'

Walter beamed and gave a hearty thumbs up. 'In that case, I'd better tell the tale about the time I rode the horse backwards . . .'

'That one I have heard,' Victoria laughed, walking away, and Dev came with her, his arm still around her.

'You're not upset us boys have taken over the parilla?'

'So relieved. Now that I don't have to cook, maybe I'll even have fun today!'

Dev laughed, pulling her in and kissing her forehead. 'It's Christmas, go, have fun with the girls.'

He turned and left, going back to the parilla, while Victoria stood touching her forehead where he'd kissed her, the place still hot from his lips. She headed back into the kitchen to finish the salads.

'Pia,' she called, 'can you come help me?'

Pia rolled her eyes and left the parilla, where she and Gabi had been hovering close to the boys, to help Victoria in the kitchen.

'Smelling good over there! Do you girls need help with the salads?' Joyce called into the kitchen. She was sitting outside with Romina, sipping wine. Only Sylvia was missing now.

'We're fine, Mom. The boys have taken over the parilla. That's a grill in Spanish, if you want to add it to your list,' Victoria said.

Joyce put her glass down, looking for her notepad.

'Back pocket, Mom, remember? I gave you that little one.'

'Got it! Wait, what's the word again?'

'P-a-r-i-l-l-a,' Romina said, as Victoria chuckled and went into the house.

'Is everyone here?' Pia asked.

'Everyone but Sylvia, I think,' Victoria answered. She opened the refrigerator to get the vegetables and salad out, along with a few more bottles of Torrontés and Chardonnay she'd picked up from Adriana's.

There was a knock at the door.

'That must be her now. Would you mind grabbing the door?' Victoria asked Pia.

She heard the door open, followed by breaking glass and a gasp of breath, and turned around to see what was wrong. Instead she saw Pia crying in the embrace of a man who was obviously Diego, with Marilena following shortly behind. Victoria felt herself flooded with emotion as she kept quiet so they could have their reunion.

'Papa, Mama, you're home! You got here for Christmas!' Pia cried.

'They just gave him the okay to travel and come home yesterday – we wanted to be here for Christmas and surprise you, bebe,' Marilena said, hugging Pia and breathing in her hair.

'You've grown taller. A foot at least,' Diego said, admiring Pia.

Pia laughed. 'Not quite a foot, but an inch or so, maybe. Do you think I can be as tall as Cindy Crawford?'

'How do you even know about Cindy Crawford in your generation?' Marilena laughed.

'We watched a lot of movies over the last few weeks, including *Clueless*,' Victoria interjected. 'Googled *everything* as we were watching it, which is why the girls have been banned from watching films with me.' Victoria stepped forward, blushing. 'Diego, I don't mean to interrupt, but I am so, so pleased to see you here today, and to meet you. I'm Victoria.'

Diego smiled and shook her hand. She noticed his eyes crinkling as he placed his other hand on hers. He reminded her of Dev.

'I have heard much about you, Victoria, and am honoured to meet you,' he said.

'Likewise. But not only from Marilena and Pia,' she laughed, nodding to them weeping with smiles in the corner. 'There is another outside who has missed you, too.'

With Marilena and Pia in tow, Diego smiled and walked on crutches out to the parilla, where all the boys were having a beer, feeding the fire.

'This the parilla for the kids? Might be able to cook a couple little sausages on that mini-fire you've got going,' Diego said.

Dev lifted his head but didn't turn around. 'Well, when it's time to cook the kids' meals, I'll let you know, seeing as that's about all you can cook.' He turned. 'Though your wife is worse, no offence, Mari.'

'None taken,' she said grinning.

Dev broke into a wide grin. He embraced Diego cautiously and kissed Marilena's cheeks.

'When the hell did you get back?'

'Just now. They let me out just in time for the holiday.'

'Mari, did you pay them off to get him here in time for harvest?' he joked.

'What a waste,' she said, pointing to Diego's bandaged-up hands and crutches.

'Surely we can find some use for him?'

'Injured or not, I'll teach you young'uns how to light a proper parilla and cook an asado for Christmas. Move outta the way,' he said, and they all laughed heartily.

Diego glanced at Marilena, who smiled up at him and kissed him.

'This is your only chance to socialise, so you'd better take advantage while you can,' she said. 'Because from this evening after the asado, you will be locked in the house with me for three days.'

'Looking forward to it, ma'am,' he said grinning and kissing her again.

'Ew, gross,' Pia said, scrunching her nose.

'Pia, come,' Diego said, putting his arm around her shoulder. 'Bring your friends over and let's build up this fire.'

Victoria ended up having the best Christmas she'd had in years. Having her own home, her parents there, sitting outside while the boys cooked the asado. She could feel the vines beneath her, also celebrating. There was laughter, good food, and a sense of community. She *belonged* somewhere.

She belonged home. At Las Viñas.

~

'Goodnight, Victoria, thank you for everything,' Marilena said. She didn't hug Victoria, but she grasped her arm, and their eyes met for an intense moment.

'Yes, thank you, Victoria,' Diego said. 'I look forward to getting to know you better soon. Bebe, are you ready?'

'Coming,' Pia said, yawning. She turned and pulled Victoria into a warm embrace. 'Thank you for the past few weeks. I've had the best time with you, Auntie Vic. Love you.'

Victoria opened her mouth to speak, but words were beyond her. *Auntie? Love you?* She was overwhelmed.

Dev chuckled, his hand lingering on her back. Was he going to stay?

'Walk us home, Dev?' Marilena asked.

'Of course,' he said. 'Victoria, good night.'

He kissed both her cheeks, his breath lingering on her cheek as his finger touched hers.

'I won't bother you when I come back to get my truck. Unless you want me to,' he added in a soft whisper only she could hear.

Her eyes looked up at his and caught, but Marilena's throat clearing released them.

'Happy Christmas, everyone,' she said, closing the door behind them.

~

Victoria cleared the back porch, bringing the dishes inside, taking a moment to look out over her vineyard. It was ten o'clock at night and the sun was lingering even now.

She felt a rush of excitement. It was all happening. She had been right to come here, to Argentina. She had her family, her vines, her children. She had a history, a past. It was as if it was all coming together. She was ready to embrace this future.

Her parents were already asleep in their room on the other side of the house. She finished the dishes, turning on some light music while she dried. But she was restless, waiting, hoping, longing.

She placed her glass on the bench in the kitchen. Finally, a light knock, and Dev opened the door.

'Do you need some help finishing?' he asked quietly.

'Perfect timing – I just finished the last dish,' she said, turning and leaning her elbows on the bench.

'Good,' he said, coming up to her slowly, reaching his arms inside her elbows as they grazed her waist.

Victoria's breath pulled, she tilted her head up as his face came so close to hers she thought he was going to kiss her.

'Come for a walk with me?'

She licked her lips and nodded, as Dev grabbed a bottle of wine and a couple of glasses. Victoria picked up her vineyard bag, a collection of blankets and Bluetooth candles she had set aside for her own nights sleeping in Las Viñas, when it called to her.

'Where are we going?' she asked, following him to one of the dark parts of the vineyard, where buds hadn't yet burst. 'Why are we heading there?'

'The darker the ground, the brighter the sky,' he answered, smiling back at her and taking her hand. 'All the dark parts are furthest away from the house.'

Finally they reached a spot that was flat enough to lay the blanket and pour wine. Victoria turned on her candles with her phone, and before she could say his name, Dev's lips were on hers.

She ran her fingers through his short but soft beard, his full lips encompassing hers over and over, his tongue delving into her mouth, hot, wet and filled with longing. They were both pulling one other closer, moaning as if singing with their longing. He lifted her legs around his waist and rolled her beneath him.

Victoria hadn't felt this kind of attraction and desire for longer than she had realised. She found herself aching in every part of her body. She didn't want to think. She just wanted.

Once they had hurriedly taken off their clothes, Dev pulled her close again, and they rolled onto their hastily made bed on Las Viñas, tangled in each other until she was on top of him, her long, dark hair creating a curtain around them as they kissed.

'I need you, Dev,' she murmured.

Dev grasped her hips and rolled her onto her back, and they made love with fervour. They were both so passionate they finished quickly, moaning and pleading and holding on to one another as the waves crashed over them again and again.

~

'Thank you for a lovely evening,' a soft, hot whisper drifted over her.

Victoria barely opened her eyes but knew it was still the middle of the night. And they made love again, the Southern Cross above them.

~

'Wake up, beautiful,' Dev whispered.

Victoria opened one eye, but it was still mostly dark, the sky a misty sort of blue.

'I don't want to,' she said with a snort, rolling back over to sleep.

'Do you really want me to leave you here? In the vineyard by yourself?'

'I sleep here all the time,' she mumbled.

He chuckled softly, and she could hear him buckling his belt.

'Alright then, lady of the vines,' he whispered, kissing her cheek and pulling the blanket over her shoulder.

'Hey, Dev?' she whispered.

'Yeah?'

'This was the best dream ever,' she said, kissing him deeply.

'I'd rather this dream turned out to be the best reality ever instead,' he said.

She smiled, rolling back over. 'Me too.'

CHAPTER TWENTY-TWO

When Victoria finally opened her eyes an hour later, a dull light was reflecting back at her. She reached out, thinking it was the glare of her phone in the December morning sun, but as she grasped it she realised it was something else entirely. She reached down to find a pair of intertwined rings that looked as though they'd been buried for quite a long time. As Victoria pulled them out, she realised they were attached to something.

'Yes!' she breathed, pulling the string, and recovering the next part of the diary. She quickly blew the dirt off and opened the pages, desperate to find out what happened to Luce and Pedro after their night in the vineyard. With a blush, she realised that this might be happening because of her own night with

Dev. Was this where Pedro and Luce had made love? Where she was now? Was that why it was buried here? There was only one way to know.

Harvest, 1968

I do not feel well today. As Maddi dressed me in my finest Spanish gown for a special harvest dinner at our house, I found myself running to the privy to relieve my nausea.

'What did you eat today?' Maddi asked me with a concerned look.

'Nothing.' I hadn't been hungry, just nauseous all day.

But then Mama came in.

'Leave us, Maddi,' she commanded, in that way that only she could. I suddenly felt sick again, but I covered it.

Mama came behind me and tied up the back of my dress, which had become slightly too small in the last two months. Her eyes met mine in the mirror as she pulled the strings tighter and tighter, almost until I could not breathe. My eyes watered. She brought her face close to mine and took my chin.

'You must get through this day as planned.'

I only nodded, feeling frightened and not knowing why.

Maddi gave me fennel to chew on, which helped my nervous stomach. I felt much better when we arrived for the harvest day. There was the ceremony as our family led the rest of the people on our land on horseback through the vineyard to the winery. I was in the lead, in the family Spanish dress, my hat on, smiling widely and waving to the crowds lining the sides. Everyone preferred the Inca costume at the Bud Burst Festival, but when the more serious people were there, Mama and I were only to wear our traditional Spanish dress. Behind me, Mama and Papa had a wagon with the last year's harvest wine to pour once we arrived, and this year's wine that had just been cellared for aging.

All my friends were there, but Papa and Mama took me immediately to a group of 'important people' tasting the wine from the barrel.

I was introduced to many people that had come from all over to meet us, the royalty of the wine world in Mendoza. There were many men there from Europe who had just moved here. They liked to converse with me because my Spanish was more understandable than others. I also speak English, which was helpful. Apparently, according to Maddi, it was also because I was beautiful. Me?! What a novel concept. To be beautiful. But I didn't care about looking beautiful to others when Pedro already thought me the most beautiful.

I think maybe I got a bit drunk on the wine, but one man I was not fond of seeing again was Felipe Ortega, who I met in Buenos Aires two years ago. Apparently he was looking at land in Mendoza now. He was the only part of the day I didn't like, but I put on my smile as my mother glared at me, until I was finally given permission to leave the winery and go outside to see my friends. And Pedro.

~

It took Maddi and me less than an hour to pack my bags and get dressed as warmly as possible for my journey. There was no option now, none, other than to leave in the middle of the night and find Pedro, and we would run away together. It wouldn't matter if we were poor, so long as we were together. For I would never, ever marry that horrible Spanish man, Felipe Ortega, that my parents had told me I was to marry in a fortnight.

I screamed. I cried. I begged. Nothing worked. At first, Papa spoke to me like an adult, explaining how this was a fine match. The money would bring new winemaking facilities like they were using in Spain. He was older, yes, but that meant he was wiser and would adore a vivacious young wife.

As I refused, begged, cried, Papa got angrier. 'You will marry him! Do you think this family can live forever off this pagan idolatry that your mother and her people brought to this family? Do you think we can expand our land and keep this beautiful hacienda without money? You think your land magic will do anything for our family?'

'But I don't love him!' I shouted over and over. 'He's cruel, I can feel it. He will be cruel to me!'

Nothing worked.

Finally Papa slapped me. I don't recall him ever hitting me before. Even he looked stunned for a moment and then he dismissed me. I looked to Mama, who had not said a word. Her face was stony, and she looked to the door, telling me without words to leave.

I did, touching my cheek, which was burning, my ear ringing. As soon as I got to my room we packed, Maddi and I.

'What will you do?' she asked.

'Pedro will know what to do. I will trust him,' I said. But my stomach was fluttering. 'Pedro said that man would die before he married me.'

Eventually the house had been still for over an hour, and I knew Papa and Mama were asleep, so we went out the back to the kitchen and opened the door, when suddenly I saw Mama there, sitting in the dark in her dressing-gown, waiting for me. Maddi ran, and I yelped, and Mama lit a candle.

'Do you know that you are with child?' she asked me quietly.

With child? That was not possible. I was still practically a child myself, and it could never happen . . .

'You and Pedro made love, yes? You have been for many months.'

I stopped breathing. How did she know?

She read my expression and nodded. 'That is how children come to be. From the act you and Pedro did together.'

I touched my stomach without thinking. Mama continued quietly. She did not sound angry.

'I know you think that you can run away, and you and Pedro will find a way, but you will not survive that way with a child. You will end up starving on the streets. I did try, when I found out, to convince your father that a local boy could learn to run the vineyard. But he was adamant. He wants the connection with Spain. In two weeks, once you marry Felipe, you will be safe. Safe from scrutiny, safe from ridicule, safe from poverty. People will think the child is his, and he will leave you alone after that first time, once he knows you are with child. He says he prefers Spain and will come back only to check on his property here. You will have much freedom.'

Tears flowed down my cheeks. 'But I want to marry Pedro. I love Pedro.'

'Unfortunately, that is inconsequential,' she said, standing. 'Perhaps one day, women will have more choice in their lives. But that day is not today. You have no choice.'

I was so angry I wanted to scream, but I did not want to wake Papa.

'I do have a choice. I can walk out this door right now and leave. I can make my own way, with Pedro.'

She looked at me with compassion. 'And what of your child?'

I touched my stomach again, suddenly recognising the life in there, within me, of Pedro's. I was fiercely protective of it, and without any reason at all, I loved it so much. I loved it more than myself, I realised, and began to cry harder.

Mama was silent for a moment, and I had to crouch down and cover my mouth to keep the sobs from coming out.

'Go to your room. Cry yourself to sleep. Things always look brighter in the morning.'

I glared at her, hating her even more than Papa, for not fighting harder for me, for us, for women. It seemed she knew what I was thinking, for she nodded, almost as if she was agreeing with me. And then she left.

I stood at that door for a long time trying to decide whether I should leave or not, but the longer I touched my belly and knew that life was in there, my sweet Pedro's baby, my child, my future, I could not.

So I did what Mama said. I went to my room. Maddi brushed my hair, and I cried myself to sleep.

But today things do not look any brighter.

~

Tomorrow is my wedding day. I sit through the festivities without emotion. I focus on breathing in and breathing out, and that is all. If I think of the truth, I will either run or cry. Neither will be acceptable. When I focus on my breathing, I have my hand on my stomach where no one can see. Every breath in is a breath of life for my child. Every breath out, taking toxicity away from her. I know it will be a girl with every part of my being. I know she is coming through me, not from me; innately I know this. I know she is mine and Pedro's, but she will never be his. This Ortega. This husband to be mine in less than a day. She will be called Camila Maria Ortega to save our family and her good soul from being tainted. But she will be mine. My Camila, an Anyas de Alveras.

Felipe has not even tried to be kind. He speaks with my papa, ignores Mama, makes speeches and talks numbers and plans. I feel relieved. Perhaps Mama is right, and he will simply leave me be. Go back to Spain and leave me alone with Pedro and my Camila. With my vineyard, and my land, things that bring me peace.

It was late when I pretended to go to sleep. Maddi had not even removed her shoes before she fell asleep in her quarters. I took them off for her. She has been so stressed, knowing everything, pretending to know nothing. She is exhausted.

I only have to get through tomorrow. That's what Mama says. The wedding, the dinner, and then I must let Felipe have me the way that Pedro does. The thought makes me feel ill. With Pedro it was unusual and uncomfortable at times, but it was so wonderful. I only wanted to be closer to him. I want nothing to do with my future husband.

Mama says to just lay there and think of other things. More pleasant things. That is how most women do it. I think that is so sad. I said to her, but Mama, if I married Pedro, I would never have to think of anything else. I would want to be together that way and make babies and feel him touch me.

She stared at me for a long time then, and I almost thought she understood. But in the end, she tightened her jaw and slammed the door, calling, 'You will marry Felipe tomorrow at noon. There is nothing else to discuss.'

So tomorrow is the day, but tonight is mine. It is my last night, in some ways. To be free. I did not try to leave at midnight this time. Instead, I lay awake all night touching my belly, talking to my Camila. I waited until the darkest part of the night to leave. When the moon set and before the sunrise. I pulled my heavy coat over my shoulders and went to meet Pedro in one of the darker parts of the vineyard.

'Amor, I have all of our bags packed. We can leave right now. Start over. Por favor, amor, do not stay here.'

'I want to leave, but what of our child? I may marry Felipe tomorrow, but then he will be gone.'

'And yet you will never be mine!' he cried, slamming his fists into the ground.

'I will always be yours! Now, tonight, we make a pact.'

'A marriage,' he amended. 'I have the rings I had made when . . . when I thought we would be a family.'

'But it won't be official,' I cried.

'It will be in our hearts,' he said.

We both wept then, saying goodbye to the hope of a future together.

'I will love you, Luce, until the day I die. You will be mine and I will be yours, in our hearts.'

'I will be yours and you will be mine, in our hearts. And I will love you until the day I die, Pedro Silvas.'

~

Now Victoria knew why Las Viñas had gifted her the two entwined bands. They had been fake wedding bands, Luce and Pedro declaring their eternal love for each other and their child. Right where she was now.

'My *mother*,' Victoria whispered to herself, staring out at the vineyard, her eyes wide, mouth open in disbelief. *Silvas*. Her true grandfather was Pedro Silvas. She knew that name. How?

The Silvas have been on the land here nearly as long as the Anyas de Alveras family and have occasionally stepped up as caretakers of the land. She remembered Santi's words.

Marilena's family name.

'Holy shit,' she said aloud, standing abruptly, packing up her blankets and candles and running back to her house.

She had to finish the story. To find out what happened between Luce and Pedro. Marilena's grandmother was Eugenia Silvas. So Eugenia must have married Pedro in the end. What happened on Luce's wedding night? Was Felipe a bad husband and as horrible a man as he seemed in the diaries? Did he ever find out about Pedro? Was this how the curse all started? She was so confused.

'Sweetheart?' Joyce said, as Victoria came into the kitchen, not realising Joyce was there. 'Sweetheart, what's wrong?'

'Mom!' she said, her eyes welling. 'I'm so glad you're here.'

Was this why she was cursed to never have children, because the land here was cursed? Ever since she was old enough to know love and desire, she had wanted to be a mother more than anything else in the world. Was this why Michael had left her for someone else? She began to cry softly, and it turned into sobs.

'Oh, darling. Shh,' her mother whispered, while Victoria cried. 'That's a good girl. These big tears are a good thing. Embrace it.'

She had to laugh, in spite of her tears. 'Why is this good?'

'Oh, sweetheart, we can only hurt this big when we love this big. And how can feeling that kind of love ever be a bad thing?'

~

That night Victoria dreamed that she was pregnant. But this time, she was pregnant with a vine, and the vine's name was Pia. In her dream she went to see Marilena, to tell her she was accidentally pregnant with her daughter, but Marilena shook her head and said, 'you are La Madre, the mother of the vines. You give them life, and I give them life. Our gift, our curse. Sisters.'

She woke with a start. And even though she knew that the dream was her brain sifting through all the information she'd been given and trying to make sense of it while she rested, it still sat with her.

It had rained all night and the temperature had risen, so it was warm in the morning, humid even, when Victoria exhaustedly got out of bed, put on her boots over her pyjamas and walked into the vineyard. She did not need to walk far or to call Dev to know that the night had brought another gift to the vineyard. In the section where she and Dev had spent their night, there had been full bud burst overnight.

But it was different, accelerated. It had already begun to flower.

She wanted to call Dev – he would be so excited – but he'd likely be there in the next half hour anyway. Besides, there was someone else she wanted to see more.

She stared past the growing vines to the still-dormant sections, knowing that was where she would find the rest of the answers. A light went on at Marilena's. But Victoria didn't have the heart to face her now, not with everything she had been through with Diego. She'd had the heartbreak of losing her dream, then the accident with her husband, and she was only just finding peace. Victoria couldn't burden Marilena with so much new information, not now. So she walked back to the hacienda and let it go for now, though she could feel Marilena's eyes on Las Viñas.

CHAPTER TWENTY-THREE

After the holidays, the true warmth of summer came, and the grapes began to grow. They seemed to glory in being alive, being in the sun.

'Look at all these beautiful berries coming in, and right on time, too,' Dev said, admiring them. 'We don't want them to get too fat too fast though; we'll have to pick them too early, and they won't be as ripe as they should.'

'I still can't believe an entire new section just flowered overnight,' Marilena said, looking curiously at Victoria, who wouldn't meet her eyes.

Victoria had not shared the diary or her secrets with Marilena, and for some reason she was feeling incredibly guilty. But every time Diego hobbled over and Marilena had to help him sit or change his bandages, Victoria simply couldn't do it. But it was sitting in her, filling her with a kind of awe. Marilena was her blood relation. They were *cousins*. She had a cousin.

A cousin who had hated her up until a few weeks ago and probably still would when she found out about their shared grandfather. But it also meant Marilena's family was tainted. The way she probably admired and loved her grandparents would now be ruined. Victoria simply didn't know what to do, or how to feel.

Diego spent every day at Las Viñas now as well, and he was more open than his wife about what their plans had been. Diego found it cathartic and healthy to share their vision.

'I think she would have wanted to keep the name Bodegas Anyas de Alveras, which was on the label back when it was a wine producer,' he'd told her. 'Silvas is her mother's maiden name, and I think that resonated with her as well, a family who lived on the land nearly as long as the Anyas de Alveras. But the asado would have been Asador Martinez, for me. I like to think quite highly of my skills on a parilla, despite the fact that I have been in mining most of my adult life.'

He laughed, and Victoria laughed with him, though it was slightly forced at the uncomfortable feeling of what she was hiding from Marilena. Diego was a relaxed and cheerful man who smiled most of the time, despite being in bandages and having a painful broken leg. He did not carry the same depth of hurt and disappointment Marilena did about her existence and Las Viñas belonging to Victoria.

'I really do feel terrible about the fact that the dream you all shared is crushed because of me,' she said to him one day.

'What on earth do you mean, Victoria?' he scoffed. 'Las Viñas is *awake*. My Mari, she is its winemaker. My Pia, she still has her La Azul room where she spends more time than at home these days.'

Victoria released an amused sigh. It was true.

'And perhaps when you open the hacienda, there will be space for me to be the asador, as you mentioned at Christmas.'

As soon as she'd seen Diego on the parilla on Christmas Day, it had been all she could think about, and she'd mentioned as much.

'Though do you have dreams to cook yourself?' he asked.

'Good lord, no! I'm not giving up entirely on honing my skills to at least make a few roasts without burning my house down, but Adriana was right when she said that it was as if I was born NOT to cook.'

Diego laughed. She stood and patted his knee as she saw the trucks pull down the long drive.

'Thank you for not hating me for existing.'

'Thank you for existing so that you could help us see our dreams. Perhaps they are not what we expected, but sometimes that can be even better,' he said. 'Mari's coming around. You wait, when your friends come down to do the video, she will be on her best behaviour.'

~

When Victoria had called Monique to tell her about her Mendoza Project, she'd had no idea that she, Levi and Ange would have jumped behind it so completely.

Monique reached out to one of her commercial clients, a woman named Callie Callahan, who was making a name for herself as a television host and was hoping to have her own show on E! News, or her dream job, her own talk show.

Monique had told Callie about Victoria's adventures in Argentina, and Callie was enamoured with the idea of doing a pilot for a new television show. She and Monique had approached Callie's agent, and they'd worked out a deal with a production company to come down to Las Viñas and shoot a pilot with a very small budget, pitching a new show Callie had come up with called *Something Unexpected*.

The aim was to make a reality television show where someone like Victoria had an unexpected gift or inheritance. Victoria did not want to be a part of anything like that, but as a pilot, it could be great publicity and there was no commitment to continue with the season.

And so it was on a warm day in January that two vans, containing Callie Callahan and a small camera crew, pulled down the drive of Las Viñas to film some video clips. All those who'd been involved with the project had been asked or offered to speak on camera if they wanted to.

'Victoria!' Monique cried, jumping out of one of the vans and waving vigorously. She ran to Victoria and hugged her tightly, looking around. 'Wow, look at what my girl has gotten herself into.'

Victoria hugged her back, squealing with delighted surprise. 'I didn't know you were coming yourself! Why didn't you tell me?'

'What, miss out on visiting my best friend and her cursed vineyard?' Monique scoffed.

'Monique! You told them it was a cursed vineyard?' she huffed. 'Now that's all they're going to talk about!'

Monique grinned unabashedly. 'Hey, whatever sells the product, right? Your words, not mine!'

'You're as diabolical as Pia and Gabi,' Victoria said, taking her hand. 'Come, let me show you to your room.'

'My room?'

'You'll see,' she answered with a grin.

When she opened the door to La Lavanda, Monique squealed with delight, looking around and falling onto the bed.

'My room!'

'I pictured you in this room as soon as I moved in. Your "signature colour" room,' Victoria said, bringing Monique's suitcase in. 'What do you think?'

Monique sat up in bed and shook her head, staring at Victoria.

'What do I think? I think, look at you, girl! You get this crazy news you've inherited a hacienda and a cursed vineyard for goodness' sake. Then your amazing ass comes down here yourself to renovate and sell the house. Instead, you found yourself a home.'

~

The next morning, Monique sat at the outside table with a young intern named Tayla.

'Your replacement, if so needed. I don't remember looking that young,' she whispered to Victoria when Tayla left for a moment. 'Or that innocent.'

'That's because you weren't that innocent,' Victoria said. 'But we were that young. Gosh, I feel old.'

'You are old, Victoria,' Gabi said, sitting down across from her and Monique. Even Monique's jaw dropped. Gabi had her long hair out in waves, her fifteen-year-old face in a perfect, if not slightly overdone, palette of gold and bronze make-up that accentuated her large features. Not to mention the sundress she wore that accentuated her other large features.

'And you are too young to be looking like that!' Victoria hissed, looking around for Marilena, who would definitely tell Gabi's parents.

Monique looked at Victoria with a bemused expression.

'You do sound old, Vic,' she said, and turned back to Gabi. 'And you are?'

'Gabriela Martina Morales,' she said, shaking Monique's hand. 'I'm here for the filming. Victoria said there were forms to sign?'

'Here you are,' Tayla said, coming back to the table and handing her one. 'It's just a permission form for being on camera and using the footage.'

'Yes, I am aware, and I have brought one of my own if you wouldn't mind signing,' Gabi said, pulling a paper out of her bag. 'This form states that I will be able to ask for a finished copy of all of my personal screen time and will be able to use the footage for, and only for, my reel, but not for any sales purposes.'

Victoria, Monique and Tayla went silent.

'I'm going to be an actress, duh,' Gabi explained.

'Oh, um, okay,' Monique said, handing the paper to Tayla. 'Can you send a screenshot of that over to Ange and check it's okay for us to sign?'

'My friend is an actress in Hollywood and she's a SAG member – she got this directly off the website, so I am sure it's legit.'

'Babe!' Julio yelled as he, Alex and Dante hopped out of the back of Dev's truck, which had just pulled up. 'You look hot!'

She rolled her eyes and turned back to Monique. 'He's my boyfriend, but only for now. If Glen Powell by any chance sees any of my footage, please pass on that I will be eighteen in two years and fourteen days.'

'I don't know that he will, honey,' Monique said, glancing at Victoria. 'I'm just a talent manager – and Callie is here on her own time—'

Gabi leaned in. 'We all start somewhere. Please keep my name in mind, Monique, when I submit my reel to you in a couple of years. Since Victoria has gone all, what's the word?'

'Homebody?' Tayla offered.

Gabi shrugged. 'Sure, if that means boring. Love you, Auntie Vic!'

After Gabi walked away, Monique turned to Victoria, her eyes wide and her mouth hanging open. 'Did that really just happen?'

Victoria laughed but quickly turned when she heard Dev's car door close. Just looking at him, seeing him, made her mouth get dry and her heart race. And it did funny things to her other parts, thinking of their lovemaking in the vineyard.

'Shit, is that him?' Monique whispered, looking over.

'Quit staring! He'll know we're talking about him!' Victoria hissed, blushing furiously while Monique chuckled, and trying not to turn back and stare at his backside longingly.

~

'Where do I look when I speak?' Romina asked.

Victoria stood beside Monique as Callie smiled and glanced at the screen of the camera.

'Turn it just a bit, Rick,' Callie said to the cameraman. 'Yes, that's perfect.'

She turned to Romina. 'I'm going to come sit next to you and have a chat, then we might walk through the vineyard. Don't pay attention to the camera, just look at me and answer as if the camera weren't on us.'

'Here, honey, let me show you,' Walter said, stepping in front of his wife, looking into the camera and slicking his hair back.

Victoria chuckled silently, and Callie, winking at her, gave the signal to Rick, the cameraman, to start rolling.

'Now Romina, remember that time Paul Newman came here and he needed to learn the ways of the gaucho, so we rode into the sunset together, he and I, while I taught him everything I knew?' Walter asked, looking directly at the camera as if to ask whether it was paying attention.

Romina rolled her eyes. 'Sure, I remember. I remember you dreamed it, you daft old man.'

'But he was quite taken with you! I had to fight him to win you forever, don't you remember?'

At this, Romina's eyes sparkled and she smiled widely. 'Now, this version I like, film this one!'

Callie and Rick grinned as they captured the scene. They could see the others lining up to watch Romina and Walter, gaining confidence to speak in front of the camera themselves.

Callie didn't have to ask many questions as the older couple told wild stories, and everyone was laughing and relaxed by the time Romina shooed Walter away, gently smacking the back of his head, saying, 'Get out of here, you daft old man.'

'Okay, who's next?' Monique called, and all the hands were raised.

~

Callie and Rick set up in the kitchen next, as Adriana prepared a late breakfast for the group.

'Adriana Lomos,' she said to the camera. 'These little delights are called "medialunas," and they are a traditional breakfast food here in Argentina.'

'So is this going to be a part of the Hacienda experience?' Callie asked.

Victoria nodded off camera. 'Sí,' Adriana said, plating the pastries beautifully as they came out of the oven. Victoria noticed that she, too, was looking quite beautiful and wondered if Gabi had done her make-up as well.

'Victoria plans to make a lovely breakfast like this, which I will likely have to make at my shop and send over for her to prove the night before and put in the oven in the morning, in the hope that she does not burn down the house in the process. Victoria, do be sure to put extra fire insurance on your project list, my dear,' she said kindly. 'Truly, Victoria and I have become great friends, but never have I seen a person worse in the kitchen.'

Callie and Rick just left the camera rolling as they laughed.

'Thank you, Adriana,' Victoria said sarcastically.

'You are welcome,' she answered. 'Now, Monique, Gabi mentioned you were a Hollywood talent manager? I wondered what your thoughts were on my doing a cooking show?'

'Oh god,' Victoria sighed, putting her head in her hands.

~

The locals all took turns being on camera with Callie. Dev took them out into the vineyard and showed them the grapes. He was so confident, his voice a low drawl, his tanned arms flexing as he pulled up his sleeves to show a thriving vine to the camera.

'Las Viñas was always healthy – she just hadn't bloomed since the seventies,' he said to Callie, looking at her and not the camera the way he was supposed to. Then he looked down at the grapes and smiled lovingly. 'Until now.'

'And why do you think that is?' Callie asked. You could hear the genuine interest in her voice.

Dev turned and looked straight at Victoria, a small smile forming at the corner of his lips. He winked, making her whole body tingle.

'No clue,' he said grinning. 'I'm just the vineyard manager.'

Monique turned to look at Victoria, her mouth agape. *Oh my god,* she mouthed, pretending to wipe the sweat from her neck. Victoria mouthed back, *I know.*

~

They had some really fun footage, but nothing yet that really talked about the cursed vineyard except for Dev's comment, so they were all excited to hear what the elusive Marilena had to say on camera. But when it was Marilena's turn, Victoria was surprised to find that she was frozen. Her brown eyes were wide open, glazed over, and she wasn't blinking.

'Uh, Marilena, I'll repeat the question. Your family has been involved with Las Viñas for a long time. Can you tell us about it?'

But Marilena remained unblinking. Monique glanced at Victoria questioningly, but she just shrugged.

'Mama?' a voice said. 'Oh, no, you Tussauded her,' Pia said, walking into the camera view.

Rick laughed and focused the camera in on her.

'Here, kid, look at the camera. What did you say happened to her?' he asked from off camera.

Pia looked up at the camera. 'You know, Madame Tussauds. The wax figures of celebrities? Look, this is my Mama, Tussauded.'

'And you are?' Callie said, coming on camera with a broad smile, her eyes still glistening with laughter. She and Pia had already met off camera, but Callie went with authentic introduction for the recording.

'Pia Martinez, daughter of the Tussauded victim being taken away to my left,' she said. Imogen, Marilena's mother and Pia's grandmother, had arrived at Marilena's side.

'She only got like this once before. Had one line in a play when she was six. Someone had to pick her up and take her offstage. She only came out of it a few hours later,' Imogen said. 'Diego!'

'Yeah, I got her,' he said, taking Marilena. 'Come on, honey, let's go light the parilla.'

'We'll come find you after this and film you cooking lunch, if that's okay?' Victoria asked Diego.

'No worries, I'll give Marilena a glass of wine, that usually loosens her up a little,' he said.

Rick winked at Callie and Monique, letting them know he was filming it all. He turned the camera back to Pia and Marilena's mother. Victoria had been so excited to meet Imogen when Pia brought her this morning, and she was dying to know what she had to say.

'This is my grandmother, Imogen,' Pia introduced.

'Imogen, do you know why Las Viñas was cursed?' Callie asked.

'Why?' she said, settling into the chair they had set up for her. 'No. But when? Yes. I have very few memories of my earliest childhood, but one. I was sitting on a little girl's lap, and she was swinging us in the tree, and as we got higher, I could see the grapes all in bloom. Apparently the vineyard was cursed just shortly after that. I was three years old.'

'Who was the little girl?' Victoria asked. Rick pointed the camera towards Victoria.

Imogen looked over at Victoria and hesitated. 'I believe it was your mother, Camila. Though it is a very distant memory and I cannot be certain,' she finished.

Monique heard Victoria's breath catch.

'Excuse me, please, I should check on Marilena,' Imogen said, getting up quickly.

'Imogen, wait,' Victoria called, walking behind her.

Rick was filming it all, but as the room cleared, he turned

back to Pia, whose eyes were focused directly on the camera. 'Aw-kward,' she said.

They laughed.

'Come,' Pia said, indicating for Callie, Rick and the camera to follow her. 'I'll take you to see La Abuela. The oldest vine. I was actually the one to wake her up, you know.'

'How did you know?' Callie asked as they followed Pia through the garden.

'She sneezed on me!'

'*Sneezed* on her?' Rick asked Callie quietly.

Callie shrugged. 'Cursed vineyard? She's a kid! Just keep rolling!'

CHAPTER TWENTY-FOUR

Dinner that night at Las Viñas was a festive affair. Monique had told Victoria's parents she was coming down with Callie as a surprise, so they'd stayed a few extra days to meet the crew, though Victoria hadn't known the reason at the time. This was their last night.

Callie, Rick and Monique had done a day of filming through the town and village, and Rick was filming at dinner when permission was given, which was more and more freely as the wine was poured.

On this occasion, Dev and Diego cooked a whole lamb over the open fire on a cross, called 'la cruz'.

'This has been a method of cooking for hundreds of years in Argentina,' Diego said to Frank as Rick came behind, filming them. 'You can do it with pork, but if you can get hold of some beautiful Patagonian lamb, there's nothing better. Smell that?'

'Smells smoky and delicious,' Frank said, before calling out, 'what are you girls making in there?'

'Salads. Again,' Joyce called, flipping the page of her magazine and taking a sip of her wine. 'You know, I'm seeing a bit of a pattern here, Bicky. You only making the salads.'

'I'm seeing a bit of a pattern with you out there drinking wine and reading magazines, Mom,' Victoria said from the kitchen.

'I'm on vacation,' she said, flipping another page of her magazine. 'Oh wait, holiday! I'm on holiday, that's what you say here, right Marilena?'

'Actually, Señora,' Marilena answered, 'in Spanish we say vacaciones, so, closer to your American word.'

'Vay-cay-chee-chonays,' Joyce repeated, pulling out her book and writing it down.

'Vah-cah-see-yonays, Mom,' Victoria corrected her pronunciation. 'And don't write it down, it will definitely not help you in a crossword puzzle.'

~

'Wow, your mom is really into crossword puzzles,' Callie said as she, Victoria and Marilena followed Adriana out to the parilla.

'Come on ladies, these vegetables aren't going to grill themselves!' Adriana called. 'Pia, Gabi?'

Pia rolled her eyes. 'I think I have to. Papa likes it when I'm closer now he's back.' She got up to follow.

'Don't you have parents, Gabi?' Callie asked her.

'Of course I do. And they are the best. But even though we have a pool, which is glorious, we live about ten miles from here. And *here* is where the action is,' Gabi explained. She leaned forward. 'So, Callie, when did you know you wanted to be an actress?'

Callie leaned back, sipping the crisp white Torrontés that Victoria had poured her. 'You really are a spitfire, do you know that? And I've wanted to be on TV since I was about your age, I suppose. What else do you want to know?'

'Have you met Glen Powell?' Gabi asked. 'Is it hard to get onto television? Would you be my fake auntie if I moved to Hollywood when I was eighteen? Does all that make-up really make your skin break out?' She took a breath. 'Is being famous awesome?'

Callie laughed heartily and leaned in. 'I'm not famous, kid, but I sure do want to be. Yes, I'll be your fake auntie, your skin sucks ass after a day of filming, it is brutal getting into television, and if I'd met Glen Powell I wouldn't be here – I'd be locked in a dungeon with him for eternity.'

Gabi grinned. 'Excellent.'

~

The table was filled with all those who loved Las Viñas and those who had come to support it. Victoria and her parents sat beside Monique. Dev, who kept leaning into Victoria when he thought nobody was looking, sat next to her, and on his other side were Diego and Pia, huddling close together. Marilena and Adriana sat beside them, with Rick, Callie and Gabi across from them.

'Where are Walter and Romina tonight?' Marilena asked.

'Sylvia is still out of town, despite not telling anyone she was going anywhere, so they are having to take Gorda and Fuego out in the evenings. They sent their regrets,' Victoria answered.

Diego leaned across the table, helping himself to a grilled fennel salad with dill and dried apricots. 'Be good to see Sylvia soon,' he said. 'Yum, did you make this, Victoria?'

'Adriana let me toss it in the end. She didn't trust me to grill the fennel or measure the dressing,' Victoria huffed.

'Victoria, if you want me to trust you, you need to start following the recipes,' Adriana said, plating some roasted eggplant and capsicum salad for herself. 'She peeled these,' she said to Marilena.

'But surely there couldn't be that much vinegar in the dressing . . .' Victoria began.

'Don't change the recipe!' the entire table called out at the same time, and they all laughed.

Victoria laughed but blushed. 'Fine, gang up on me, why don't you?'

'Hey, I'd much prefer to gang up on you with love and humour – the way Michael used to do it was all passive aggressive and humiliating, but acting like he was being supportive,' Monique said to her, as she reached forward to pour herself more wine, realising that the table had gone quiet and they had all heard what had been meant for Victoria's ears alone.

'Who is Michael?' Pia asked.

Victoria made herself a small plate of food and forced a smile for Pia. 'Michael was my former fiancé, back in LA. We parted some time ago now.'

Monique bit her lip and mouthed 'sorry' to Victoria, who shrugged. It was impossible to live a life without bringing him up eventually.

'He sounds like a total douchebag,' Gabi said. 'You're better off without him, Victoria.'

'Hell yeah,' Pia confirmed. 'Victoria, if you were still with Michael, you wouldn't be here.'

'And here is where you belong, Bicky, I can feel it,' Frank said.

'You should become an Antiguan for real!' Joyce announced, spilling her wine as she toasted no one in particular.

'Argentinian, Mrs Bishop,' Dev whispered politely.

Suddenly Callie snorted indelicately, trying to cover her laugh. But then Rick joined in, along with Adriana, Diego and Dev. Frank and Joyce started in next, and Pia and Gabi. Finally, Victoria let out a breath of laughter and Monique joined her, wrapping an arm around her shoulder. And the last person Victoria looked up at was Marilena, who looked at her curiously.

Soon, she thought, and raised her glass to Marilena. When she raised her glass back, the wind shifted. Marilena and Victoria were the only ones to notice as they looked up. Las Viñas was waiting.

~

The following day was one of goodbyes. Callie, Monique and Rick left before sunrise to get their rental van back before their flight. Victoria took her parents to Mendoza for lunch and a stroll before their flight at 9 pm. So it was late at night when she arrived back at the hacienda and unlocked the front door, stepping into silence for the first time in weeks.

After such an exciting few weeks, an overwhelming loneliness settled over her. She found her eyes threatening tears as she started turning on as many lights as she could to try to alleviate how overwhelmed she felt.

There was a sudden sound at the window. Was Dev here? As she opened the window, she realised it was simply a growl of dissension, the vines sneaking in towards the house for a peek, seeming as unhappy as Victoria that the house was empty.

Victoria slammed the window shut. 'Oh, leave me alone.'

'Sorry,' she heard a voice mutter from the other side.

Quickly, Victoria opened the door and saw Marilena standing outside.

'Mari?'

'I didn't mean to bother you,' she said.

'You weren't,' Victoria said. 'I was yelling at the vines. They won't leave me alone.'

'You were yelling at the vines?' Marilena asked, her lip quirking.

'Probably the same way you yell at Pia. Teenagers, right?' Victoria chuckled. 'Come in.'

Marilena came in hesitantly, closing the door behind her. 'You're wonderful with Pia and Gabi,' she began. 'But you . . .'

Victoria had gone to the refrigerator to grab some wine but paused. She was not in the right place to have this conversation now, but she didn't seem to have a choice. It was going to happen eventually.

'I can't have children, Marilena. I have a condition that prevents me from having them.'

'Oh,' she heard Marilena sigh. '*That* is it.'

'What is it?' Victoria snapped, hating the way her voice sounded pleading.

'The curse. I thought it was when the last of the line died. But it was . . . you *are* the last of the line,' she said, as if waking from a dream. 'It makes sense now.'

Red fury was in Victoria's gaze. 'Yes, Marilena, I am the last of the line. I am barren. What, are you happy now? This makes sense to you now? I can't have children – does that mean you can stop blaming someone else for your life and why this land isn't yours?'

Now it was Marilena's turn to rage. 'You don't know anything about this land! You may be its blood, but you are not its heart. You know *nothing* about my land, I can see that now,' she yelled, her face red with anger.

'*Your* land, Marilena? This is *my* land! I AM THE ANYAS DE ALVERAS. YOU ARE JUST—'

Without warning, the air suddenly turned, and the end of Victoria's sentence came out with a frosty breath.

'What the—?'

Suddenly all the old sirens went off in the vineyard. Victoria did not recognise the sound but knew in her very being that something was wrong.

Marilena's eyes met hers, wide and terrified.

'Frost!' she cried loudly, running towards the winery. She turned back to Victoria. 'Frost!'

'No!' Victoria cried, and they ran to the winery together.

'Quickly, we must find the torches,' Marilena said. 'They'll have torches for frosts. It's an old technique, but it might work.'

Victoria and Marilena opened the winery doors and ran into the back, finding as many torches as they could.

'Mama, we're here!' Pia said, running in, with Diego limping behind her.

'What happened?' Diego asked.

'Frost!' Marilena called. 'Pia, find the wings. You know what they look like from the old photos?'

Pia nodded and ran off.

'Diego, when she finds them, we need to spread the warmth.'

Marilena and Victoria ran back into the vineyard, planting as many torches as they could into the freezing earth and lighting their fires.

'I'm here, Mama! I have them!' Pia yelled, out of breath, as she gave each of them a set of 'wings'.

'Spread the heat, Victoria! But don't cause a fire!'

'I don't know how,' Victoria called.

'Like this, Victoria,' Pia said, and pulled the fairy-like wings onto her arms, gently moving them up and down like a bird.

'Slowly,' Diego said, joining them. 'We move the heat around, gently.'

And all through the night, Victoria, Marilena, Pia and Diego walked the vineyard, trying to keep the frost off their precious vines. And they did not stop until the sun came up, and the warmth from it allowed them to rest their weakening arms.

They walked to Victoria's slowly, checking every row. But nothing they had done had worked. The whole vineyard, it seemed, had frozen. As if it were stopped in time.

Victoria let the tears run down her face, as Marilena muffled her cries and called Dev.

'What do you mean a frost? That's impossible! There wasn't a frost last night, not anywhere in Mendoza!' Dev's voice was so loud Victoria could hear it through Marilena's cell phone.

'Okay,' Marilena responded quietly to something Dev said, and then hung up her phone. 'He said he'd come soon. I don't understand what happened. We were so close. What happened?!'

Victoria stopped and dropped to the ground, putting her head in her hands.

'Fine!' she yelled, 'you win!'

Victoria could hear Marilena crying behind her as she went inside, gathered all the parts of the diary and put them into Luce's leather-bound journal. She didn't bother with the tiara or any of the other little gifts that Las Viñas had been giving her, but she did tie the two little gold wedding bands to the strap.

When she came back outside. Las Viñas seemed to look up, see the journal.

Victoria shoved the diary into Marilena's hands.

'Look, she has it!' she yelled at the vines. 'So thaw, okay? Just thaw now!'

Marilena turned, confused, but the vines were all still frozen, looking no different. She looked back at Victoria worriedly.

But now that the diary was out of her hands and in Marilena's, Victoria felt calm again.

'You need to read that. Don't ask me any questions, just go home and read the diary. When you are finished, text me. We'll have somewhere to be.'

'Victoria, should I call Dev? I'm actually worried about you now. You're sounding crazy.'

Victoria sighed. 'I know. But I'm not, and you'll see why soon. I think we need to do the rest together. That's what Las Viñas wants.'

'Do what together?' Marilena nearly growled.

'You'll see,' Victoria said, turning back to the house. 'Text me when you're done. And don't take too long.'

CHAPTER TWENTY-FIVE

Where do I meet you?

Victoria jumped as her phone finally dinged, about two hours after Marilena had left.

Look out your window to the part of the vineyard that hasn't bloomed yet. Meet me at the start of it in ten minutes.

Victoria watched the dot dot dots with bated breath.

Yes, see you then.

She let out a sigh of relief and headed out the door.

~

Less than ten minutes later, she and Marilena met at the edge of the last part of the vineyard that had not yet bloomed. Victoria realised that it was directly between their homes.

'Hi,' Victoria said, awkward now that she was in front of Marilena.

'Hi,' Marilena replied, obviously feeling the same.

They were quiet for a long time.

'So, does that mean we're cousins or something?' Marilena finally said.

'I know that finding out you are related to me is unfortunate, but . . .' Victoria said, shrugging, but she couldn't hide the feeling in her voice. Just when she was starting to figure out who she was, she suddenly wasn't. A lump formed in her throat.

'You are the first blood family I have ever had,' she finished.

Marilena's hand rested on her arm, and Victoria raised her head, surprised.

'You are an Anyas de Alveras, Victoria. The gift through the mother, to the daughter. That is how it always was and always will be. You are Camila's daughter, and she was Luce's daughter, the daughter's daughter of the Anyas de Alveras line since the first Anyas married the land, the vines. That is who you are. I am not your only blood relative.'

The lump in Victoria's throat got tighter and moved to her eyes, filling them with tears.

'What does it even matter what line I carry when I can never pass it on? Never have a daughter.' She could barely get the words out before she was sobbing, dropping to her knees and letting go of the grief she hadn't even realised was still in her. So strong, so relevant.

'You are the mother of the vines,' Marilena said softly, as Victoria cried from her soul.

It took her a long time to stop, but when she finally did, taking gulping breaths through her mouth because her nose was all stopped up, the first thing she felt was Marilena's hand on her shoulder. Her family. She felt it seep down into her veins, to her hands, to the earth of Las Viñas. The ground began to shake slightly under her hand. She reached into the earth, and there was a signet ring carrying the Ortega family crest from Spain. Victoria pulled it out of the earth, and with it came the next pages of the diary.

They looked at one another and began to read.

~

Wedding, 1968

Tonight was my wedding night. Mama told me to stay still, to let him . . .

But what he wanted was different than with my Pedro.

I have been violated. I have been abused. By a man I am married to! Married to! For the rest of my life.

When Mama came in this morning, even she was startled by my black eye still swelling, the bruises on my body, the breathing that was difficult because he cracked my rib.

I heard her breathe in, and I prayed, prayed to myself, that she would help me escape.

When she sat beside me with a cold towel for my face, she whispered, 'Did he have you?'

I was so angry I wanted to scream. But I knew what she was asking. Will your child be safe?

'Yes,' I finally whispered, my throat so hoarse she had to tilt water onto my lips.

She touched my stomach then. Lovingly. 'She is our future.'

And in that moment, I vowed that our future will be cursed if I have anything to do with it.

~

1969

Pedro married Eugenia today. I was her maid of honour. I focused on my breathing for the whole ceremony, only letting myself be distracted by Camila and her endless beauty. She does not know that she is the sacrificial lamb of my love with

Pedro. Of our home. Of our land, our vines, our family. She only knows she is happy, alive and beautiful. I love her so much it is almost enough. Almost enough to keep lying to Eugenia, who is glowing at finally having the man she has loved since she was twelve. Almost enough to turn away when Pedro hesitated at his vows and looked at me, because in his heart and mine, we are married to the vines and to each other.

But then Felipe comes home, my husband, more often than he should, and he violates and desecrates me, and I will never let him have this. Us. Any of this.

And yet I would have kept it all our great secret if Pedro would have stayed mine forever as he was supposed to. But it was getting too suspicious, which is why he married Eugenia. Uncle Pedro, my childhood friend, come to visit me and our Camila, the doting uncle. I hired him as the vineyard manager. The family, the Silvas family, will forever be connected to the Anyas de Alveras. On the nights my husband was away, Pedro would sneak into my bedroom, and we would make love for hours, swear devotion to each other for the rest of our days.

Until he decided to marry Eugenia. Today. I watched him swear himself for the rest of his life to Eugenia, his new wife, my best friend. She turned to hug me. I hated her. I hated feeling the warm touch of a woman that will spend the rest of her life in bed with my love, my true heart husband, even though she loved him first. I hated that she will have children he will dote on more than my Camila, his Camila, who he can never admit to. And yet I love Eugenia so much, my best friend, that in some ways I am almost glad that she will be the one to have him, that she will be happy, even if I will want to die. I love her, and she can never know. She can never know.

'I can't wait until our daughters are truly sisters,' she whispered, her fingernails digging into my arms. And I cannot release my arm, and my breath is shattered, and she smiled at me, and I don't know if she said that out of love or because she knows our secret.

~

1973

'We are leaving,' Pedro whispered to me this morning in the vineyard. 'Eugenia and Imogen and I. Next week.'

I tried to keep my lip from quivering, my eyes from pooling, my heart from aching. To lose Pedro when I married was enough. To lose him when he married was worse. To lose him from my life . . .

But to lose Eugenia? No matter what she has said to me, how she hates me. And she should hate me, and in some ways, I still hate her, too, for what she said, for how cruel she was.

She found out eventually about me and Pedro. I couldn't stop loving Pedro, and he loving me. But she ended up having him. And I know it is so hard for her to look at my Camila every day and see that she is our daughter – it must be awful. But as awful as her telling me she hopes my husband does kill me? Knowing what he does to me? She is the only one who knows, and I haven't told her everything, but she does know. So how could she be so cruel?

She is my blood sister, a child of the vines with me, Caro and Sylvia. But more than that, she is my best friend. We have hurt and wronged each other. But we are still connected. She is still . . . she is still my soul sister. And she is leaving.

'Luce,' he whispered, trying to place his hand on my shoulder, but I shrugged it away, leaving the vineyard to go home. The vines followed me, dying a little bit as my shoulders drooped, my soul withered. I wanted to touch the soil and tell them to wake up, to be free of me, but I could not. We are too connected.

Camila was at her desk, colouring after her nap. A Disney colouring book and she was on the Sleeping Beauty *page, looking very serious. I sat beside her, pulling her silky hair out of its mess from her nap and starting to braid it. She hummed with pleasure.*

'Sleeping Beauty, huh?'

'It reminded me of us,' she said.

'Oh!' I said, putting on my Mama voice. 'How is that, bebe?'

'That is the bad king. He is keeping the princess hostage. And there is the prince, to rescue us.'

'Us?'

'Me and you, the princesses being held captive. And the prince is Uncle Pedro.'

'And who is the bad man?' I asked, bile in my throat.

She didn't answer, just went back to colouring, but I felt flooded with relief that Felipe wrote recently and said he was not coming back this year.

~

1973

This is the last entry I will ever make, and I ask anyone who reads it to burn it immediately, as it will ruin the lives of myself and everyone I love.

Felipe came from Spain yesterday. When I saw his driver, I felt sick, so sick I wanted to die, but I pretended everything was fine. Camila hates seeing me upset. Last time her 'father' was home it took months for my broken ribs to heal.

This time, he ignored me. I have never been so pleased. He ignored me! Camila seemed okay. Perhaps I imagined it when she said there was a bad king. Perhaps she didn't mean Felipe.

Tonight was cold. Colder than it should be in May. The 1973 season has been bottled, and it is looking like our best one.

I had lit all the fires in the rooms used. Felipe had gone down to the local village drinking at the bodega, which suited us fine. I was on my way to bed when I went to top up the fire in Camila's room.

Felipe was in there, on her bed. Camila sat looking at the fire, stiffly. He was rubbing her lower back. My five-year-old daughter. Who wasn't even his. I stared at his thumb.

'Camila, get out of the room,' I said. She turned, looking at me gratefully.

'You don't go anywhere until I tell you to go,' Felipe said, but I pulled her behind me and shoved her to the door.

'Run to Uncle Pedro and Auntie Eugenia's,' I said, 'and stay there until I come get you.'

I didn't turn but heard her little feet running. I knew he was going to hurt me now. But she was nearly safe. I would protect my child with everything inside of me. Including my life.

'Why didn't you tell her to run to her papa's house?' he sneered. I couldn't help the look of shock on my face. He laughed, cruelly, spitefully, and spit at me. 'You think I don't know? Just because she looks like her whore of a mother and no one else?'

I said nothing, but my face must have betrayed my hatred, for he hit me then, hard, across the face. I didn't care. I needed time. Time for Camila to get away. Time for her to be safe. I smiled at him, and he hit me again. And every time, I smiled, and every time, vhe got angrier, and hit me harder, until finally I had to spit out a tooth. I couldn't see out of one of my eyes. I began to get woozy. Once more and I was going to pass out. He seemed to know that. For that is when he came to me gently, and laid me down on the bed, pulling my hair off my forehead, and then pressing the pillow over my face.

I think it came as a bit of a shock that he was going to kill me. Truly kill me and suffer the consequences. I wanted to go peacefully, to be brave, but Camila's face was in front of mine, and suddenly I needed to fight. I fought with every ounce of my strength, but I had no more oxygen, and the life was leaving me . . .

And suddenly I heard a sound of rage so great and feral I didn't recognise it, but there was now a dead weight on me, and then it was gone. I pulled the pillow from my face and looked down at the dead body of Felipe, bleeding profusely. And there as my saviour, the one I loved . . .

Victoria and Marilena sat side by side, silent, not speaking.

'A sound of rage?' Marilena asked, looking at Victoria.

'The one I loved . . . ?' Victoria continued, looking at Marilena. 'Good god.'

'My . . . our . . . grandfather . . . killed Felipe Ortega,' Marilena whispered. 'What have we gotten ourselves into?'

'The curse. We've gotten ourselves into the curse. And we are the only ones who can get us out. We can save Las Viñas now. And we can free everyone of this curse. Maybe even me,' Victoria whispered softly.

Did Luce's curse cause her to be barren? It sounded as though she'd wanted to end the line.

Marilena looked at her. 'But how? How do we lift the curse?'

'I think we have to find the body.'

They both looked up. The vines around them had bloomed. Only one patch of land stood still dead.

'Only you and I together can.'

'Yes, it seems that way,' Marilena said. 'I always wanted to be an Anyas de Alveras, you know?' She looked at Victoria, who nodded.

'And it turns out I was a Silvas. I don't really think my brain has quite computed it yet. My brain hasn't computed anything that's happened in the last year,' Victoria admitted.

Marilena glanced at her. 'Do you want to talk about it?'

'With you?' she asked. 'My enemy up until five minutes ago?'

Marilena snorted. 'Yeah, I don't really want to hear it either. Just because we're like, related, doesn't mean I like you.'

'I don't like you either,' Victoria said.

'Good.'

'Good.'

CHAPTER TWENTY-SIX

Victoria and Marilena arrived back at the hacienda covered in dirt, Victoria's face smeared from wiping her tears.

'Jesus, you girls look like shit,' a voice said.

'Sylvia!' they cried in unison.

Sylvia had pulled up to the hacienda in her car and was walking towards them to the back door.

'Where have you been?' Victoria asked. 'We were expecting you over the holidays.'

'You missed quite an exciting couple of weeks, Sylvia,' Marilena said, looking into the car. 'Is someone with you?'

The passenger door opened and a small woman around Sylvia's age stepped out, tilting her head as she looked at them.

'I'm Caro,' the woman said, stepping forward.

Victoria gasped. 'Caro? But what are you . . . I mean . . .' She looked to Marilena.

'What's happening here?' Marilena asked.

'That diary you girls found has a lot in it I'd love to read for myself, honey,' Sylvia said. 'And a lot more that happened later that you may or may not want to know. But we don't have a choice now. Las Viñas is on hold until we finish off this curse. And we, as always, are her servants.'

'We?' Victoria asked, weakly. She had an idea forming of what exactly was happening now.

Suddenly a tall vine close to Caro started glistening, as if it were melting in warmth. Caro turned and looked at it, shaking her head and smirking.

'Flirt,' Sylvia said to the vine, chewing her gum. 'Go get cleaned up and get dressed, girls. We've got one more to pick up before we do this thing.'

'But . . .' Marilena interrupted.

'No buts,' Caro said. 'Jesus, you're just like your grandmother. She's going to have a heart attack when we all show up today.'

'My . . . my grandmother? Nonna Gen?' Marilena choked. 'That's who we're going to see?'

Caro's face softened. 'Get dressed, you girls, and the answers will be revealed. We were all happy to die with the secret, but Las Viñas wants to live. You know, Victoria, your grandmother had the old magic in her blood, the land magic. She was one with the land, she could speak to the vines. But even she told us one night, a long time ago, a night we'll go through later, that we were only asking permission. Even one like her couldn't demand anything from the land, only ask nicely. The vines have just taken kindly to us and kept her end of the bargain, and that was keeping the secret. Up till now. Now you girls are here.'

'Why us?'

They looked at each other.

'We'll go get Eugenia. This is something that must be done together.'

~

'Your mama wouldn't remember, of course,' Caro said to Marilena as they drove towards San Juan province, a couple of hours north of Mendoza. 'She was just a baby. But my oh my, did little Camila dote on Imogen. Didn't know she was her half-sister by blood. Just knew she had a little baby to love. She was just barely three of course.'

'Actually, she does remember, albeit vaguely,' Victoria said. Marilena turned her head. 'When Callie and Rick were here filming, she mentioned a memory of being on a swing before Las Viñas was cursed, on the lap of a little girl. She thought it was my mother, Camila.'

'I don't remember her saying that,' Marilena said.

'You were, as Pia said, Tussauded by the camera,' Victoria said with a smirk.

Marilena put her head in her hands and groaned. Victoria couldn't help but laugh.

'So how much do you girls know, anyway? Or how much, I should ask, has Las Viñas shared?'

Sylvia turned back to them with an eyebrow raised as she popped chocolate into her mouth, offering the bag to Caro. 'Well?'

'We know a little about you all growing up. And about Luce and the land, too,' Victoria said, glancing at Marilena. 'And we know that Luce and Pedro were in love and that my mother, Camila, was Pedro's child, and that Luce was forced to marry Felipe Ortega – money for the family – and that . . .'

But she couldn't finish.

Marilena reached and took her hand. 'That she was raped by her own husband.'

Caro and Sylvia both let out horrified gasps.

'We didn't know how bad it was,' Caro said, bringing her hand to head, covering her face. Her shoulders began to shake. 'Had we known . . .'

'Had we known, perhaps we could have done something. Helped. Oh god, Luce, I'm so sorry,' Sylvia whispered.

'She didn't tell you,' Victoria said to them, leaning forward and placing a hand on each of their shoulders, 'because she was too embarrassed, she said in her diary. I know you would have helped her if you'd known. She knew that, too.'

'We knew some,' Sylvia admitted. 'It was the sixties. The world had different ideas then. And her parents, I know they knew about it.' Her voice rose. 'I think she would have spoken to us more had it not been for her rift with Eugenia. Poor girls, it was impossible to know who to side with, so we just stayed out of it.'

'I went to work at the newspaper in Buenos Aires,' Caro said, 'and Sylvia ended up going to Córdoba for a degree in veterinary science. She was very advanced for our day,' Caro smiled.

'Oh hush,' Sylvia said, taking the next exit. 'Besides, I wouldn't talk. Our Caro got herself a typist job at the newspaper in Buenos Aires, just to get in and listen to how it all worked. Then one night she goes out and follows a lead everyone else ignored. Wrote one of the most provocative articles of the early seventies about women's rights and the rebellions. We were so proud.'

'What was it called?' Victoria asked.

'"The Second Wave,"' Sylvia answered proudly. Caro rolled her eyes but smiled.

'Hey!' Marilena exclaimed. 'I know that article. I read it in a history course I did in school – Women's Studies. But that was written by a man, wasn't it? What was his name again?'

'*Her* name was Car Wilson,' Caro laughed. 'There was a moment when I went to sign it Carolina Silvas, but at the last minute, as I finished typing C-A-R, I knew this article was too important to risk my own ego, and it would never get published if it was written by a woman. A secretary at that. I pretended to have it sent to me by someone undercover. I was the only one he would speak to, I told the publishers, as Car Wilson was in trouble with the government, and on the run. From that day on, all my articles got published,' she said smugly.

'Wait, *you* are Car Wilson? *The* Car Wilson?' Marilena asked. 'But that's impossible.'

'That's amazing, Caro,' Victoria whistled.

'Even I didn't know at first,' Sylvia said. 'Just like we didn't know what was happening with Luce and the abuse, or Eugenia and . . .'

'What?' Marilena said. 'What was wrong with my grandmother?'

'It was another of those things no one talked about then. Depression. She was already so sad that Pedro never loved her the way she loved him. She thought that if he married her, even though she was his second choice, that he would love her and she would be happy. Ah, Pedro, none of this was his fault. Your grandfather was actually a very, very good man. Had no idea Eugenia ever had feelings for him until she asked him to marry her,' Caro said.

'She did what?' Victoria and Marilena asked at the same time.

'Hush now, Caro, this isn't our story to tell,' Sylvia admonished. 'Girls, the rest of the story is Eugenia's and Luce's to tell. There is still much we don't even know, to be honest. So hold your wee horses now and wait. We'll be there shortly. And I have a good idea as to where the rest of that diary ended up.'

'We think that Felipe Ortega is buried in the vineyard. We think that's the last secret,' Victoria said, looking to Marilena, who nodded, her eyes wide. They both turned back.

Sylvia kept driving. 'That's exactly why we're here.'

'So you know he is buried there?'

There was silence for a moment.

'We helped your grandmother put the curse on the land. We had to,' said Sylvia.

'All three of you?'

They looked at one another.

'Just the two of us, and Luce,' Sylvia continued. 'By that time, she and Eugenia were no longer speaking. We thought Eugenia was just being jealous. She was always jealous of Luce, and of course we all knew about Camila. But Pedro was loyal. Or so we thought.'

'What do you mean?'

'The night Felipe Ortega left us . . .'

'You mean was murdered?' Victoria asked.

Sylvia winced. 'Luce called me, whispering fiercely that I had to come straight away, and not to tell anyone.'

'She said the same to me,' Caro said.

'When we arrived at the vineyard, she and Pedro were there, together. Covered in blood and dirt. Luce was so distraught; Pedro was holding her while she shivered. He looked calm. Felipe was a horrible man, to be sure, but to know that he was dead. That they killed him.'

'It was truly frightening,' Caro agreed.

'We asked Luce why we were there, and she told us we needed to do a ritual at Las Viñas,' Sylvia said.

'I remember,' Caro interrupted. 'She said, "She will hide this. She will protect us. Las Viñas will protect us. They can't blame anyone if there is no body."'

Sylvia nodded. 'Luce looked at Pedro and he nodded, and kissed her forehead, and we knew then that the affair we'd thought was over had continued. That Felipe had perhaps walked in on them, or he'd been hurting Luce and she called Pedro and he killed Felipe.'

'I remember asking why Eugenia wasn't there,' Caro said. 'She was his wife. She was Luce's best friend. It shouldn't have been like this. It was wrong.'

'"No!" they both yelled at the same time,' Sylvia remembered. 'They said Eugenia could never know and to leave her be.'

'Luce told us that Felipe wasn't meant to be home, but when she went to check the fire, she saw him with Cami. On her bed, rubbing her back,' Caro finished. She shook her head.

'I remember feeling the bile rise in my throat. And I was glad he was dead.'

'But then she screamed, Luce did. Over and over she just kept saying, "my daughter, my baby, I lost control!"'

'Jesus,' Victoria whispered, and Marilena took her hand. It surprised her but steadied her too.

'And that's what we know, bebe,' Caro said. 'We don't know if Luce killed him right then, or if she called Pedro. We don't know if Pedro walked in. We don't know which one of them killed Felipe. We do know that we got our Inca dresses, and we sat with Luce, and we spilled our blood, and we cursed the land.'

'But the land doesn't want to be cursed,' Sylvia said. 'Which is why we're here.'

'But why here, Sylvia?' Marilena asked, opening the car door after they had pulled up to her grandparents' house. 'My abuelo, Pedro, is in a nearby home with dementia. He's not even here, not that he'd remember anything anyway.'

'And even if he did remember, he wouldn't tell you,' a voice said from the door.

'Gen!' Caro and Sylvia said simultaneously, smiling.

Eugenia smiled, then looked over at Marilena, brightening. 'Mari! What a pleasure!' She came and hugged her granddaughter.

'But Gen, we know you don't know this, but we . . .'

'Cursed the vineyard, yes, I know,' she said breezily. 'I was the one who called Pedro to the hacienda. To bury Felipe.'

'You?' all four said at the same time.

'Yes,' Eugenia answered calmly. 'We asked my husband to help us bury the man I had just killed.'

CHAPTER TWENTY-SEVEN

. . . Eugenia!

I have never heard such rage before, such primal protection. She was crouched, her face like a huntress, and I knew the Inca blood we all shared was in her now. In her hand was the poker from the fireplace, cast iron and heavy, yet she wielded it as if she was a warrior. She was covered in blood but didn't seem to notice.

I realised then that adrenaline was running through her as it was through me, and that when it left her, she would be distraught. The poker began to shake and fell out of her hand.

I ran to her then and took her in my arms. We held each other tightly, as the rage and fear and adrenaline came down and we began to tremble in each other's arms.

'Oh my god, oh my god, oh my god,' she whispered.

'Shh, I'm here, Gen, I'm here.'

She pulled away, and we both looked down at Felipe.

'Is he . . . is he dead?'

I bent down to feel his pulse. I didn't have to – as I saw his face his eyes were open, glassy, without life.

'Yes,' I whispered back. 'Gen,' I said, standing to turn to her, sure she would lose it now. But instead she stood taller, took a breath.

'Good,' she said, her voice clear. She looked at me. 'I never meant it when I said I hoped he'd kill you. I was so angry with you, for so long. But even then, I loved you. I would never let anyone hurt you.'

I swallowed. 'And I will never let anyone hurt you. Go, call Pedro, tell him to come here now. Go home and don't let anyone see you. Clean yourself up. Look after the girls. Make Camila believe nothing bad happened.'

'But . . . ?'

'You can never know anything else about this night. We will bury the body. There is no crime without a body,' I said to her.

Eugenia ran back home barefoot in the dark, and Pedro was here in less than fifteen minutes.

'Dios mío,' he cried when he got into Camila's room and saw Felipe's body. 'What happened?'

As I looked at Pedro, the man I thought was the great love of my life, I realised that while I would always love him as a man, my love was too broad, too much for that. I could feel Eugenia's blood running through mine, through Las Viñas. Though I hated to involve them, I knew that because of the journey I took us on at twelve years old when my friends came with me to marry the land, they were part of this. There was a reason Mama had allowed them to come, I knew that now. There was power in our blood. There were too many of us to silence. We were one with the land, and the land would protect us. Las Viñas would protect us.

'We must get the body to the dark part of the vineyard,' I told him. 'I will call Sylvia and Caro.'

Thankfully he asked no questions and rolled Felipe into a sheet. I called the girls and told them to come, in their dresses, and where to meet us.

We carried the body through the vineyard as best we could but had to drag him at times. Las Viñas covered all of our trails, and I knew she would cover Eugenia's, and Caro's and Sylvia's. Las Viñas would protect us.

We had finished digging the hole and rolling Felipe's body into it when the girls arrived over an hour later, both thankfully home for the week.

'Why are you here?' Sylvia asked Pedro, looking between him and me. I wanted to say more, but there was too much to do in too little time.

'Pedro, go home, clean up, try to get some rest. You and Eugenia and Imogen were planning on leaving town – you must stick to your plans and not alter them, or it will look suspicious. The whole town knows. You have a new life waiting for you. Go as planned.'

'But . . . ?'

'Anything outside of the normal is too dangerous. Life goes on like normal. Go, now.'

Pedro hesitated, looking at all of us, but he left in the end.

'Here we are,' I said to my friends.

'Luce . . .'

But I silenced them as I knelt on top of the grave. They followed my lead. I took the same knife my mother had used the day I turned twelve and cut my own palms. They did the same.

'Take hands,' I said. I remembered everything and yet it did not feel like me. I believe something was working through me, as mother once said.

'The blood that runs through us is the keeper of the vines. The blood that runs through me is the mother of the vines. Las Viñas, serve us.'

The vines started to move around, as if listening, waking up, questioning.

'Put your palms to the ground now,' I said.

We did.

'Las Viñas, protect our secret. Let what is buried remain buried. Let us protect those who we love, let us . . .'

'Do you not love us?' Caro said, but her voice was different. I looked up. Her eyes were white. She was not Caro.

'Do you not love us?' she said again.

'Yes,' I whispered, 'yes, I love you. My lifeblood . . . But Camila.'

'Will you give us up, in exchange for the secret?' Sylvia spoke now, her eyes white like Caro's.

I died inside at that. To give up my land, my vines, who I was, to protect Camila. Eugenia. Pedro. Imogen. I began to sob.

'You want me to give up Las Viñas? My land?'

'We are not your land,' Las Viñas hissed at me through Caro. 'You are of us, part of us. We love you the way you love us. We will protect your secret.'

'You will?' I asked, relieved. 'Thank you.'

'We will go to sleep, be a vineyard no more. Until the last Anyas de Alveras comes to wake us up, so shall we sleep, and with it, your secret will be safe.'

'But . . .'

'It is done.' Caro's eyes closed.

We must have passed out then, for when we came to in the vineyard just before sunrise, none of us could remember anything past that moment. As we looked around, we realised a frost had come onto the land. The sirens went off and we all lay, trying to recollect what had happened, until the workers found us.

In my grief, I became feverish. It was another two days before the fever broke and I woke in my bed, surrounded by staff. I could see the mourning, the grief in them. I remembered everything and sat up quickly.

'What happened?' I asked.

'Las Viñas,' I heard a voice crying. 'We lost her in the frost.'

'What do you mean?' I asked. 'Show me.'

'Mrs! No, you cannot get out of bed now. You have frostbite and have been very ill.'

'Camila,' I cried, standing up.

'Mama, I am here,' she said, taking my hand. 'I am here.'

I could see from her eyes, worried but not wild, that she knew nothing of what had happened to Felipe.

The staff walked me to the door, to the porch, to look at my land.

It is gone. All the grapes. The flowers. I feel the pain in my soul.

Camila comes to stand beside me. I suddenly see her, the vivacious beauty of my daughter. My love.

'Mama,' she says.

They were all silent for a long while.

'Eugenia,' Sylvia whispered, handing the pages back to her. They were the only pages not buried in the land, but held in the safe hands of Eugenia. 'I can't believe you never told us. All this time.'

'There are things you simply cannot tell. No matter what happened between Luce and me, when your friendship is that strong, you can forgive. You cannot forget, but you can forgive. And you can fall on your sword for that person. And you can . . .'

'You can kill for them,' Caro whispered.

The others looked at Caro.

'I have been a reporter for a long time. You'd be surprised how many crimes are for love. For protection. You protected Luce, Gen. He would have killed her.'

'And then he would have done god knows what with Camila,' Sylvia said.

They were quiet again.

'What was up with all that possession mojo? Do you remember that?' Victoria asked.

'No!' Caro replied. 'Do you, Syl?'

'Nope. You don't reckon we were high, do you?'

They laughed suddenly, a light part in a very dark day.

'So what now?' Marilena asked. 'What do we do now?'

Victoria stood, knowing exactly what to do, feeling the power of the vines flowing through her even now.

'Now we lift the curse. All of us. Together.'

'But how?' they asked.

'With a little bit of magic,' Victoria said, a smile on her face.

CHAPTER TWENTY-EIGHT

Later that afternoon, after a long drive back to Las Viñas, Caro and Eugenia went to Sylvia's place to have a siesta, while Sylvia dropped Marilena and Victoria back at the hacienda.

'I have to get something out of Luce's old room,' Sylvia said, parking the car. 'Come, girls, follow me.'

They followed Sylvia to La Azul. 'This was Luce's room?' Victoria asked. 'But Pia has renovated it so much, I would be surprised if there was anything from the old room left.'

But it turned out Pia had kept it much the same, just refreshed the curtains and soft furnishings.

There was a drawer under the daybed that pulled out, but

when they opened it, it was filled with Pia's things – her clothes, a few books and magazines.

'Oh,' Sylvia choked, disappointment lacing her sigh. 'I thought . . .'

'What were you looking for, Sylvia?' Victoria asked.

'Wait,' she said, putting up her hand and pulling the drawers from the daybed entirely out. 'Move those aside,' she said, reaching under the bed and feeling along the floorboards. 'Aha! Come on, you young girls, help me pull this up.'

Marilena and Victoria slid the drawers to the far side of the room and moved the bed out of the way, seeing the loose floorboard Sylvia had found. They loosened it further and finally lifted it up, and then another and another, to reveal what looked like an old trunk underneath.

'Ah,' Sylvia said, smiling softly and opening the trunk, pulling an old frock out. 'Our Inca dresses. Luce's mama left them for us to wear during the first ceremony, the night the vineyard was gifted to Luce. I thought they might be appropriate for your ceremony tonight.'

Victoria was speechless. 'My ceremony? What do you mean?'

Sylvia's brow creased. 'Well, who else would lead us to uncurse Las Viñas but its mother?'

The word 'mother' made Victoria's stomach turn.

'See you at midnight,' Sylvia said, carrying out some dresses.

'But . . .' Victoria called, but it was too late. Sylvia had gone, leaving two Inca dresses behind.

~

Just after eleven, Victoria and Marilena sat on separate settees in La Azul, wearing the thick Inca dresses and feeling overly warm on the summer evening, despite Las Viñas still being under its frost.

'What are you going to do when we get to La Abuela? Do you know a spell or something? Has it been passed down to you?' Marilena asked.

Victoria shook her head. 'I know nothing. I'm going to look like a fool.'

'The Inca people believed there was something like a collective unconscious, things that were either passed down through blood or heritage,' Marilena said. Victoria looked at her curiously, and she blushed. 'Remember I wanted to be an Anyas de Alveras more than anything. I did a lot of research into the Inca history.'

'I don't know if I believe in a collective unconscious,' Victoria said.

'So how did the vines wake up when you arrived? *Only* when you arrived.'

'Probably because of climate change and too much rain,' Victoria sniffed. 'I used to be pragmatic.'

Marilena rolled her eyes. 'Even tried-and-true sciences like biodynamics are less pragmatic than you think. It's almost . . . magical.'

'I wanted to believe in magic. I came here thinking that being a part of something I was born into, something bigger than me, something greater, that would heal me. But here I still am. The same me, broken in the same ways.'

'You've got it wrong,' Marilena said. 'You are not here to be healed; you are here *to* heal. Humans are ridiculously selfish creatures. We want and take but never give unless it suits our purposes. Well, let me tell you something, Victoria Bishop. You want to be healed, because you feel lifeless, broken. Look around you! For whatever reason, Las Viñas, who was lifeless and broken, is living and thriving. They are awake. You are breathing life into Las Viñas.'

'How can a barren woman breathe life into anything?' she whispered, admitting her greatest fear.

'There are ways to bring life other than by having a child. Look around, Victoria. Stop waiting for the world to heal you. You will heal fine on your own. Focus on what you can do to heal the land. When you learn to take the focus off yourself, you will find your peace. Your purpose. And perhaps your place, too. Tonight, you will finish this curse and bring Las Viñas back to life.' Marilena took Victoria's hand. 'And I'll be there with you. As family.'

~

Victoria, Marilena, Sylvia, Caro and Eugenia began to walk through Las Viñas to the dark part of the vineyard where the body of Felipe Ortega was buried. They wore Inca dresses and carried old lanterns. Marilena was carrying a box of candles Victoria had found for the ceremony, and the ritual knife as well. She was feeling very nervous. They all were – no one spoke as they walked.

'Wait for me!' a voice cried, breaking the eerie silence. They turned to find Pia running to them, wearing Marilena's old festival dress and the tiara from Las Viñas on her head.

'Pia! What are you doing out here?' Marilena hissed, then stopped. 'And what on earth are you wearing?'

'You looked dressed up,' she managed, catching her breath from running. 'I made do.'

Sylvia snickered while Caro laughed outright.

'Well, I think you look just the part, sweet pea,' Eugenia said, reaching to hug her.

'Nonna Gen!' Pia exclaimed, hugging her back. 'What are you doing here?'

'What are *you* doing here, young lady?' Marilena asked again, her voice stern.

'I . . . I don't know,' Pia answered truthfully. 'I just woke up, wide awake. And I looked out my window and saw you walking. And I knew I had to come, too.'

'You can't, sweetheart,' Marilena said softly, putting her arm on Pia's shoulder. 'I'm sorry, but . . .'

'Yes, she can,' Victoria said firmly. 'Come, let's continue.'

'But Victoria,' Sylvia said, 'she is just a child.'

'So were all of you,' Victoria reminded them. 'Marilena, you are Pia's mother, it is your decision ultimately. But I think she belongs there with us.'

Marilena looked at Victoria, her eyes piercing. And she nodded. 'Yes, this is her story too.'

The vineyard was covered in a low mist as they walked through, and Victoria realised it was Las Viñas, thawing in their wake. The air got colder the closer they got to the dark place, and when they finally arrived, it was as cold as winter. The land was hard, the vines here without any bloom, frozen solid. Victoria was glad she was wearing the warm winter costume of the Inca women, who had dressed for the mountain life. Even still, she was cold. Pia looked freezing.

They stopped in what looked like a large circle of dead ground, for nothing grew here, not even a vine. It was larger than she'd remembered.

'This was where we found the . . .' Victoria began, but Marilena coughed loudly, her eyes reminding Victoria that Pia was there. '. . . this,' she finished instead, holding out the ring she and Marilena had found with the Ortega insignia.

'I know that crest. I'll never forget it,' Sylvia said, looking at the ring in Victoria's hand with disgust.

'The number of times we could see the insignia branded into Luce's skin,' Caro said.

'Ortega,' Eugenia finished scornfully. 'He is here.'

They all looked down to the dead space beneath them, which had no vines, no leaves, just dead frozen earth.

'No!' Pia said after a few moments of silence. 'Are you telling me there's some dead guy buried under here? Is that why you have shovels, to dig him up? That's disgusting!'

Suddenly Marilena snorted, covering her face. Victoria followed, and they all began to snicker, then giggle, until finally they were laughing out loud, crying with laughter.

'Oh, Pia,' Victoria laughed, hugging her, 'I knew you were meant to be here.'

Pia was laughing, too, but looking at all of them like they were crazy.

'Well,' Victoria said finally, as their laughter ceased, 'this is it.'

They formed a circle around the dead space.

They were all silent for a few minutes, until they looked at Victoria.

'I have no idea what to do,' she admitted.

'Well, we do, at least a little bit,' Caro said. 'But when Luce cursed the vineyard, she was already its mother. I was thinking, or Sylvia and I were thinking together, that maybe we need to perform the ceremony we did when Luce was twelve. That's why we brought the clothing out.'

'Okay,' Victoria said, nodding. 'Let's see, in Luce's diary, you all drew blood and then made a circle around Luce and held hands, or something like that.'

'Luce's mother said something about the past,' Sylvia remembered.

'And then the women began to chant,' Eugenia said, nodding. 'And Luce's hands were cut, and she had to put her hand in the earth and wait to see if a bud bloomed. If it did, the land belonged to her.'

'Well, I don't know what to chant and no one who knows is here,' Victoria said, 'so I suppose we just do the rest and ask nicely?'

Marilena finished lighting the candles in a circle and reached for the knife, but it was gone. 'Pia!'

'Here goes nothing,' they heard Pia say, as she twisted the knife into her palm, cringing as a drop of blood came out.

Caro took the knife from her as Pia kept her palms facing up and did the same to her own palms. Sylvia took the knife next, and then Eugenia, and finally Marilena took it. She looked at Victoria and they both knew exactly what to do.

Marilena came to Victoria and put the knife into her palm, drawing the blood, and finally to her own.

'Come, take hands,' Marilena said. 'Victoria, place your hands into the earth. If Las Viñas gives you a bud, she will be yours.'

With wide eyes and bated breath, they joined hands and Victoria placed hers in the earth, the others joining her. They waited. And waited.

'Please,' Victoria whispered to the land, her eyes filling. 'Please.'

But nothing happened.

No one moved, nor said anything, as Victoria began to cry softly, her hands in the dirt, the disappointment washing over her, over all of them. She couldn't give life to the vines. She couldn't heal.

'What is that sound?' Pia asked a few moments later.

Hers was not the only head lifted. Marilena heard it, too, and Caro. It was a buzzing, or a humming, they couldn't tell.

'It's getting closer,' Sylvia said, and they were all alert now, looking around.

Victoria finally lifted her head. And that was when they saw it. Lanterns, dozens of them, coming from all parts of the vineyard, the women holding them from the mountains, the women of Luce's heritage, of Victoria's, chanting the words they'd done so many years ago with Luce. Suddenly Marilena,

Pia, Sylvia, Eugenia and Caro were standing, chanting too, though they didn't know the words. It was as if they were coming through them, as the women descended upon Las Viñas.

Victoria placed her hands into the soil again, her heart full. And when she looked down, a new vine came out of the earth and bloomed.

'La Hija,' they named the new vine. 'The Daughter.'

And the women celebrated late into the night.

CHAPTER TWENTY-NINE

March 2025 – Harvest

'Hurry, Joyce, or you'll miss it!'

Joyce opened the bathroom door in La Amarilla in a panic.

'I can't quite fit into this damned Spanish dress Victoria gave me!' she cried, tugging at the red shoulders. 'Turns out women then weren't so well endowed,' she said.

'No, they were not,' Frank said with a whistle, smiling appreciatively.

'Frank!' she said, blushing. 'Not now! I don't know if I can run in this thing. It's got some sort of corset underneath. You'll have to carry me.'

'I am your slave, milady,' he said, turning around. 'Quick, hop on my back.'

'Run fast, Frank! I've wanted to do this ever since that episode of *I Love Lucy*,' she said, hopping on Frank's back.

He started to jog. 'You've never even seen that episode of *I Love Lucy*. You only know about it from *Pretty Woman*.'

'What does that matter?' she scoffed, holding on tight. 'Oh no! It's starting! Run, Frank!'

'It matters because last week you answered the crossword clue, "TV sitcom character who crushed grapes" as "Julia Roberts"!' he yelled, running faster.

'But it was Julia Roberts in *Pretty Woman*!' she argued.

'Dios mío,' Frank muttered, running faster.

Victoria was laughing as she watched her dad run as fast as he could with her mom on his back. Her parents really were the best. She'd loved nothing more than having them here again the past week.

It wasn't just them who had turned up for the harvest. Monique flew down from LA with Levi and Ange in tow, looking well out of place on the vineyard. And yet they worked as hard as anyone and never stopped smiling. Callie Callahan came with Rick the cameraman, and they filmed a few sequences to follow up the pilot. Sylvia brought her long-secret partner, Laura, who had finally moved in with Sylvia. Caro came back from Buenos Aires, and Eugenia brought Pedro, who, despite his dementia, was in good spirits and seemed to remember what to do on a vineyard, even if he didn't really know where he was. Which, Victoria and Marilena agreed, was for the best.

Diego was on the parilla, Pia and Gabi were helping Adriana in the kitchen, and Dev was walking up with the first bunch in his hands to give to Victoria.

He fed her one grape, and as the Lady of the Vines, she approved, gaining a cheer from the crowd, and then she and Marilena began the ceremony of taking the small bunch and stomping on it with their bare feet, as the rest was poured into the vats for the harvesters to crush in the ceremony.

Dev's large family had also come. Victoria thought it would be weird at first, meeting Dev's family. For not only was she meeting them for the first time as his colleague on the vineyard, but as his girlfriend as well. But they all embraced her with enthusiasm and joined the festivities.

Since they'd lifted the last of the curse from Las Viñas, she'd been producing so many healthy grapes it was as if she was making up for the years she was asleep. Dev and his team had worked nonstop over the last two months to keep the grapes healthy, the vines thriving, the right amount of moisture and water. But Las Viñas was out to party. Turns out she might have been a magical vineyard even before she was cursed.

'I watched one of the vines today smack a bird who pooped on it,' Pia had said over dinner one night. 'Then she wiped the poop off herself. It was so weird.'

They laughed with the rest of the table, but Marilena and Victoria looked at one another and shrugged. It likely did happen just as Pia had said.

Dev made the call for the harvest to start in the second-to-last week of March. He and the boys did a survey of the land.

'There are just so many grapes, and they all look beautiful. We need hands, Vic,' he'd said, putting his arms around her as she burnt dinner. 'Smells great, babe.'

'Liar,' she'd laughed. 'I'll send out word to the brigades. And don't worry, I won't cook.'

'You mean tonight?' he'd asked hopefully.

Victoria had laughed. 'Too late. Burnt provoleta – again.'

He'd sighed dramatically. 'I'll scrape the black off – again.'

Adriana and Eduardo came together for the week, setting up food every morning that they replenished through the day. Victoria had seen them accidentally bumping into each other so much she wondered if it was an accident. Then one morning she'd grinned as she saw Eduardo *finally* kiss Adriana on the cheek.

By the week they started, Victoria had assembled quite a group, albeit one that had never done what they were there to do.

'Remember that time I made the award-winning wine for Trapiche?' Walter asked Romina one day as they picked.

They all laughed.

'Of course I do. That's where we fell in love,' Romina said, smiling fondly.

'Wait,' Victoria said, halting her grape-picking. 'Of all the tall tales you've told, you actually did make the award-winning wine for Trapiche? Which put Mendoza on the map?'

'Yes,' Walter and Romina said together, nonchalant.

'Would have been nice to know,' Victoria muttered under her breath, but when she caught Marilena's eyes, she was laughing so hard and silently that Victoria joined her and could not stop for a day.

~

For one full week, the ragtag team picked the thousands of grapes on Las Viñas. They hand-picked full bunches and brought them in wheelbarrows to the winery, dropping them on the sorting table and heading back out. The days were so hot that they mostly scheduled the pickers to go out after 7 pm, and into the evening. It wasn't rare for the group to have dinner at 1 am or 2 am. Adriana and Eduardo either left something to warm up or left Victoria to do the cooking. Thankfully, she was usually saved by the boys lighting up a fire and doing an asado, leaving her to the salads. She couldn't burn those.

Those who weren't out picking were at the sorting table. They had to do everything by hand this first year, but Victoria was planning to get a machine sorter for the next vintage. Marilena had to train the sorters and oversee this process to be sure the grapes were de-stemmed properly and that no damaged grapes were going to press.

They did have a machine press. It was very old, but that was good, because they had decided to keep only the first press free run juice and sell off the rest from the second and third press.

And that was where they were today. At the final Harvest Party. The grapes were all in, the sorting was finished, and now they were pressing the grapes. And they decided together that one whole section of the vineyard, which they called 'el último,' or 'the last,' was going to be foot pressed in the traditional way. No machines, no hands, just the women, their feet and a festival.

Marilena and Victoria led the women to the large vat to foot stomp the grapes. Julio began to play the guitar. It was a very traditional song for harvest, and though none of them knew it, they all suddenly did.

When the party was finished, Victoria and Dev's boys took the second and third press juice and got it ready for pick-up the next day.

Marilena and Dev took the free run juice and lovingly put it into barrels.

It was nearly sunrise; they were ravaged, exhausted, but filled with hope.

'What do we do now?' Marilena asked.

Victoria looked around at everything they had accomplished and smiled. She took their hands.

'Just like Las Viñas – now we just live.'

EPILOGUE

Sixteen months later

Victoria, Dev, and Marilena sat together outside of the hacienda, a bottle of champagne on ice, a plate of cheese and nibbles in front of them. The plate remained untouched; the champagne unopened. They sat, instead, in silence, staring at Victoria's phone, which was in the middle of the table.

'What time is it?' Marilena asked.

Victoria looked at her watch. They each could have looked at the phone, but they were too afraid to touch it.

'Nine twenty-three,' she said.

'And they're calling at nine thirty?'

'Yes, Mari, same time they were always calling, same answer as one minute ago when you asked the time,' Dev said with a sigh.

'Not really,' she huffed. 'One minute ago, it was nine twenty-two.'

Dev smirked. Victoria wanted to, but her face was frozen.

'Oh, come on, ladies!' Dev said. 'Whether we get this phone call is not the end all be all. We made a great wine, absolutely. I mean, Las Viñas was really showing off, if you ask me. A vineyard that hasn't produced grapes in fifty-odd years producing something of that quality. It's like she's just been waiting,' he continued, looking awed like he always did when he gave this speech.

'Yes, and we've had a second amazing vintage. I reckon next year will look even better. We've really found our style this year, I think,' Marilena agreed.

'Plus, we were able to make quite a bit more since we didn't have to sell off the extra juice. You know, I reckon that second run juice was just as good,' Victoria said.

'Yes, but I still want to keep the free run and the second press separate in barrel,' Marilena said nervously.

'We know,' Victoria and Dev said, together.

They were silent, then.

'What time is it now?' Marilena asked.

Even Dev looked at Victoria, not berating Marilena again. He was, in all actuality, just as anxious. They all were.

'Nine twenty-six,' Victoria said.

They did not feel the need to fill in any more time. Instead, the three sat in silence as they watched the cell phone clock get to 9.28, then 9.30. They held their breaths then, but the phone did not ring.

'It's not like, an automated system or anything, right?' Victoria asked. 'I mean, the International Wine Challenge is done by a series of judges. They'll have a person call, right?'

Dev nodded. 'Yes. If we've got a medal or placed for an award. They won't call if we don't.'

'I know that,' she whispered. Dev took her hand and squeezed it. Marilena grabbed her other hand. 'That kinda hurts, Mari.'

She let some of the pressure off.

When the clock passed 9.35, they let go of one another's hands. At 9.42, they each felt their souls crumble, just a bit. But they looked up at one another and smiled.

'I say we open the champagne anyway,' Victoria said cheerfully, even though it was hard to swallow the lump of disappointment in her throat. 'We celebrate that we lifted a curse off a vineyard, made a beautiful wine and have had a successful second vintage.'

'I second that,' Dev said, standing and taking the champagne from the ice bucket, pulling the cork out with a hurrah. He poured them each a glass.

'A toast,' he said, and they all stood, lifting their glasses. 'To the best winemaker in Mendoza, Marilena.'

'The best winemaker in Mendoza,' Victoria repeated, lifting her glass.

Marilena blushed fiercely but smiled and nodded. 'To me!' she said, and they laughed and each took a sip, feeling lighter, happier. 'And to the best damned viticulturist in the southern hemisphere,' she said, toasting to Dev.

It was Dev's turn to blush. 'Sheesh, Mari, that's a pretty heavyweight award there.'

They each took another sip.

'I didn't say the northern hemisphere,' she scoffed. 'Get over yourself.'

They were all laughing genuinely now.

'And to Victoria,' Marilena said softly. 'For making this all happen.'

'To Victoria,' Dev repeated, kissing her neck and pulling her in.

'To me!' she laughed with a little cheer as they sipped. 'And, of course, to Las Viñas. Long may she not be cursed.'

'Las Viñas!' they said together, pouring the last of their champagne to the ground.

Victoria sighed and looked at the phone. 'Ah well, next year, perhaps.'

'Or the year after, even,' Marilena said.

'Or never,' Dev said. 'Wine isn't about an award. It's about stories. The stories of the land, its history, the people who make it, the bottling, the year, and finally the people who drink it.

Sitting with friends at a restaurant, or at the vineyard, or taking a bottle home to share. Wine has been in our blood for as long as humans have existed.'

'Seven thousand BCE, remember,' Victoria reminded them. '*Wine Folly*.'

They took the bottle and began walking to the vineyard to finish the rest when Victoria's phone rang.

They stood frozen for a moment, and suddenly all three ran back to the table, where Victoria picked up the phone and quickly put it on speaker.

'Hello?' she answered.

'Victoria Anyas de Alveras Bishop?' a British voice asked on the other end.

Dev, Marilena and Victoria looked at one another, eyes wide.

'Yes,' she finally answered.

'Bodegas Anyas de Alveras has received a Gold Medal from the International Wine Challenge. We look forward to seeing you in London. You will be emailed details shortly. Congratulations.'

They stared at the phone for a long time after the call ended, before they started jumping and cheering.

Finally, Victoria stopped cheering and took their hands, smiling at them. 'Well. Now *that* is a good story.'

ACKNOWLEDGEMENTS

Thank you to everyone at Moa Press and Hachette Aotearoa New Zealand and Australia. To Dom Visini, Angela Radford, Sacha Beguely, Suzy Maddox, Tania Mackenzie-Cooke, Sharon Galey, Nic Faisandier, Angie Williams, Mel Winder & Cyanne Alwanger – I am honoured to be part of your team and cannot thank you enough for all you do.

Thank you to Dianne Blacklock, editor/copyeditor extraordinaire – I've loved working with you on three books and hope we work on many more together!

To Theresa Crewsdon, thank you for your amazingly thorough and enjoyable copyedit on this book.

Special thank you to Stacey Clair for her eagle-eyed proofread.

I would not have this wonderful career as a writer without Kate Stephenson. Kate, thank you for your wisdom and vision and your unwavering support. Working with you is a joy and an honour.

Writing can be a very solo journey and one not easy to navigate, so I am forever grateful for the Mighty Moas. You women are amazing writers and friends and knowing you has been a highlight of this ride so far.

A special thank you to Gary and Rach for your insights about the vineyard and the winemaking process, and also to Bianca Grinovero for your help with the Spanish language.

Dan – you are a true partner and my biggest champion. Thank you.

At the heart of all my novels are the bonds of friendship, love and strong familial ties. I feel grateful every day for all the people in my life that have made those the core values in both my books and my life. To all my family and friends, thank you for being supportive, inspirational and uplifting. I hope that my novels lift people up the way you do for me.

Erin Palmisano is the author of bestselling novels *The Secrets of the Little Greek Taverna* and *The Secrets of Maiden's Cove.* A dual NZ and US citizen, she lives in Nelson, New Zealand, where she and her partner are restauranteurs. She loves writing stories where her passions of food, wine and travel come together, often with a hint of magic. *The Secrets of the Lost Vineyard* is her third novel.

www.erinpalmisano.com
Instagram: @authorerinpalmisano
Facebook: @authorerinpalmisano